Nancy Sparling was born in South Carolina, USA and grew up near Detroit, Michigan. She moved to the UK in 1991 and now lives in Hertfordshire. She has a degree in politics.

FREE LUNCH

Nick Reed pretends to be related to famous people. But Nick isn't a bad man; he's a purveyor of happiness. For who wouldn't want to meet Goldie Hawn's baby brother or John Travolta's son? And in return for letting those he encounters revel in the pleasure of befriending the brother of Brad Pitt, Nick is given lots of freebies. His hotel rooms are paid for, dinners are on the house, beautiful women fall at his feet. Never quite the charlatan and not always the con man, Nick Reed has a set of rules to live by. But rules were made to be broken, and when they are, trouble begins . . .

NANCY SPARLING

FREE LUNCH

Complete and Unabridged

ULVERSCROFT
Leicester

First published in Great Britain in 2003 by
Hodder & Stoughton
London

First Large Print Edition
published 2004
by arrangement with
Hodder & Stoughton a division of
Hodder Headline
London

British Library CIP Data

Sparling, Nancy
    Free lunch.—Large print ed.—
    Ulverscroft large print series: general fiction
    1. Imposters and imposture—Fiction
    2. Large type books
    I. Title
    813.6 [F]

    ISBN 1–84395–295–5

Published by
F. A. Thorpe (Publishing)
Anstey, Leicestershire

Set by Words & Graphics Ltd.
Anstey, Leicestershire
Printed and bound in Great Britain by
T. J. International Ltd., Padstow, Cornwall

This book is printed on acid-free paper

To John and to my parents

Acknowledgements

With thanks to: Eugenie Furniss, Wayne Brookes, Tracy Fisher and Lucinda Prain.

CLINGING TO THE
COAT-TAILS OF FAME

Have you ever wondered what happens to the children of famous people? No, I'm not talking about those sensationalised sob stories of neglect and abuse. I mean the day-to-day lives of the relatives of an adored celebrity, when people like Audrey Hepburn's daughter, Steven Spielberg's brother, Russell Crowe's sister meet Joe Public. Well, I'll tell you. It's a world of freebies and instant popularity. Free breakfasts, free lunches, free dinners, free drinks, free hotels, free clothes, free holidays, gifts and smiles everywhere you go. And I like it. It's a good way to make a living.

Or it was until I broke the rules.

Sit down, all you sue-happy litigation lawyers. Get off the phone. I'm merely giving examples here. I'm not saying these particular relatives — I don't even know if they exist — act like me, I'm just saying they could. With names and connections like theirs they could do anything they wanted.

I did. And it was great. I had the time of my life.

1

Until I got carried away.

There are simply some things you shouldn't do. Times when you should say no. Even when what's on offer is free.

Trust me. I should know. Just look at me now.

LUXURY VACATIONS FOR REAL MEN (IF I'D SEEN THE BROCHURE FIRST I WOULDN'T BE HERE)

It's like that scene at the start of a movie when the characters are introduced and you see them sitting around in what is obviously a combat training room, looking decidedly wimpy and pathetic next to the ex-Marine instructor, and you just know that they're all going to die. Not right away, of course: they'll survive the training and their last days on earth will be filled with dirt and sweat and pulling muscles they never even knew they had. (Ex-Marines always think suffering is good for the soul.) It's only after the end of the training that they'll die, when they're sent off on a mission that's meant to be easy but something goes disastrously wrong.

It always does.

I know how it is. I've seen the films. I've sat in countless cinemas watching groups of weedy men and women get tough and strong — or at least try — only to be annihilated on their great adventure.

Well, I'm one of those sorry soon-to-be-dead fools, and my only consolation is that my pale, pasty British skin is camouflaged by a healthy-looking American tan so I won't immediately be typecast as a cute but confused pre-*Bridget Jones*, Hugh Grant type. The sweet, slightly bumbling man is never the first to go — he's there for a much-needed dose of light-hearted relief — but in this kind of movie he'll be the second or third to die, for he's expendable. The audience needs to know that if the nice guy gets it, then what hope is there for the others?

The best I can hope for is the chance to play the cool Steve McQueen character and, glancing round the room, I think I'm the only one who could possibly fit the role. That doesn't mean I'll live, I'm not expecting to, but I'd be one of the last to go and, most importantly, I'd be able to die in style.

Funny how that matters. Dead is dead, but it would be a pity to let the side down. And I have to live up to my name, after all. Must be all these cinematic thoughts influencing me, trying to make sense of my death, turning it into some kind of heroic statement when in reality it'll be bloody, messy and downright undignified. Body fluids all over the place, stinking, putrid and revolting for that poor sorry person who'll stumble across the lot of

4

us after we've been shot to shit and massacred like sheep.

Our esteemed instructor has already introduced himself. Name: Ted Bradenton. Age: forty-two. All-time favourite weapon: M-16 assault rifle. Occupation: ex-Marine.

Ex-Marine. Like what he's doing now doesn't matter. That it's just a day job, that it doesn't define him, that it's not who he is, merely what he does to pass the time until the military realises its mistake in forcing him to retire and recalls him for one last mission that only he can do.

Looks like Ted's about to start the motivational introductory pep talk. I suppose I should pay attention — I might be wrong, this could be one of those movies where the hero and one or two of his buddies survive despite the odds. And, if that's the case, I may as well give myself a fighting chance.

'This,' says Ted, from the front of the room where he stands straight and tall, looking exactly as an ex-Marine should, 'is not just a bounty-hunting training school. This is Arizona's *finest* bounty-hunting training school. So if any of you civilians don't plan on giving it everything you've got, now's the time to leave.'

What Ted doesn't mention is that this is a training school for tourists, for anyone who

5

wants to spend a week of his or her life pretending to be a bounty-hunter.

He stares at each of us, meeting our eyes, measuring our worth and, no doubt, finding us sadly lacking. (I find us sadly lacking so Ted certainly does.)

I want to raise my hand and shout that I don't want to be here. (I don't want to be here.) But I can't leave. It's too late for that.

'Good,' says Ted, when none of us moves. 'I hate cowards. Now, before we get started, we're going to have some introductions. Brief and to the point. None of that crap where each of you has to tell us your name and some goddamn boring fact about yourself. We just don't care.' He points at me and smiles — and what do you know? His face isn't made of glass so it doesn't crack into a million pieces. 'This, ladies and gentlemen, is Nick Schwarzenegger. And, yes, Arnie is his daddy so pay attention to your lessons. I don't want to look a fool in front of Arnie's son.'

Arnie, that's right. As in the one and only Arnold Schwarzenegger.

So what the hell am I doing here if I'm the son of Arnold Schwarzenegger?

That's just it. I'm not Arnie's son. But *she* thinks I am. Ted thinks I am. They all think I am now.

It wasn't inevitable, it didn't have to get to this point, there's no logical reason why I'm here. The truth is, I got sucked in: first by lust and longing, and then by some crazy sense of misplaced honour. Once I met Holly, once I knew her, once I liked her, I couldn't let her come here alone. It's laughable, but I thought I'd be able to protect her.

Protect her, when my being here makes it obvious I'm not even very good at looking out for myself? What a joke.

I'd like to be able to stand up, grab Holly's hand and take us both far away from here, but she won't leave. And if she won't leave, I won't leave. I can't.

EVERYONE'S A WINNER
WHEN I'M AROUND

I took my first personality test when I was ten. My school went through a phase where they thought answering questions such as 'Would you like to work outside?' or 'Do you like animals?' would help us determine our career paths. They didn't realise that we were still at the stage where the thought of working in an office, sitting at a desk all day, was dreadfully boring, not at all like the glamorous lives we were planning. We hadn't yet discovered that working outdoors entails a great deal of hard, demanding physical labour and hours of standing around with your hands shoved under your armpits for warmth.

We were the first year to be tested so young, the guinea-pigs of our district, and I think they were genuinely surprised when the results came back and we were all told that we were best suited for employment as tree surgeons, zoo-keepers, marine biologists or, my personal favourite, forest rangers. (They told us they didn't want us to harbour unrealistic expectations, so all sport and

8

entertainment careers were excluded. Otherwise half of us would have favoured becoming professional footballers while the others would have been seemingly destined for pop stardom, Hollywood or the London stage.)

Images of wrestling crocodiles and bears, tending injured flamingos and patrolling vast tracks of virgin forests entertained us for weeks. And this was in the days before the *Crocodile Hunter*, when Steve Irwin hadn't shown the world exactly what playing with crocodiles entails. If he'd been around when we were children we would have been amazed by him, we would have thought he was so cool, we would have wanted to *be* him. 'If Steve can do it, we can do it,' we'd have said, oozing confidence and determination. We'd have gone to the zoo to see those crocs move and watch those jaws snap together. Our teachers, feeling guilty, and our parents, increasingly concerned, would have tried to convince us it was better to become doctors or lawyers, but we wouldn't have listened. They'd have warned us that we could lose an arm or a leg or, worst case scenario, a head. But nothing would have swayed us from the desire to become just like Steve.

Our dreams of being Tarzan-like guardians of the jungle would have held even greater lure and lasted much longer if we'd had him to look up to. The inevitable disillusionment would have been devastating. It was bad enough as it was when it dawned on us that working outdoors in Britain does not involve crocodiles or flamingos, jungles or palm trees. Rather, it involves tramping around in the mud after badgers in the middle of the night, worrying that mould might be growing between your toes because your feet have been wet for weeks.

As awareness slowly dawned with its acid tang of disappointment, I realised that I wasn't cut out for a life of toil and physical labour. That realisation left me with no other option and no real choice. I was more suited for life inside an office.

An office would tide me over while I was waiting for fame to find me. To be discovered. Ah, from one dream to the next. I no longer wanted to be a forest ranger: I wanted to be famous.

I accepted the office as a necessary evil until stardom came my way. I had the suit and tie, the desk in a cubicle and the fluorescent lighting. For six long years I had a proper job. At first it was easy to keep on dreaming, but then real life sucked me in and visions of rock 'n' roll and Hollywood faded. Then, about six months ago, I was promoted to a cubicle with a window. And I was happy about it. A window. Wow. Yes, I had to keep the blind closed most of the day to keep the sun's glare off my computer screen, but it was still a window. I was proud that I'd achieved something. All those late nights and extra hours had been rewarded.

It was only when I went home that evening and saw my guitar in the corner, dusty and unused for weeks, that I knew I had to do something.

Life wasn't working out as I'd planned.

I was never going to be famous.

I was never going to be famous, but I didn't want to spend the rest of my life shackled to a desk, a chair and a computer monitor. There had to be a better way.

And then I found it. I think it suits me.

I don't work outside, nor do I work indoors. Both had their drawbacks. I work wherever and whenever it pleases me, and not in an office at all.

And what exactly do I do?

I'm a purveyor of happiness. I bring joy and sunshine to people's lives. That's my aim in life, my job description. I'd put it in my passport if I didn't think they'd stop me at Immigration or Customs, thinking I was some kind of spaced-out deliverer of happiness drugs or an Ecstasy smuggler and want to subject me to all kinds of unpleasant

11

internal examinations.

I'm not a wise old philosopher, I've never claimed to be a guru, but I have a handle on the purpose of it all. I can't lecture the masses about the divine and the great plan for the universe, but I do know how each of us should spend our lives. It's all about happiness.

The purpose of life is to be happy and to make others happy. There's nothing more to it than that. Leaving the world a better place for our descendants is but a side effect. A good one, perhaps, but not the main point.

And I don't feel bad about lying. There's nothing wrong with a few lies here and there, especially when they serve to make someone feel better. Just imagine what a cold, hostile place the world would be if everyone had to tell the truth — the absolute and de-euphemised truth — at all times.

'White is such an awful colour on you, it's so unflattering.'

'Your skin looks blotchy and those dark circles — shouldn't you try to get more sleep?'

'What on earth have you done to your hair?'

'That spot on your chin makes me feel sick.'

'Yes, you *do* look fat.'

'Don't get mad, you asked for my opinion.'

'Sorry, but no, you're not as good in bed as she is.'

No, it wouldn't work. We'd all be miserable, more miserable than we are now. Give me a basket of rose-coloured glasses and I'll hand them out to everyone I can find. I'll hunt high and low until every single person on this planet has his or her very own pair.

Maybe I'm being too vague, maybe I'm trying to gloss things over by saying I'm a purveyor of happiness. For what is a purveyor of happiness? I could be a ride attendant at Disney World, a billionaire philanthropist, the author of the Harry Potter books (don't I wish), a magician who performs at children's parties. But I'm not.

I pretend to be related to famous people. That's my job, the one thing that suits me and that I can do well. But it's not all fun and games. It's hard work. I have to be witty, entertaining and patient. I'm on call twenty-four hours a day.

Yes, I tell people I'm Russell Crowe's brother, that I'm the son of Robert Redford, that I'm Bruce Willis's baby brother. Not all at once, of course. That would be just plain stupid. And I don't do impersonations in a Matt Damon Mr-Ripley-goes-psycho way. It's not like that at all.

I'm not exactly truthful. But so what? Does it really matter?

I don't consider myself a con-man, that's too harsh a word for me and what I do. I don't swindle people out of money, I don't take what people can't spare. I accept gifts, but only in proportion to what my patrons — that's how I think of them, as patrons to my artistry — can afford.

No one is harmed, no one is pauperised. I'm charming and kind. I make people feel special. I bring glamour and excitement to their lives. Most of them will be able to live for years, even for the rest of their lives, off the tale of how they met Kevin Costner's younger brother or the son of Anthony Hopkins. People smile when they catch sight of me and continue smiling as I leave, hoping they'll see me again. They're all excited and happy. I make everyone so very happy.

And my relatives come out well. I give them free publicity — *good* publicity. I always say how wonderful they are, what a great mother Jessica Lange is, what a fabulous big brother Tom Hanks is, how lucky I am to have Gwyneth Paltrow for a sister.

It's what my public wants to hear. It's what I want to tell them.

I make them happy. And so the world goes round and round.

THE BORING TRUTH
(A BRIEF ACCOUNT)

I didn't grow up in Hollywood and I'm not related to anyone famous. (Except the Queen, although the link is a bit tenuous: she and I, along with millions of others and not just the Royal Family, are descendants of William the Conqueror.)

I'm from that jewel in the crown of suburban London known as Surbiton. (Or Surbiton, Surrey as the more refined like to point out, hoping to disassociate themselves from south-west Greater London and summon up pictures of healthy rural living, green fields, rolling hills and flower-strewn meadows.)

I'm not complaining. It's a lovely place despite the snide comments of urbanites and country-dwellers alike. It's a nice, safe, not unfriendly spot to live. It has the Thames, wide and relatively free of boats so there's plenty of room to practise your rowing or sailing or whatever takes your fancy. Hampton Court Palace is just across the river and the delightful Kingston-upon-Thames is only a mile or so up the road, providing a modest nightlife and all the shopping possibilities you could need.

My parents are good, decent folk. I wasn't abused or made to feel bad about myself, they gave me a pleasant upbringing. We weren't super-rich, nor we were super poor, we were in the middle. Middle-middle class, that's us.

At school I achieved reasonable but not outstanding results. I never had an inspirational *Dead Poets Society* teacher, but I can't grumble about my education.

My free time was filled with alternating months of Shakespearean recitals (I played Hamlet, Puck and Othello all in one year) and being lead guitarist and songwriter for the all-male band, Lesbians In Portugal. LIP for short. I was only fifteen when I came up with the name, and we thought we were being so funny, clever and witty when all we were being was pretentious with a rather unbecoming dress sense and a bizarre taste in hairstyles. Looking back, I'd say that LIP was a cross between Limp Bizkit and John Fogerty. Imagine that, if you dare.

And, even then, I wasn't doing it just for fun, though it *was* fun, I was doing it to make something of myself. I was going to ride the high road out of the nice but dull suburbia that surrounded my life like a fluffy white cloud, comforting and cosy but limited on fame opportunities. I thought I was unique. But now, from my lofty perspective of a few years ahead, I can see that I was only normal. How many teenagers do you know who have the same dreams? Every single one of them? Exactly.

But I was determined to make it. Laurence Olivier I wasn't, but I had natural talent and I was a quick learner. I had the necessary ingredients. I had potential. I was going to be famous. I was going to be marvellous. Bloody marvellous.

At university I worked hard, I really thought I was going somewhere. I acted on stage and wrote dozens of songs. I was going to be famous. I knew I was. Afterwards, my student years behind me, I moved to Wimbledon — four train stops closer to central London than Surbiton. Wow, what an adventurer. I got a job as a sales consultant selling insurance to multinational companies. We dealt in everything from the mundane to anything imaginable — I once arranged a policy to cover the life of a seahorse mascot against three specific kinds of fungal infection. It wasn't what I wanted to do, what I dreamed about, but it was okay.

My life was acceptable, more than

tolerable, but it became ordinary. I became ordinary. I was plain old Nick Reed the insurance salesman.

Yawn. Yawn. Big yawn.

I had only taken the position in insurance because I couldn't find anything more appropriate and because it satisfied my father. Most of all, it would pay my bills while I was waiting to be discovered.

I told myself I could pretend to be a salesman while I was working towards my real future. And, besides, any time spent as one was to be chalked down to experience. It would allow me to hone my acting skills and work on those emotions of sincerity, regret and friendliness no matter how I was feeling inside at the time. It would make me an expert at improvisation. 'Mumble, mumble, duck and swerve,' my colleagues and I called the response to an awkward question. 'Of course cover can be arranged,' we said aloud. Or, depending on the circumstances, 'I'm pretty sure it's covered. Better check the policy.'

I don't mean to sound conceited, but I know that I'm good-looking. I'd never admit it aloud, of course — I'm English, for goodness' sake — but I'm at the attractive end of the spectrum. (Especially under optimal lighting when seen from the left.) I've

18

got light brown hair that turns blond with a bit of sun, my eyes are a deep, dark blue, not the stunning azure I'd like, but they're not bad. My nose is neither too small nor too big. I'm tall but not too tall, I'm well built without being a body-builder. My skin, normally pale under the weak British sun, tans well with a bit of gentle coaxing.

My looks would have helped, if only I'd had that one big break.

While I was waiting for fame to find me I kept on acting, trying to get into the London fringe scene. I formed a new band and we played in pubs. I started writing a screenplay for a low-budget film I could produce and direct myself. At first it was easy to keep myself motivated. Yet as time passed I grew busy with work, playing football with my mates, going out on the town and socialising. It became harder to stay focused on my goals.

For six long years I was a salesman.

I kept telling myself that my experience would help, that as long as I made it before I was thirty I'd be okay. Now I'm in my late twenties, young enough to be called young, but old enough to have seen a bit of the world, and I still haven't made it. But I'm finally wise enough to face facts.

Being a purveyor of happiness is the nearest I'll ever get to fame. The nearest I'll ever be to living in that magical world of success, stardom and acclaim.

I'm never going to be famous. I've accepted that. I'm not glad about it, but that's the way it goes. I'm never going to be famous.

THE ROUTE TO ADVENTURE

So how did I end up where I am today?

The easy answer is to point to my redundancy as the turning point. No, I wasn't brave. I didn't sit at my desk until one day I experienced enlightenment and resigned in one big, flashy gesture. My pleasure at promotion to a cubicle with a window was a wake-up call, and I knew I had to do something, but even that didn't make me take action. I went to work the next day, adjusted the blind to keep out the sun, and got down to business.

I needed a good kick in the rear to change my life. When my company offered voluntary redundancy because it needed to cut the staff by a third, I knew that it was my last and only chance. If I didn't get out while I still could I would never escape: I would be there for another thirty years, moving to a bigger cubicle and maybe one day to an office of my own when enough people above me had retired or died.

That's what brought about my transformation. It was the one identifiable catalyst that separated the two phases of my life: Before the Lies and After the Lies.

Before the Lies I was boring. After the Lies I started living.

I wanted one last great adventure, a final fling to celebrate youth and frivolity before settling down to real life for good. And because I'd decided to have an adventure, I wanted an Adventure with a capital A.

Despite anything I might have implied to the contrary, this was never intended as a permanent career move. It's not something you could do for ever. Or not something *I* could do for ever. To live off lies properly I would have to stop being a purveyor of happiness and become a true con-man. And that's a whole lot more ruthless than I could ever be. I'm not greedy — well, okay, maybe I'm as greedy as the next person, but I'd never steal someone's life savings or swindle a granny out of her nest egg. I wouldn't want to do it. My calling is all about happiness, and that wouldn't make anyone happy.

My mother would be horrified if she knew what I've been doing.

For her sake I'd like to be able to say that this was all accidental, that I didn't have a devious plan in mind from the start, that becoming a purveyor of happiness was something I fell into, but that wouldn't be true. I knew exactly what I was doing. I even drew up a list of rules to follow so that I wouldn't be tempted to make foolish mistakes. Oh, I was so sure of myself, so cocky. I knew I could do it, I knew that nothing could go wrong. And it didn't. Not at first. Not when I lived and breathed the Rules.

THE RULES
(OR FRIENDLY HINTS AND INSTRUCTIONS FOR IMPERSONATING RELATIVES OF THE RICH AND FAMOUS)

1. Head straight to America. The British are too shy and self-contained to support you in the lifestyle you deserve. (Please note, this applies to everyone. If you are British or European or of any other nationality, go to the USA. If you are American, stay there. It's the ideal country in which to live the life of a purveyor. Luxury is readily available and Americans will talk happily to strangers.)
2. Don't make friends. Be friendly at all times but don't get too attached. All interaction and conversation has to be kept superficial.
3. *Never* stay in contact. Not even for a woman. You cannot get involved.
4. Have autographed photos of your most frequently used stars ready to hand out to those who support you most. These

are usually fairly easy to obtain: do a few searches on the Internet and shop around for the best prices. Sometimes you can even get them free.

5. Stay no more than two weeks in any one place. One week is better but two weeks is permissible.

6. Use your real name when hiring cars or flying. You don't want to do anything illegal, and the FBI would get pretty touchy if you start trying to board aircraft using fake IDs.

7. Charge nothing to your credit cards while you're working. They'll be in your real name unless you get hold of some fakes and, believe me, you don't want to go there. Authentic cards under false names are also out. (Figure it out for yourself. Hone that common sense: you're going to need it. The food and lodging might be free in prison, but that's not the kind of 'free' you're after.) You must, therefore, carry enough cash to cover any bill you run up in case you should be so unlucky as to have to settle it.

8. Exception to above credit card rule: when booking hotel rooms, phone ahead pretending to be the assistant of the relative. Use an American accent or, if that's not possible, at least an accent

different from your own. (Though do avoid mimicking the characters in *Trainspotting*, if you want to be understood.) Book room in the relative's name, always using the famous surname so the hotel reservations clerk will know instantly and can spread the word. If a credit-card number is needed, which it probably will be, give your real credit-card number in your own name. You are the assistant making this reservation for your employer. But don't worry: if you do your job right, it'll never be charged. Someone else will pick up the tab. And if it goes wrong, hey, well, there goes some of your savings, and you'll just have to work a bit harder next time, won't you?

9. Impersonate no more than one relative in any given location. (Don't get carried away. You're not training to become a pathological liar: you're there to do a job.)

10. Always do some basic research into your chosen relative's past and true family circumstances. You're not pretending to be a real-life son or brother, you're not impersonating an actual person, you never assume someone else's name, but you should double-check to make certain that he or she is not well known for being

an only child or for having no children. You can lie and cover up most things, but you should avoid glaring untruths that could make potential patrons uneasy or instantly suspicious. The Internet is a good source for basic information.

11. Don't accept any trips, jaunts or holidays that aren't instantaneous.

12. Make your patrons feel special.

13. As a purveyor of happiness, your job is to be smiling and cheerful at all times. You must spread joy and happiness — that's what you're being paid to do, even if others might not see it in quite the same way.

14. Never allow yourself to be photographed. Claim it's because you love your famous relative and don't want any photos of yourself to be used to embarrass him or her. Not that your patrons would do such a thing, of course, but there are all those people who develop the film. And photos can get lost. Think of additional excuses. You're going to need them.

15. Don't go where the celebrities are. That means no excursions to LA, Palm Springs, Aspen, etc. Or, at least, no working trips to such places.

16. Avoid people who might know the famous person or about their family. This

includes all celebrities, and those working in PR or the media.

17. Don't spread gossip, just say nice things about your famous relatives.

18. Get hotel, bar and restaurant employees on your side ASAP. They're great at spreading the word of your arrival and providing validation of your identity. In return for their hard work on your behalf, you must tip well. It's only fair. (Tips are the exception to rule 19.)

19. Pay for as little as possible. Always accept free meals, free outings, free lodgings (when safe, of course, but you should have a good, practical head on your shoulders to make judgements about such things).

20. If something goes wrong, leave immediately, without waiting for someone to pay your hotel bill, without saying goodbye. Settle your own account and slip away without fanfare.

21. Don't tell the truth to anyone. Not old friends. Not your real family — heaven forbid. Not new acquaintances.

22. Sell off unwanted presents for cash, for those times when you really need your own money.

23. Don't let the popularity go to your head. It's not really you they're crazy about.

24. Make no mistake, you'll work hard for your money. The hours are long and sometimes lonely.
25. Most importantly, remember that it's all about happiness. Yours, theirs, everyone's. It's what lifts us above the common con-man.

IN THE BEGINNING

Atlanta, Georgia, five months ago. I was fresh off the plane from England and Atlanta was my starting point, the gateway to the vast interior of a country I'd always longed to explore by car. My head was filled with romantic images of empty roads, five-litre engines and sunglasses worn because you have to, it's so bright, and not only because you're trying to look hip. I'd been to LA and New York on previous holidays, I'd done Orlando and the theme parks twice, but I wanted more this time. I wanted to capture the elusive spark and thrill of an American road trip for myself.

To finance this great expedition and keep myself in style I set off on my new career as a purveyor of happiness. I like to think of it as backpacking round the world for the more discerning traveller. Forget the gigantic rucksack, forget the budget hotels. It's plucking glasses of champagne and caviar from party trays rather than picking grapes under the blazing sun to keep you going.

I could have waited until I was settled in

— I could have pretended to myself that jet-lag was a good excuse — but I knew I had to get that first time out of the way. As soon as I got to the hotel, the lie I'd been repeating in my head, over and over for the last ten hours, found its way smoothly past my lips — and after that it was easy.

'May I help you?' asked the woman behind the desk.

I smiled at her, in instant charm mode. 'Yes, I have a room booked. The name's Nick Carrey.' Nick, my real name, short for Nicholas, of course, which I'd decided to stick with throughout my travels to make things less confusing for me.

'Let me just check our records,' she said, typing something into the computer in front of her. She frowned. 'Sorry, I can't seem to find the reservation. How do you spell your name?'

I spelt it and waited for her to pick up the bait. Would it work? Would it be that easy?

'C-A-R-R-E-Y,' she repeated after me. 'Ah, with two Rs.' She looked up and smiled. 'Like Jim Carrey?'

'Exactly like Jim Carrey.'

'Any relation?'

I knew that she was only mildly curious, asking the question because it had to be asked, because you never know, but I could

31

hardly disappoint her, could I? I was a purveyor of happiness, and my answer would make her very, very happy. I glanced to the left and right, flashed her a grin, then said in a low voice, 'He's my brother.'

At this revelation her smile turned into a megawatt beam, and she showed off those pearly whites like I was a casting director. 'Really?' she asked, in a dramatic whisper.

I shrugged like it was no big deal and managed to look a bit bashful. 'Yep.'

'Wow.' She looked at me, really looked this time, studying my face, searching for any resemblance. 'Jim Carrey's brother.'

She was no longer whispering and I knew she wouldn't be able to keep it to herself, but that's exactly what I wanted. It would be more believable if people heard the gossip about my identity from someone other than myself, and especially from a member of the hotel staff. That would give my name official confirmation and people wouldn't think to question it.

The woman was still studying me. 'But you're British,' she said.

This was the question I'd been waiting for. I'd thought long and hard, but decided that my skill at mimicking an American accent was limited. I could do an acceptable Cary Grant at parties, when everyone was really

32

drunk and less judgmental, but there was no way I could keep it up for days on end. I thought that being British while my famous relative was American helped my case: surely no one could think up such an outrageous lie. (The three weeks of judo class I attended last year taught me to convert my weaknesses to strengths. I like to think that although I walked away without a black belt — indeed, without any martial-arts skills at all — I left with a great new philosophy to apply to life and with every bone still intact.)

'Guilty as charged,' I said. 'Jim and I are half-brothers. My mother was British and I grew up there.' I had a more elaborate story prepared to answer further questions, but the woman behind the desk seemed satisfied.

She nodded. 'You know, I didn't think you looked anything like him at first, but now I can see that you've got the same cheekbones. It's amazing, it really is.'

Just for the record I look nothing like Jim Carrey. Other than having two eyes, ears, a mouth, a nose and, oh, yes, cheekbones. It's that human factor. Makes us all look so alike.

'And the ears,' I said, turning my head so she could see my profile. 'Jim and I have the same ears.'

She chuckled. 'I'll have to pay attention the next time I see one of his movies. I'm usually too busy laughing to notice his ears.'

'I know what you mean.'

'So, is Jim working on anything at the moment?'

'He's been on the set of his latest project for months. Shooting's supposed to be wrapping up soon, and if it finishes on schedule he's hoping to meet me here in Atlanta for a few days.'

She looked so excited that I almost expected her to burst into delighted giggles.

'And how many days are you planning on staying with us, Mr Carrey?'

'I asked my assistant to book five nights,' I said.

I'd decided on a short visit but not so short that I couldn't find someone to pay my bill. And to get someone to pay my bill I had to stay in the best hotels: however kind ordinary folk may be, the thought of paying for someone else's hotel room wouldn't cross their minds — particularly when they would assume I was much, much richer than they were.

She checked the computer again. 'I'm sorry, Mr Carrey, but I can't find anything in your name.'

'Perhaps it's under my assistant's name by mistake. His name is Reed.' (I'd followed Rule 8 when I made the reservation, holding the room with my real credit card.)

She typed this into her computer. 'Yes, here we are, we have a room booked for five nights for Mr N. Reed. You're listed as an additional guest. I'm so sorry, Mr Carrey. Please accept the hotel's apologies for the confusion. I'll put you in our best suite to make up for our mistake.' She flashed me a dazzling smile. 'At no extra charge, of course.' She called over a bellboy. 'Please escort *Mr Carrey* to the presidential suite,' she said, giving the bellboy an intent look.

She didn't ask for my credit card and that suited me perfectly. Unless I had to, I did not want to go into my carefully prepared tale of how I'd lost my wallet to explain why I had no cards in the name of Carrey. She had Mr N. Reed's details on file from when the booking was made, and the credit-card (my real name, my real card) was valid. I'd always vowed not to do anything illegal, and I'm not a thief. The room was going to be paid for one way or another, it's just I wasn't planning on footing the bill.

She smiled as she handed me the key. 'I hope you have a wonderful stay, Mr Carrey. Please call if there's anything you need.'

'Thanks,' I said. 'And I'll let you know if Jim needs a room.'

As soon as the elevator doors closed the bellboy turned to me and asked, 'Carrey?'

LEARNING MY NEW VOCATION
(IT'S LIKE BEING A SALESMAN: YOU JUST TELL THEM WHAT THEY WANT TO HEAR)

And it worked. All that planning and scheming and hours spent acting out scenarios in my head, practising the reactions and responses that would be expected from me as a celebrity's relative, had paid off. I'd passed the first test. I'd been believed.

I was Nick Carrey, Brother of Jim. And I'd been given a suite. (Luxurious, twice as big as my flat in Wimbledon, wonderful, just wonderful.)

It was the start of my glory days.

An hour later, I entered the hotel restaurant — I'd lingered in my suite to allow time for those rumours to spread. My arrival was truly an Entrance. It's not that they all knew instantly that I was the man they were waiting for, but there was an element of excitement in the air, electricity and eagerness in the way everyone was sitting up and watching that told me the hotel staff had been busy. They were waiting for someone.

I could only conclude that they were waiting for me. Waiting for the Brother of Jim.

The *maître d'* confirmed this for me when, on catching sight of me, he all but abandoned the wealthy-looking couple he was showing to their table and rushed at once to my side, beaming as he crossed the restaurant. (The receptionist must have given him a description.)

'Mr Carrey,' he said, not shouting, but loudly enough for some of the other diners to catch his words and swivel in their chairs to stare at me. A moment later everyone, even those who hadn't heard him, was aware of the commotion and knew that I was The One.

'Good evening,' I said, smiling, gracious, inclining my head as a good Relative of the Rich and Famous should.

He was closer now, quieter, his words for me and me alone, and no longer for the benefit of half the dining room. 'Mr and Mrs Davonport have requested the pleasure of your company at their table, should you care to join them.'

What else could I do? I nodded, smiled and accepted the invitation. I followed the *maître d'* across the room, carefully noting all the glances sent my way, judging every one a success, wanting to leap into the air and celebrate that it had worked. I'd been accepted. I'd been studied and found suitable. I'd been believed. But I allowed nothing of my joy to pass across my face. I was the epitome of the suave sophistication that should come with being the brother of a Hollywood star.

And so my first few days in America passed without a hitch. I was fêted and dined and would have been the belle of the ball if there'd been a ball and I'd been a woman. I was Mr Popularity, and I could do no wrong. I told jokes and they were always amusing. I cleared my throat and a drink was instantly offered by whoever was with me at the time. It only had to get near lunch- or dinner-time and I was besieged with offers of free meals.

It was fabulous. I was fabulous. Life was fabulous.

Superficial. Comfortable. Luxurious. Exactly what I wanted. Enjoying the benefits of fame without the pesky need for actually doing anything to earn or maintain that status.

What had been born as the whim of a late-night drinking binge a month before my redundancy had turned out to be the best thing I'd ever done. And who says alcohol isn't good for creativity? It obviously turned normal old Nick into a genius that night, and when opportunity had struck I'd had to see if my idea would work.

And it did. Five months of constant success were mine.

Until I met Holly and broke the Rules. Until I messed everything up.

WHEN I MET HOLLY

Holly. The stuff of instant infatuation and the only reason I'm at this crazy bounty-hunting school. (She's my reason, and Holly, well, she's not insane, this isn't her idea of a good time, she has a valid reason for being here. Unfortunately.) I've been smitten since the first second I saw her. She is 100 per cent gorgeous and there's something about that twinkle in her eye and her wicked sense of humour that makes me want to stay glued to her side.

I know the Rules state that I shouldn't get involved with anyone. I know I'm supposed to remain friendly but superficial, flitting here and there unfettered by past acquaintances. I know I'm allowed casual flings — a man like me who believes that happiness is the most important thing in life knows that celibacy is not good for the soul — but nothing serious. And I know I'm not supposed to remain in touch with the people I meet on any of my outings.

I understand that I can't maintain the façade of my identity for ever, that it's vital I change my name and head on to new places after a week or so.

I knew all that when I saw Holly sitting at that bar.

I knew that. I told myself to keep walking.

I should have kept walking.

I felt that instant attraction. I knew that she called to me physically. But I should never have stopped to talk to her. I should have known better. I *did* know better. I'm a professional. My job requires me to remain sensible and in control at all times, and allowing myself to talk to a woman I'd want to know in my old life wasn't sensible, however you look at it.

So why did I do it when I knew, even in that first instant, that I shouldn't?

I just couldn't help myself.

I've come up with a little test that will explain my actions once and for all. Imagine Liz Hurley. (Voted Most Sexy Woman in the Universe by me, but you can insert another name if that will make it more appropriate to your own personal taste. Perhaps Kylie Minogue, petite perfection, or Salma Hayek, a love goddess with a mind-blowing purr in her voice.)

Now, imagine yourself seeing a woman as gorgeous as Liz Hurley sitting less than ten feet away from you.

And she's sitting alone.

Next thing you know you're turning towards her, the word 'sensible' no longer in your vocabulary, and then you're meeting her. And liking her. (Self-evident, I know, but I'm trying to make things crystal clear here.)

Then imagine her liking you.

Your Liz Hurley turns out to be American and she's wonderful. Her voice is husky and sexy, and that accent, you've been hearing it all around you for months, yet hers is different somehow, American, yes, but it's as if hers is straight off the silver screen, embodying all the sexiness, fantasies and promises of Hollywood. And she seems to like you.

You know that you're hooked. It's impossible for you not to like her. It's impossible for you to walk away.

You talk, you get on really well. You know she's the one for you. Suddenly you find yourself thinking that commitment is desirable and you can't remember what all the fuss was about. All that fear of stability and monogamy seems like a bad dream, a nightmare forced on you by society because that's how young men are meant to feel. You know then that it's all a lie, that the clever ones have figured it out, that when you meet a woman like Liz Hurley, like Holly, you do anything and everything to keep her.

To make her yours.

I met her in Phoenix, but it could have been anywhere. It was at one of those ultra-deluxe resorts that always look lush and tropical, wherever they are in the world, even in the middle of the desert.

Holly was sitting alone at the poolside bar when I saw her. I fiddled with my Rolex in a daze, tempted, undecided. Then she looked up and our eyes met. I was lost. I had to meet her. I approached and asked if I could join her, my heart pounding in my chest, willing her to say yes.

And she did. I introduced myself as Nick. I didn't want her to know my full name. I didn't want to impress her with false credentials. I just wanted to talk to her. I wanted her to like me. I didn't want her eyes glazing over with images of fame and glory and the hope of meeting, actually meeting, Arnold Schwarzenegger if things went well.

I wanted her to see *me* when she looked my way, not Arnie's eyes, cheekbones or jaw superimposed on to my face. I wanted to be Nick. Just Nick.

She was cute and funny, flirtatious and sweet, vivacious and charming. She was the sexiest woman I'd ever met. It was too early to think about love, but I knew that she and I were meant to be. I bought her a drink. And then another.

Now back to the test. You and your goddess chat for an hour until some obsequious waiter comes along and spoils everything by calling you Mr Schwarzenegger. But your real-life Liz Hurley doesn't mind, she doesn't let it faze her, she's starting to feel she knows you by this time. You're no longer just Mr Schwarzenegger, you're not even Nick Schwarzenegger, not really, not quite: you're Nick now. Or nearly. (Remember she's not actually Liz Hurley, Holly's not used to associating with Hollywood stars — this is only an example.) You invite her to dinner and she says yes.

Holly said, 'Yes, I'd love to.'

And you chat for another hour, then two, and you both say you should clean up for dinner, that you should change, but neither of you wants to part. You end up having a casual meal at the resort's family restaurant so you needn't be separated for a moment.

It's like a dream.

And you're happy.

I knew I'd broken the Rules, that I'd smashed them, that they lay in smithereens at my feet and I was jumping up and down on the broken shards, but I didn't care. I wasn't going to waste time searching for a patron,

44

hunting for someone to pay my bills and treat me to dinner. I wanted to treat Holly to dinner. I didn't care about anyone or anything else.

Even that first night I wanted to tell her the truth, that I was not Nick Schwarzenegger but I was in fact Nick Reed. I longed to confess that I wasn't related to Arnie, but I knew I couldn't. It was too soon. I needed to give her time. A chance to get to know me.

But I *was* going to tell her. When the time was right I would. And then I'd have to retire from my career as a purveyor of happiness, but I was ready for that: I wanted to retire, to rejoin the real world. I wanted a lawn to mow every Saturday afternoon, if it meant Holly would share it with me.

And then, later, after dinner, after drinks, when we were on a moonlit walk, we kissed. We stayed up most of the night talking. Just talking and talking and kissing.

We met for breakfast, then had lunch together too. We explored the resort in the morning and she took me abseiling in the afternoon. She reminded me of a couple of my ex-girlfriends, only Holly was a hundred times more exciting. And sexier.

It was a glorious day. After dinner, when we were alone, outside, away from the hotel, away from everyone, and I was feeling mellow, relaxed, just happy to be alive and holding Holly's hand, she said, 'There's something I have to tell you.'

She had something to tell me?

'I haven't been honest with you,' she said.

Fantastic. That was great. If she'd been fibbing to me she couldn't hold my lie against me. Or not when she'd had time to calm down and think things through logically.

My second thought: Uh-oh. What hasn't she told me?

'I'm not here on vacation,' she said, lowering her voice. 'I'm working.'

'Working?'

'I'm a reporter.'

Gasp, shock, horror, disaster.

Rule 16 specifically states that I should avoid anyone working in the media. She was the last person I should have spoken to. I was doomed. We were doomed.

(It's not odd that this hadn't come up before. I'd purposely kept the conversation away from careers: I hadn't wanted to deceive her any more than I had to, and obviously she'd felt the same way. She'd not lied to me. She just hadn't told me what she did for a living. Like I'd not told her.)

I felt sick. My gut twisted and I was shivery and shaky inside and I didn't know what to do.

Holly must have misinterpreted the look on my face because she grinned and squeezed my hand. 'Don't worry. I'm not going to ask to interview your father. I don't do those kinds of articles.'

'Oh, right.' I laughed weakly. If only that was all I had to worry about.

'I'm a travel reporter,' she said. 'Freelance. For newspapers and magazines. Undercover, of course. I shouldn't even be telling you, but I felt guilty, like it was a dark secret I was hiding. But you're not allowed to say anything. Not to this resort. Not to any restaurant. No one can know who I am.'

'They try to bribe you?' I asked, aiming for a tone of nonchalance, pretending I didn't have a care in the world now that she'd reassured me she wasn't attempting to use me to get to Arnold. I adjusted my Rolex, feigning unconcern.

'Like you wouldn't believe. Free drinks, free meals, upgraded rooms. Spa sessions, massages, facials, the works.'

'Really? That sounds fun. I should try it.'

Okay, okay, so I should have withdrawn, kissed her goodnight, said I was leaving the next day and bidden her farewell. I should have ended it, but I couldn't.

So we continued talking and I found myself losing my heart and my mind to a woman I should never even have met. I ignored the alarm bells and decided instead to be flattered that she'd trusted me with the truth.

She liked me.

So I'm a sorry sucker. So what? You would have done it too. Your brain, like mine, would have sunk to trouser level and your heart would have overruled that brain anyway, wherever it was located.

I mean, my own Liz Hurley? Gorgeous, funny, charming and wonderful. And she *liked* me. What would you do? Exactly.

But it's not over. That doesn't quite explain why we're here, why Holly and I ended up in a bounty-hunting training school.

Or does it?

Imagine Liz Hurley — sexy, lovable, fabulous Liz Hurley — telling you she's going on a bounty-hunting training course as her next assignment.

What would you do?

I couldn't let her go alone. Not when she was looking up at me with those vulnerable puppy eyes. Not when she'd explained what she'd be doing. And why the hell is it legal?

Holly is my flesh-and-blood, touchable, knowable Liz Hurley. She's mine and I'm not going to let anything happen to her.

CONFESSION

No. Cut. Stop right there. I can't leave it like that. It might be the glossy, child-friendly explanation for why I chucked it all in and became a purveyor of happiness, but if I left it there I'd be lying. I know I've said I've got nothing against lying *per se*, and I haven't, but skimming over the facts and making me sound so bold and confident just doesn't sit right with me. It wasn't like that at all.

Oh, sure, the night I realised I was unhappy with my job and that I'd actually become an insurance salesman rather than being a man who merely worked in sales, I longed to do something dramatic. I wanted to make a grand gesture, be noble and brave, embrace passion and excitement. I wanted to be like Kevin Spacey's Lester Burnham in *American Beauty* and grab life by the balls, but I did nothing. It was outside influences that eventually spurred me on.

I'm not brave, I'm not noble; I'm just a bloke who wants to have a life he can be proud of. I want my deathbed to be like a poem. I want to look back on my time and be able to say, 'I have lived. I have truly lived.' I'd rather not die at all, but as I doubt I'll be able to come up with a way to avoid it — I'm no mad scientist so there'll be no last-minute experimentation with alchemical longevity drugs or cryogenics for me — I'll settle for the poem. I want to know that I lived a good life, fought a good fight, or whatever corny phrase is in vogue at the time. I don't want to live in a world where everything exists on a scale of grey. I want to smell the roses and the lilac, the lilies and the lavender fields. I want to feel alive and full of joy.

There's nothing wrong with that, is there? So what if it was one of the seven deadly sins that goaded me to action? So what if it was only jealousy — pure unadulterated envy — that finally made me do something? I did it, didn't I? And that, when it comes down to it, is what counts.

THE BEGINNING OF THE END
OF ORDINARY

That day a month before my redundancy was a day just like any other when my boss, Nigel, called me into his office and told me I was being promoted. 'Congratulations, Nick. Your quarterly sales figures are the highest in the company,' he said, shaking my hand in a firm, managerial manner. 'We're so impressed with your performance that we're making you a Grade Eight.'

Wow. That was really something. And I'm not being sarcastic when I say that. I'd been a Grade Seven for less than a year and hadn't been expecting a promotion, even though recently I'd made some complicated and lucrative deals. I was suitably enthusiastic and all smiles when Nigel told me my new salary and led to my new cubicle. A new cubicle that was larger, more private, and had the coveted window. (The cubicle had been vacant for two days after Duncan had left to work in Australia, and we'd all been speculating about who would get it.)

But, no, I did not see that window and

instantly lose my smile. I did not see the sad irony in my smug self-satisfaction that I was doing so very well for myself. On the contrary, my smile widened. I was happy. I'd been given the window cubicle. How could I not be happy? Wasn't I such a success?

After work I went out drinking with my colleagues. It wasn't a spur-of-the-moment celebration of my good fortune, just coincidence that my promotion happened to occur on the same day as our weekly Thursday-night pub crawl — but I felt like I was celebrating anyway.

Well, one pint followed another, as it does, and I was in love with the world and everyone in it when I caught a cab back to my flat in Wimbledon. I unlocked the door, switched on the lights and stumbled to the sofa with a silly grin on my face. I yawned and stretched, twisted my head to the side, and then I saw it. My guitar sat in the corner of the room. It was dusty and neglected and I hadn't strummed so much as a chord in weeks. I probably couldn't even get my fingers into a Gm7 any more. My smile fell.

I hadn't been celebrating a recording contract or a part, however small, in a film or a play. No, my triumph of the day had been nothing like that. Life wasn't working out as I'd planned. Yes, I had a decent job and I was good at it, and most people would have been thrilled to be where I was that day, but it wasn't what I'd always wanted. I'd only been working to pay the bills while I waited for my real life to start. But somehow I'd forgotten that.

I was living Plan B.

I can't pinpoint an exact moment when I had given up on my dreams, when I'd accepted that the suit and tie were mine, that I would never have glory or fame or make a difference to the world, but I had. I was just like everyone else, after all. I was ordinary, one of the many. Responsible, respectable, reliable, resigned to the way things were, accepting without complaint the hand fate had dealt, I'd become complacent, focused on daily pleasures at the expense of grand plans. I was turning into my father.

I sat on the sofa and stared at my guitar. I didn't stalk to my bedroom in disgust, or go to that corner, pick up my guitar and start work on a new song. I brooded.

My eyes roved over the frets, the strings, the tuning keys, and I wondered which riffs I'd be able to play without stumbling. Ten minutes later, perhaps twenty or thirty, my flatmate returned home.

'Hey, Nick,' said Richard, slurring, grinning, inebriated. 'Good night?'

'I got promoted.' My voice was grim.

Richard collapsed on to the chair opposite me. 'And that's a bad thing?'

'I don't want to be a corporate worker for the rest of my life,' I said.

' 'Course not. You're going to be a rock star.'

'No, I'm not.'

'What?' Richard's grin faded. 'But you've always wanted to be a musician.'

'And I'm never going to be one. I'm a failure. I might as well end it all right now. I'd save myself the misery of getting old and having to look back on the glory days of my youth and remember the night I celebrated because I got promoted to a cubicle with a window.'

'A window? I've always wanted a window,' said Richard. 'That's great.'

'Yeah. Great.'

Richard stared at me, then stood up. 'If we're going to have this conversation I need a beer. Want one?'

'Sure.' A beer would dull the pain. 'I might as well drink my sorrows away.'

Wisely, Richard ignored me and returned from the kitchen with two cans. He passed me one and I opened it, took a long drink. 'I don't want to sell insurance policies for the rest of my life,' I said.

'Well, what about that screenplay you wrote?'

'No one in the industry wants to read it. I'm obviously not cut out to be a writer.'

'Then what are you going to do? What do you want to do?'

'I want to be a rock star or a movie star, but that's not going to happen. It's time for me to face up to reality. I've worked hard at it, but I'm not going to get that lucky break. And my film studies degree hasn't helped. I just have to accept defeat and tell my father he was right. It was all a waste of time.' I had another drink of beer. 'You know, they always say that if you work hard at something you'll succeed, but that's a load of bollocks. Just think about it for a moment. Fame, success, wealth. We all want those things, but not everyone can have them or there'd be no need for the words. Or if the words still existed the dictionary definitions would be different. What would fame, success or wealth be if everyone had them? They'd be the average, and then we'd all be back to square one.'

'So you're saying a good job and a great salary isn't enough? That it doesn't mean you're successful?' asked Richard.

'I don't want logic. I know my life sounds good on paper. I've just been made a Grade

Eight. Whoopee. But I don't want to be a Grade Eight. I want to be unique, special. You don't get the Mozarts, the Shakespeares and the Marlon Brandos of this world having to suffer the indignity of being categorised by a grade number. If everything worked that way, where would geniuses be? Would they have to work their way through the ranks, or would the great and good jump in somewhere near the top, say at Grade Thirty or Forty? The highest you can be in my company is a fifteen. And that's the MD. So where does that leave me?'

'Half-way to the top.'

I shrugged, took another sip of beer. 'Half-way to the top of a sales career.'

'If you don't want to be a salesman and you've given up the idea of music and films, what are you going to do?' Richard watched me and had a drink from his can.

I sighed. 'I don't know. That's the problem. And I don't think flipping through the employment pages of the *Evening Standard* will give me any ideas. I want to do something amazing.'

'You could always start working on your dotcom idea again.'

'The timing's all wrong. It's not so easy to make a quick fortune now. And, besides, I'm fed up with desks and offices. I don't want to slog my guts out in front of a computer screen. I want more. I want to be Indiana Jones.'

'You want to be an archaeologist? But you're allergic to dust.'

'No, not an archaeologist. I want to be suave and savvy and have lots of adventures. And I want to be the hero.'

Richard laughed. 'Oh, that's easy then. What's the going rate for a hero these days? A thousand pounds a week to strut your stuff? And does the job come with a cape or do you have to supply your own?'

I smiled, relaxing for the first time since I'd seen my dusty guitar. 'You know what I mean.'

'You, Nick, are an idealist. You want everything.'

'No,' I said, 'I've just been thinking a lot about death since my grandmother died last month. I don't want to spend my life wishing I'd been daring and bold. I want to do something, be something.'

'Let me get this straight. You want adventure, excitement, success, fame, and money, presumably?'

'Not necessarily. I just don't want to be ordinary.'

'Maybe you need a new girlfriend. Sexual withdrawal's a nasty thing. It can do a man's head in.' He grinned. 'Or so I've heard.'

I snorted. 'It's only been three weeks since Georgina and I split up. I think I can cope with the deprivation.'

'You could always tell her you've changed your mind and want to move in together. I wouldn't hold it against you. I could find a new flatmate. Maybe I'd get a girl who'd watch TV in her nightie.'

'And you could offer her sexual favours in exchange for her doing all the cooking and cleaning.'

Richard nodded, his eyes alight with possibility. 'Maybe you should move in with Georgina.'

'I'm not feeling this way because of her.' We'd only been going out for six months when she said she wanted to live together or end our relationship. She was way too serious for me so we broke up. 'I just want to do something different with my life before it's too late.'

'You could dive for pearls and make your fortune,' said Richard, giving up trying to reason me out of my mood. 'Or mine for diamonds. There's a programme on one of the Discovery Channels called *Treasure Hunters*. We could watch that for ideas.'

'I don't want to be tied down to one place. It might get boring after a few months.' I took a sip of beer. 'I could be a mercenary instead. Or a bodyguard'

We both burst out laughing. 'But you've never been in a real fight,' he wheezed. 'And you want someone to hire you to protect them — or blow up a bridge or something?'

'Okay, okay, not a mercenary or a bodyguard. I could become one of those men who get hold of things for people, like hard-to-find gems, rugs or antiquities, things like that.'

'Or you could become a helicopter pilot and spend your days taking billionaire tourists on luxury chopper rides in dangerous but scenic areas of the world.'

'I could be a racing car driver or a courier for the rich and famous and spend my days flitting from airport to airport.'

A few minutes later we were laughing and joking and I was feeling better if not content with the way things were. Eventually we said goodnight, and it was only when I was on my own, lying in bed and staring at the ceiling, that I had my one moment of genius: I came up with the idea of becoming a purveyor of happiness.

I'd like to be able to say I went in to work the next day, resigned and set off on my new-found path, but I've already admitted that I did nothing. I went to work, adjusted the blinds, picked up the phone and got back to selling.

So if that didn't do it, what made me take up that offer of voluntary redundancy? It doesn't make sense, does it? If I didn't do it immediately, why did I give up my job a month later? Why would a reasonably successful man renounce his career just like that to become a drifter on a bizarre extended working holiday?

The day before the redundancy offer an article in *The Times* caught my eye.

William Templeton, bully, cheat and downright bad egg in an otherwise good school, had just made £22 million after he'd floated his electronics company on the Stock Exchange. William Templeton, the man behind the boy who'd made our lives hell, was now retiring to Bermuda — in his twenties. He'd worked hard for a few years and now he had the rest of his life to enjoy himself. He could tell people what he'd achieved and they'd all pat him on the back and say, 'Well done,' like he'd accomplished a miracle. He'd been a bastard as a boy and I can imagine he's a bastard still, though I have no proof.

If I'd thought of him at all in the intervening years, it was to picture him as poverty-stricken, bloated and old before his time. It was what he deserved to be: fat, grey and unhappy, sitting on a lumpy, faded sofa in a dingy room watching TV, day after day after day. Sitting on his sofa wearing a string vest stained with food and sweat marks that he hadn't bothered to change in weeks. He'd have seventeen children screaming, fighting and swarming through his crumbling house. And another on the way. His heavily pregnant wife would yell at him, maybe even hit him, and she would be the one to rule the house with an iron fist. William would sit there, watching TV and dreaming of his youth when he dominated the schoolyard. He would sit there in silence and his wife would bully him. His car would be perched on bricks in the front garden, without tyres, without a windscreen, ruined, vandalised — not because it was nice to start with, just because it was there — never to be driven again.

Not to go on, but it's what he deserved. A childhood spent terrorising others should earn a man a miserable adulthood. It's only fair. It's only just.

But William Templeton is not sitting in his sweaty string vest with a beer belly the size of a small dog. No. He's in Bermuda buying a secluded mansion with his supermodel wife.

Supermodel wife. I went straight out and bought a copy of *Vogue* — never wasted on a

61

single guy — to verify the article's claims of her beauty. And there she was. She was gorgeous.

William Templeton is the reason I'm here. William Templeton and his supermodel wife. If he could have a good life, an extraordinary life, I wanted one too.

My boss tried to talk me out of redundancy but, in the end, he couldn't refuse my request as there hadn't been enough volunteers. I allowed myself a week between resignation and leaving for America. Any longer, and I knew I'd get cold feet and end up back in Wimbledon. Or, worse, stuck in my old bedroom at my parents' house in Surbiton because Richard would have found a Scandinavian exchange student to take my place in the flat an hour before I decided to stay.

And just like that I was out of a job, out of my flat and out of the country. I had become a purveyor of happiness but I was under no delusions. I knew I couldn't live off my freebies for ever, but I wanted to do it for a year, maybe two. I just wanted to be able to say that I'd done something exciting in my life.

Then I met Holly and she's so wonderful that I didn't mind that those days were over. I still don't, Holly's worth it — but now that we're at the bounty-hunting training school it's like we've entered some sort of alternate reality. It almost feels like we're in a film. For how can this be the real world? How could I have ended up training to become a bounty-hunter? I'd rejected the idea of becoming a mercenary because I knew my very first client would shoot me in the head in disgust at my incompetence. Is the presence of a woman I fancy going to turn me into a top-notch action man? I don't think so.

So there we have it. An early mid-life crisis led me to America, which led me to Holly, who led me to Ted's classroom.

I'll just concentrate on the film imagery. I'll need it to fill my head with visions of victory if I want to be a hero. If I want to pretend to be a hero. Just picture that swelling music, Nick, keep your back proud and straight, and you might just squeak by. Don't wait for the music warning of danger to tell you that everyone is doomed before you act or it'll be too late.

And if this is one of those movies where everybody dies, at least I've had five great months of adventure and excitement. Not long enough, not nearly long enough, but it's a better way to go than having a heart-attack while making a cold sales call on the day you finally make it to Grade Twelve.

REMEMBERING THE GLORY DAYS: BEACH BABES AND INSTANT POPULARITY (THANKS GOLDIE)

Oh, glory days. Oh, happy days.

It'd be impossible for me to choose just one impersonation from my months of fun to pick as the best, but the week I spent on the beach near Sarasota, Florida, has to rank near the top.

It's a time I'd like to remember until my dying breath. I could have spent the next three, four, five, even six years of my life in that place, with those people, with everything remaining the same: it was that good. I was tempted to stay longer, but back then, when everything was fresh and new, I was still wise, religiously following the Rules, and Rule 5 states specifically that one can stay no more than two weeks in any one place. One week is better but two weeks is permissible. (The longer one stays, the greater the odds of being exposed as a fraud.)

If I could think of a way to tell the story to my friends back home and make it sound realistic, while skipping over the fact that everyone thought Goldie Hawn was my half-sister, I would. But I don't think a yarn like that would work. Without the Goldie factor no one would believe that I was the star of the beach. Without Goldie I *wouldn't* have been the star of the beach. Oh, sure, I would have had fun, I would have made friends, I would have had a good time, but being Nick Reed is not the same as being Nick, Brother of Goldie. Of course it isn't. Being Goldie's baby brother meant beach babes and instant popularity. Thanks, Goldie. You're a gem. (I'd like to write and tell her how much everyone loves her, but without explaining how I know that she's universally adored, it'd be just another gushing fan letter, so what's the point?)

From Atlanta I headed straight to the Florida beach. I shed my identity as the Brother of Jim Carrey as I checked out of the first hotel and assumed the mantle of Brother of Goldie Hawn as I arrived at the next. It was midnight when the porter finally showed me to my suite and I was tired so I went straight to bed. I woke early the next morning, excited about what the day would bring. I was no longer shackled to my cubicle and life had regained its zest. I was happy. It was all so simple back then when I followed the Rules.

Before the day's proper work began I went for a long jog on the beach, running barefoot along the edge of the sea, letting the waves splash against my calves, feeling free and so alive. As I ran I thought of another maxim to add to my list. Rule 26: look after yourself and keep your body fit. A purveyor of happiness does not have to be a sex god or goddess, or reach Hollywood standards of perfection: you are, after all, a mere mortal or you would have taken that fame route in the first place. But you must pay attention to your appearance. If you're decent-looking in your own right, you're that much easier to believe. And it'll only take a few minutes of excited basking in your presence and sharing in stories about your famous relative for your new companions to realise you're not merely attractive, you're gorgeous, sexy and oh-so-shaggable.

As it was my first day at a new location, I spent the rest of the morning lounging by the hotel pool, dividing my time between the shaded and sunny areas, not wanting to turn into a sunburnt lobster-impersonator only hours into my début as the Brother of Goldie. I'd yet to acquire the playboy tan that better suits my image, but those few days in Atlanta and a couple of visits to a tanning salon while I was still in England had given me a sun-kissed look, so I wasn't out of place.

I knew I had to establish myself, get my identity known so that the freebies would begin. That's the hard part: once the word has spread and people know who you are they come to you. Get the gossip started as soon as you can: you can't very well *ask* a perfect stranger for a free drink. A con-man asks for things. A true relative would never do that. They'd just graciously accept what's freely given. And that's what I do — did.

My patrons were always delighted to buy me food and drinks, to give me gifts, what they saw as little tokens of affection so that I might remember them and possibly, just possibly, think to mention them to my mother or father, brother or sister. Everyone likes to think that someone important in Hollywood might hear his or her name.

They were happy, I was happy, everyone was so very happy. No one was ever grumpy or rude when I was near. I was the ultimate pick-me-up. I could have been patented as a cure for depression. Okay, okay, maybe not. My particular charm wouldn't have worked for the clinically depressed, but I could have revived those with flagging spirits, given them hope and joy to carry on. I would have cheered them up, if only during the time they were talking to me.

The poolside bar opened mid-morning and I was tempted to rush right over and get a drink (it was hot and I was thirsty), but I knew I had to wait until it was crowded so that as many people as possible would hear my name and see my face. While I was waiting, I watched a trio of bikini-clad babes frolic in the shallow end of the pool and the minutes flew by. I was thoroughly entertained, wanting nothing more than to join them but knowing I couldn't. It's not just about lust and popularity, it's about finding patrons to pay your way before you can even think about mixing pleasure with business. Finally, I judged that the bar was busy enough and I strolled over, with a gait that was not conceited but proud and confident and declared to the world that I was a man to be reckoned with. (These are my memories so I'm allowed to coat everything with a golden tint and say how wonderful everything was, including me.)

'I'll have a martini, please,' I said to the bartender when he turned my way, 'and could you add it to my room tab?'

'Sure thing,' he said. 'What room are you in, sir?'

'The Roosevelt Suite,' I said.

The bartender stopped what he was doing, looked at me and smiled. 'You're Goldie Hawn's little brother?'

Ah, the joy of hotels and the reliability of the staff in spreading the word of my arrival.

I smiled, nodded, offered him my hand. 'I'm Nick.'

'It's great to meet you,' he said. 'I'm Paul. I'm a huge fan of your sister.'

'I'm sorry to interrupt,' said a woman in her forties, 'but did he say you're Goldie Hawn's brother?' Her voice rose excitedly as she spoke, and more than a handful of people glanced our way.

I shrugged. Bashful. 'Yes, I'm her half-brother. Same father, different mothers.' Inwardly I was thinking, Yes, yes, yes. It was working. I wouldn't have to let my name slip out 'accidentally' to get the ball rolling.

'Wow.' She pumped my hand up and down. 'I love Goldie. You tell your sister we all love her. Tell her that she's a credit to women everywhere.' She turned to Paul the bartender. 'I'm buying him a drink.'

'Nonsense,' I said. It's always good to throw in a token protest. 'You don't need to do that.'

'I insist. I'll buy you a drink, and then you won't mind me talking your ear off about how wonderful your sister is. I'm sure you get this all the time.' She smiled and held out her hand. 'Let's start again and do this properly. I'm Mary Winterton.'

'Pleased to meet you,' I said. 'I'm Nick.'

And just like that I'd found my first patron of the week. We stayed at the bar for an hour, chatting about this and that well about Goldie and Goldie's movies really, and how Mary Winterton's favourite Goldie films were *The First Wives Club, Housesitter* and *Overboard*, but that all of them were great. We kept coming back to how much Mary loved each and every hair on Goldie's blonde head. It was not a particularly stimulating conversation but, then these things never are. It's all about happiness. I was happy, she was happy, we were all happy.

It was then that Rule 27 occurred to me: when you're choosing your famous relative, pick only those stars you really, really like. It's much easier to gush about them and agree with your patrons that, yes, she is so very beautiful, or that, yes, he was wonderful in *Gladiator* when you admire them too. The celebs who first pop into your mind when you decide to do this are people for whom you feel an instinctive fondness so it's not normally a problem. Just keep in mind that you will be talking about your mother or your father, your brother or your sister over and over and over again. Fortunately I realised this while I was on the second leg of my journey and as I'm a fan of both Jim Carrey and Goldie it was never a hardship to talk about them. In actuality it was fun, especially back then when it was all so new to me. And it was my job too. It's what was expected. It's what I was being paid to do. It was easy.

An hour later, an invitation to dinner with Mary and her husband duly accepted, three drinks down and twenty new acquaintances under my belt as the Brother of Goldie, I bid farewell to my bar friends and went for a swim in the pool. As I walked barefoot across the path I could see people turning to watch me. Word had spread further. Game, set, match. I was in.

And when I waded into the pool, which luscious women should approach me? Why, the trio of babes I'd seen earlier. Life was grand. I was so happy not to be selling insurance policies to companies concerned with protecting their shipping cargoes from rare stink-beetle infestations. This was all so much better. I wasn't a rock star, I'd never be a rock star, but I was having the time of my life.

'We heard you were Goldie Hawn's brother,' said the beach babe in the tiny blue bikini, twirling a long strand of auburn hair around her finger.

My libido rocketed into warp speed. Fortunately I favour loose swimming trunks rather than skin-tight Speedos. 'I'm Nick,' I said.

'I'm Julia,' said the beauty. 'This is Lisa.' She indicated the blonde in the red bikini.

'And I'm Cathy,' said the blonde in the green bikini.

'Hi.' My smile widened. 'It's a pleasure to meet you.' And it was. That was certainly no lie.

'We're organising a volleyball game down at the beach, and wondered if you'd like to play on our team.' Julia gazed at me hopefully.

And what could I do? I couldn't be cruel and deny them my presence. That would make them sad. It was my duty to make them happy. So I agreed and off we went towards the beach, chatting about Goldie and her movies.

The afternoon passed as afternoons do when you're young and single and a purveyor of happiness. I played beach volleyball and it was fabulous. Not that I was the only male among a bevy of beauties, but I was one of the group. I was popular. I'd acquired instant friends without even trying. Strictly speaking, I suppose I should have spent more time finding patrons, but I'd already acquired a dinner invitation and this was a holiday, albeit a working holiday, so I was entitled to enjoy myself as long as my work didn't suffer. And, besides, all my new volleyball buddies knew about Goldie. I could count on them to spread the word. It's natural for people to want to brag about their new mate, the Brother of Goldie. Everything was going according to plan.

When I said reluctantly that I had to leave as I had plans for dinner, Julia looked so sad that I didn't have the heart to deny her for long. I made arrangements to meet her for a late drink.

Dinner with the Wintertons was lovely — or it was after that first split second had passed and I knew by their welcoming faces that they hadn't found out the truth, that they weren't going to call me a liar.

They were an attentive audience as I regaled them with endless tales of the adventures my dear sister and I had had together: shopping excursions in the souks of Istanbul, a cruise down the Nile when I was twelve, a masked ball in Venice, Goldie teaching me to ride horses, Goldie visiting me three or four times a year in London. Then there was that time she surprised burglars in the house and managed to sweet-talk them into leaving without taking so much as a spoon, and they had driven away feeling guilty and ashamed that they'd broken in. The stories went on and on and I was able to recycle the things I'd made up in Atlanta about my life with Jim Carrey, altering them as needed to fit in with my new relative.

(The trick is to pretend to yourself that you're an actor and that this is your starring role. That's what I used to do when the stories became repetitive. If I had become an actor on the London stage, I would have had to say the same lines night after night. I didn't allow myself to become bored when talking about my famous relatives and our lives together. It was just part of the job.)

'I was looking through some old family photo albums last week,' I said. 'There were all these pictures of my sister when she was in high school. Did you know that she was not only Homecoming Queen but also the president of the student council? And she considered a career in the diplomatic corps in case the acting didn't work out.' I had no idea what Goldie had done in high school, or what career alternatives she'd considered, but it didn't matter: my patrons just needed to hear things that might be true. As long as what I said was believable my imagination was allowed free rein.

'And she did all her own stunts in *Bird on a Wire*. She and Mel Gibson became great friends and he's still a regular guest at dinner.'

Mary and her husband drank their wine, their faces flushed and excited as they listened to me, commenting occasionally.

'My sister's an incredible dancer. Ballet, ballroom, modern, you name it, she can do it. The tango's her favourite.'

'I like dancing too,' said Mary. 'I never knew Goldie did.'

'She's always loved it.' I lowered my voice confidingly. 'In fact, she's working on a new script with Bette Midler and Diane Keaton at the moment. I can't tell you what it's about, but it's going to be phenomenal. And don't be surprised when the movie comes out to see my sister dancing like you've never seen her dance before. She'll probably direct it too. And Bette might produce it, but she hasn't decided yet.'

Dessert came and still the tales continued. Goldie this, Goldie that. They couldn't get enough of her.

'What do I do? Oh, I scout movie locations for some of the big studios,' I said, answering Mary's query. 'I'm always on the lookout for houses, hotels, shopping areas, interesting buildings, streets, anything that might look great on screen.'

When the bill came I refused to allow the Wintertons to pay for the meal, but they were so persuasive that I had to give in gracefully. That's the best way to handle these things: initial protest then gracious acceptance. They wanted to meet me for drinks the following afternoon, and who was I to refuse them? They were my patrons, it was what I was there for.

After dinner I headed to my rendezvous with Julia. On the way I stopped to buy some condoms — you never know, and it's best to be prepared. Unfortunately, the only packet left was a novelty variety pack, a lucky-dip box where every condom is wrapped in the same colour foil and you don't know what you'll get until it's opened, and by then it's too late. Knowing they were in my pocket threw me off my stride and I spent the rest of the evening worrying about what would happen if we did go to bed. We might end up with a glow-in-the-dark condom. That would be fine. But what if we withdrew one from the box and unwrapped it to find it decorated with little mouse ears and a nose 'to add that extra dimension of play to the bedroom'?

I should have been enjoying Julia's company. I did enjoy it, but the novelty pack made me postpone things until the next day. Laughter is all very well in the bedroom, but not on your first night. Then you want things to go according to plan. And at least she thought I was a gentleman when I bade her goodnight with just a kiss.

The next morning, I went to a larger store and stocked up with a few standard packs so it wouldn't happen to me again. I had a great week in Florida. Julia was so very accommodating. We even tried out that novelty box.

On my last day, when I went down to the beach to say a silent farewell to the ocean, as I always do, I couldn't stop smiling. It was early, barely mid-morning when I was finishing my stroll, but already the beach was crowded with sun-worshippers.

'Nick. Nick. Hey, Nick,' called a breathless female voice from behind me that I recognised as Julia's. 'Wait up.'

Unable to ignore such a plea (no male could), I stopped and turned, pushing up my brand-new sunglasses as I waited. (Thanks for the Ray-Bans, Mrs Winterton, it was really so kind of you and, yes, I'll be certain to tell my sister all about you and your delightful yacht that she's welcome to use any time.)

Julia, dressed as always in a skimpy bikini, was racing across the sand. She was clasping a sunscreen bottle and one arm was still covered in the stuff, all white and greasy.

It was wonderful being popular.

'I just wanted to say goodbye,' she said, coming to a halt beside me, her eyes sparkling, her cheeks flushed becomingly. 'I know we said 'bye last night, but I wanted to wish you well.'

'Thanks,' I said. (I've never claimed to be witty. Fortunately, a purveyor of happiness just has to smile a lot and be friendly: everyone already likes you so you don't have to be funny for people to think you are. They're predisposed to think you're wonderful.)

'It was great getting to know you.'

'And you,' I said, smiling. It's easy to be polite when you're speaking the truth. She was a babe. Of course I was glad to know her.

Julia kissed me on the lips, then the cheek and stepped back. 'Goodbye, Nick.' Then she smiled and laughed. 'I can't believe I've slept with Goldie Hawn's brother.'

My smile slipped a little. Ah, yes. The Goldie factor. I wondered if Julia would even remember my name in a few weeks' time or if I'd been rechristened for ever in her mind as Goldie's Brother. Star-shagger. Bet she won't even remember what I look like soon, I thought.

But then it hit me. Did it matter? One doesn't normally recall much about holiday shags: name, face, height, body, all that slips away, fading into the cracks in one's memory until the temporary lover becomes just part of an excellent holiday. Julia and I will both think, Wasn't Florida great? And at least she'll remember me, even if she's recalling the Goldie factor and not me at all.

I kissed her again and I wasn't sad to leave — Julia and I didn't have that kind of relationship. She smiled and waved, then ran back to her two friends. (They weren't as close as I'd originally hoped but, hey, one beach babe is enough: two or three is greedy.)

My smile was back in place and I walked on. I nodded, greeted the people I knew, waving to those too far away for words, meeting yet more of Goldie's fans. Everyone knew who I was, and being Americans they weren't shy about letting me know it. They all wanted to share in that Goldie magic.

'Nick,' called a man who'd bought me lunch the day before, 'call me if you want those tickets.'

'Front row to see the Dolphins? You know I do.' And I did. I would have killed to see the Dolphins play. I would have liked to sit in the front row and hear all those grunts and groans and watch the cheerleaders bounce around and jump up and down at close range, but I couldn't. It was a pity, it really was, but the game was three weeks away, and I never allowed myself to accept tickets to things that weren't happening immediately: Rule 11 forbade it.

'Well, call me,' he said, 'and I'll arrange something.'

'I'll do that,' I said, knowing I never would.

And then I continued walking down the beach, greeting my fans but not lingering with anyone.

'Hi, Nick, don't forget to stop by and see us next time you're in Cape Cod.'

'How ya doing, Nick?'

'Nick, thanks for joining us at dinner the other night. It really meant a lot to me that you met my daughter and gave her all that advice about Hollywood. I really appreciate it.'

'Will I see you in Paris next month?'

'Don't forget to call, Nick. You've got our number. Any time you want to stay at our place in the Caymans you're more than welcome.'

And on and on and on.

It was a week I'll remember for ever, the sort of dreamtime every man longs to have: beautiful women, friends everywhere, I'd had it all. I was popular. I was loved. I knew it wasn't me they loved: it was the idea of me, the whiff of glamour and fame surrounding me not for myself but for a quirk of fate and a clever mind.

But still. It's always fun to be popular. And I loved being loved. It's only human nature.

AND JUST WHAT WILL HOLLY
THINK, EH, NICK?

Suddenly I feel a flush sweep across my face and I feel deeply, thoroughly guilty. Holly's going to hate me. I'm not fool enough to tell her everything I got up to during my purveyor days when I'm eventually able to reveal the truth about who I really am. I'll leave out the likes of Julia, but Holly's an intelligent woman, she might realise the potential that rests in every purveyor of happiness. Holly's going to see me as a seedy womaniser, using lies to entice women into my bed.

It wasn't like that, really it wasn't. Julia was the sort of woman I'd have shagged on holiday anyway. Oh, all right, the sort of woman I dreamed about shagging on holiday. Maybe if I hadn't been pretending to be the Brother of Goldie Julia might have picked someone hunkier or richer, but I would have slept with someone. I was never a monk. I've never claimed to be.

Besides, all that happened before I met Holly. It didn't mean anything and I'm sure

Julia's shagged plenty of men who weren't related to anyone famous. It was just one of those things. But I can't tell Holly that. She'd hate me. And I do not want Holly to hate me.

I'll have to come up with some other things to confess to when I tell Holly the truth, so that she won't think about what I might have done — what I did.

HOW TO TRAVEL FOR PRACTICALLY NOTHING, OR DRIVEAWAY, TRANSPORT FOR MISERS LIKE ME

If I couldn't fly on a fake name, I couldn't hire a car on one either. I worked all that out in Rule 6 when I decided that the FBI wouldn't like it. And if the FBI wouldn't like it, I wasn't going to do it. This means, this *meant* — I suppose I should be thinking of all this as the past now that I've met Holly and I'm planning to give it up — that if I wanted to travel anywhere I had to use my real name. That, I'm sorry to say, entailed spending my own hardearned money: savings, redundancy pay, that last month's salary I hadn't squandered on rent, food and alcohol.

Selling off small gifts like aftershave, jewellery, fancy pens or designer-brand beach towels given to me on my travels could only keep me in pocket money. It couldn't finance my wheels. Not counting accommodation costs, which would — hopefully — be covered by patrons or highly discounted by the hotels I graced with my presence, transport was my one big expense. Even if I had the money or the inclination to pay a rental-car company a small fortune for the privilege of driving one of their cars across the country, it was impossible. As a professional purveyor of happiness I couldn't be associated with a car registered under my real name. It was too big a risk. What if I had an accident in the hotel car park and had to show my licence and insurance documents? I would instantly be labelled a fraud.

And if I was going to be Nick, Relative of the Rich and Famous, I'd have to have a super-expensive sports or luxury car. There's no way a purveyor should have that kind of money for more than a week or two to splurge — I didn't — and if you do, then you're in the wrong line of work. You've already made it. (Perhaps not famous, but at least you're rich. And, believe me, that counts for something.)

But you don't need a car when you're working.

You don't need a car? In America?

Of course a man needs a car when he's in America. Everyone knows that. It's the land of the automobile. Yet you don't need a car. I know what I'm talking about. When you're staying in one location, being Mr Cruise or Mr De Niro, you'll always have plenty of friends and they'll always have cars.

But how do you get from one city to the next?

I have the perfect solution: driveaway. A wonderful concept for all involved.

Driveaway schemes exist all over the country and here's how they work: owners of cars — sometimes individuals, sometimes companies — want their vehicle to get from point A to point B but they don't want to drive it themselves or bear the cost of shipping. Adventurers, freeloaders (not merely purveyors of happiness), the less wealthy or the just plain clever sign up. Once you're a registered driver it's easy. You can pick and choose and only take the cars and routings you want, all you have to pay for is the petrol. And no matter how much Americans may complain at the price, when you come from Britain you know, even with those gas-guzzling cars they have in America, it's still damn cheap.

You don't have complete freedom to drive the car wherever you want. You work out a basic route (including major roads, mileage, number of days the journey should take) with the driveaway branch involved, but you're allowed to stop off and see the sights, and you're not allowed to drive more than eight hours a day. (In the US driving for eight hours is not abnormal, and when Americans do it they don't spend the rest of their lives talking about how far they once drove. It's nothing. They've all done it).

You can pick and choose your cars. Each vehicle, of course, has to reach a particular destination (those pesky owners have made up their minds), but if you're free to roam it's a luxury. You can zigzag back and forth across the country all you want. (Or you can do it just when money's running low. That's the joy of this gig. You've no one to answer to but yourself. You're at liberty to follow your whim however and wherever it may take you.

Your only structure is the Rules and you can amend those as you go, fine tuning them as you discover what does and doesn't work for you.

That was my life until a few short days ago.

Five months of amazing adventure and fun.

WOMEN JUST WANT TO SHAG YOU WHEN YOU'RE BRAD'S BROTHER (AND WHO SAYS I'M COMPLAINING?)

Oh dear, oh dear, oh dear. I was such a rogue in the days before I met Holly. A lovable rogue, I hope, but a rogue none the less. I may not have Brad's looks, Brad's finesse or Brad's charm, but you wouldn't have known it from the week I spent in Boulder, Colorado, as the Brother of Brad Pitt. I guess I was the next best thing to Brad. Not the real thing, not even *like* the real thing, but the closest anyone I met was likely to get.

I can guarantee that none of the women will remember me as Nick. They'll remember Brad Pitt's brother, but not my name or my face, and their memory of me will become more and more like Brad himself as time goes by, until one day they'll convince themselves we were identical twins. (Sorry, Brad, brother-mine, but don't worry, they'll all make favourable reports. I worked very hard to maintain your good reputation.)

Not, you understand, that everyone is a

star-shagger, but it makes sense that the people who were less impressed by my claim to fame as a Relative of the Rich and Famous weren't the ones pushing their way to the front of the pack to make my acquaintance. And this goes for all the celebs I was claiming as my own. The star-struck were the ones who felt they had to meet me, and then they just had to buy me a meal or two as a gesture of goodwill. Those who weren't in awe of the Brother of Bruce Willis or the Son of Harrison Ford didn't bother me: they just kept to themselves if they weren't particularly interested in saying they shook the hand of so-and-so's little brother or son.

The type of reception I received varied. Women became noticeably cooler when I claimed Pamela Anderson as my sister, but she was always popular with men — useful if I wanted to hang out with the guys for a few days and do some fishing. Believe me, those anglers wanted me along on their trips. The kudos they achieved with their mates was off the scale. The Brother of Pammie? Wow, wow, double wow.

People always stared at me — I was used to that — but when I was the Brother of Brad they were always there, gawking, practically panting. I could see them. I could see their staring eyes. I could feel their intensity burning into my back. No one bothered to disguise the interest. Or the lust. Not for me, of course, but for my brother, and given to me by my claim of association.

And they wanted every snippet of information I could give them.

'Remember Brad in *Twelve Monkeys*? At home we were really worried about him,' I said. 'He lived that part for months, practising every twitch for hours to get it exactly right. Sometimes he'd just sit on the sofa and go into one of his rants. He was so convincing that it was a tense time for all of us. We were glad when he finished filming.'

'He wore his own tux in *Meet Joe Black*. The costume department thought he looked so good in it they didn't bother ordering another.'

'Yes,' I'd say, responding to the inevitable questions, 'he works out a lot. Two or three hours every afternoon, plus an extra twenty minutes before breakfast just on his abs.'

'The whole family's meeting for Christmas in Australia this year. We want to go diving on the Great Barrier Reef.'

I invented tale after tale and they loved me.

There was only one sticky moment (outside the bedroom, I mean). I'd gone for what I thought would be a nice, quiet swim in the pool when Helen Thomas — the cute, friendly thirtysomething who, with her husband, had treated me to dinner the night before — introduced me to her sister.

(See, Holly? It wasn't all about sex. I was working, hunting out my patrons same as always. I was a good boy, really I was. The sex was just a side effect, a perk of the job, an unwritten, non-taxable benefit. And I'm so very sorry, Holly. Really I am . . . Hmmm . . . I think the apology needs some work. Perhaps I should just skip over my time as Brad's brother when, after my confession, I'm telling her about my travels. Tricky to know.)

I'd done no more than lay my towel on a chair, planning to let the sun dry me, when Helen and her sister approached.

Helen was smiling. 'Nick, I'd like you to meet my sister Abby. Abby, this is Brad Pitt's brother.'

I smiled and shook her hand. By then I was used to being introduced as Brother or Son and hardly ever as Nick. It's the price one pays for being in this line of work. And I didn't mind. I needed to be viewed as the Relative. It's how I made my living.

Abby nodded at me, frowning. She tilted her head to one side and studied me as if I was a bug about to be sprayed with insecticide. 'You don't look like Brad Pitt,' she said.

'Ouch,' I said, laughing, trying desperately to stop myself flushing. I had to make her feel like she was insulting me — she was, obviously, even if she hadn't meant it that way.

'I didn't mean to imply you're not attractive. You are.'

Helen sighed and rolled her eyes and I shared a secret smile with her. After all she was a believer.

'It's just that Brad is beautiful,' continued Abby. 'He's not only handsome. He's beautiful.'

I remained silent, merely raised an eyebrow. I'm the first to admit that I'm not beautiful, but it was fun to see her squirm.

'I'm a sculptor, you see,' she said. 'I study people's faces. Yours is very nice, you know, but your bone structure is quite different from Brad's.'

Really?

'That's why he's the mega-successful actor of the family,' I said. 'I'm afraid it's only our feet that are identical. And our ears, maybe. We've both got Dad's ears.' I let her stumble on for another minute or two until she was reassuring me that I'm just as attractive as Brad. (I'm not. Of course I'm not.)

And what could have been a messy situation, if I'd spluttered and been awkward, was all smoothed over. She might not have thought I looked like Brad Pitt, but she couldn't say we weren't related. And after insulting me and telling me I wasn't beautiful, she was hardly going to go around spreading the word that I looked nothing like Brad. Everyone else saw the similarity, even if it was merely imaginary.

I had a new rule for my list. Rule 28: If anyone doubts that you are who you say you are, don't argue with them, don't try to convince them, let them do the talking. Let them keep digging their hole deeper and deeper, and embarrassment will do the trick: they'll believe you if for no other reason than that they've got their foot in their mouth and are looking for an easy way out. They may still doubt you, but they can't prove you aren't who you say you are. Most people won't go screaming it from the rooftops.

Even if, later on, they check magazines or books then accost you with their scepticism and say that so-and-so doesn't have a British brother or whatever, you can shrug and say something like, 'Guess I'll have to break the news to my mother. She'll be devastated to hear it.' You don't deny their suspicions, you make them feel foolish. And even if they still doubt you, they'll doubt themselves too — for there is just a chance that you are who you say you are. So what's the harm in being friendly when you're being so charming?

And, besides, you're also following Rule 29 so it doesn't really matter who you are. Or aren't.

Rule 29: Don't ask for anything. No gifts, no favours, no free meals. No one can claim you're conning anyone if you're just easy-going and let the freebies come to you. Solicit nothing and even the doubters won't spread their ill-will too loudly.

And Abby herself? Well, let's just say she had ample time to make it up to me. After the first day it was easy to overlook her having been the cause of the one black spot on that perfect week. If her sculpting is anything like her performance between the sheets she's going to be the next Michelangelo.

Cheers, Brad. I owe you.

I'd definitely recommend him as a relative. Just keep in mind, if you do claim to be Brad Pitt's brother, be prepared for everyone to say, 'That Jennifer Aniston has lovely hair, doesn't she?' And you, of course, will smile and nod and agree, for she certainly does, and even if she didn't you'd agree anyway, for you are always warmhearted and say nice things about your relatives. A purveyor of happiness can only spread joy. That's what makes the system work.

STRUTTING MY STUFF
ON THE DANCE FLOOR

From Colorado I drove to Louisiana, stopping off in Arkansas to see the Ozarks and a couple of sights along the Bill Clinton tourist trail. I didn't have to claim John Travolta as my father when I rang the hotel in New Orleans and made my reservation. I could have chosen a different name. But once I'd checked in and my assumed identity got out, there was no way I could avoid the pleas. All those feminine eyelashes fluttering at me, those coy smiles, I had to make them happy.

I ended up at a nightclub, posing as the Son of John Travolta.

My companions, six dolled-up women, pulled me on to the dance floor as soon as we arrived. I wiggled my hips and I like to think I held my own, but I'll be the first to admit I'm no genius with the moves. I'm not in John Travolta's league. Who is? The girls danced round me and, after a few minutes, I noticed something odd: not only were the other dancers watching me, they were trying to imitate my moves.

Just like that I became the star of my very own version of *A Knight's Tale*. I was the peasant pretending at knighthood. I was the impostor showing my mettle on the dance floor when I didn't have a clue what I was doing.

They watched me. They copied me. I floundered for a second. With all my dreams of fame I'd never aspired to be a dancer. I knew my limitations. I was tempted to flee, but I couldn't. Not if I wanted to keep my women happy. They'd be sad if I left. So I stayed. After four or five beers — cheers to all those strangers who kept buying me drinks — I was feeling more confident. With an alcoholic buzz in my blood but not enough to affect my balance, I began to strut my stuff.

I shook my hips and so did my crowd. I did a spin and so did they. I laughed, I called out, 'This is popular in the clubs in London,' and waved my arms above my head. They followed me. I was a leader.

'This is my dad's favourite move,' I shouted. I spun round in a circle. And so did they.

Drink flowed and we all laughed. We became friends, but we didn't have to speak. We didn't need trivial smalltalk. We just danced and danced and danced.

'I'm not my father,' I said, 'but you've already seen that.'

They chuckled. They loved me. They were happy to settle for me. They would be able to live off the tale of how they bought John Travolta's son a drink and boogied the night away with him in New Orleans.

We whirled and spun and followed the beat, and when the DJ dusted off his *Saturday Night Fever* album we tried out some of the less complicated moves.

This is a memory I could share with Holly. It was all innocent fun. I made everyone so very happy.

'Just follow me,' I said. And they did. They all did.

ALL HAIL THE *STAR WARS* HEIR
(CAN I BE A JEDI? CAN I?
PRETTY PLEASE?)

Nick, Son of George Lucas, hit Seattle like a rainbow. Smiles and bursts of joy followed me wherever I went. My presence brightened the lives of everyone I met and the world was instantly a better place.

It's important to choose your identities with care, vital to match them to the locale, even if it's only a personal association for you alone. I'd always longed to visit Seattle. And when I think Seattle I think grunge music, Frasier Crane and Microsoft. I'd ruled out pretending to be Kurt Cobain's long-lost brother. That would be too complicated and way too sad: a purveyor should never choose anyone who'll depress their intended patrons. As for *Frasier*, I love the TV series, but I don't know if it's filmed in LA or Seattle, and I couldn't risk pretending to be related to an actor from the show. Not when they might be in town.

It came to me in a moment of inspiration

as I was driving through Kansas on the way to Seattle. I would be the Son of George. Seattle would love me. And they did.

'I want to be in the next *Star Wars* film.'

If I had a dollar for every time I heard that line I'd be rich, and I'd have retired from being a purveyor of happiness long before I ended up on this damn bounty-hunting course. (But, then, maybe I wouldn't have met Holly and, whatever else happens, I am glad I did.)

'I want to be in the next *Star Wars* film. Can I be in the next *Star Wars* film?'

It's Joe and Tracy Wilson I remember best, though all my patrons that week were the same: thirtysomethings who'd adored the films the first time round and adored them still. Affluent men and women who were all too happy to spread their wealth around if it meant meeting the Son of George.

'I want to be a female Jedi,' Tracy said, again and again, her eyes shining. 'A Jedi Knight.'

'I want to be a Jedi Master,' said Joe, with a big smile. He waved his breadknife around as if he were holding a sword, making swishing sounds like a blade slicing through the air, dreaming of holding his very own light saber. 'We don't need big parts. We don't even need any lines.'

(Joe had made a killing on the stock market and fortunately had sold his shares before the technology crash of 2000. He was used to getting what he wanted. Money was not a problem.)

'I don't get a say in Dad's films,' I said, looking apologetic, discouraged and disappointed all at once. 'He doesn't even let me be an extra unless I put on an alien costume so no one recognises me.' (A spur-of-the moment line and one with which I was quite pleased. It would explain why they'd never seen me in any of the background shots, and even if they went home and watched all the *Star Wars* movies frame by frame they wouldn't spot me. Was I cool under pressure or what?)

'We could help fund the next picture,' said Tracy. 'We could be independent investors. Would your father let us be extras then?'

I broke it to them gently. 'Dad wouldn't accept your offer. The studios always cough up the cash. They give him everything he asks for. He never accepts private investment.' I was talking bollocks, but it sounded believable. George Lucas would have no need to go cap in hand to potential investors. Why should he? He'd have plenty of offers available. Studios must salivate at the thought of being able to thrust money at him and

100

share in all those tasty profits at the end of the day. Or so I think. And it sounds right. And that's what counts in the end when you're only trying to impress your patrons. I created another rule right then and there. Rule 30: You don't have to *be* right: you only have to *sound* right.

'But,' said Joe, earnest, 'I'd give any-thing — '

'They told me you're Nick Lucas. They told me you're George Lucas's son,' inter-rupted the loud, slurred voice of a man approaching our table.

He wasn't smiling. People always smile when they see me. I didn't like his frown. I didn't like his attitude. How dare he come near me in such a loud, obnoxious manner?

'Yes, I am,' I said simply, calm under pressure. All those years as a salesman dealing with the occasional quarrelsome customer had been good for something after all.

'So you say.'

The restaurant quietened noticeably, as those nearby strained to overhear. Tracy and Joe glanced at me, then worriedly at one another. The thought of doubting me had probably not occurred to them. I'd been introduced to them as the Son of George by a reliable third party. Why should they doubt me?

I shrugged. 'I am,' I said again. What else could I say? Oh, all right, fair call, guv, you've caught me? I think not.

In my head I pictured myself giving an eloquent little speech and smiling a Hollywood smile of gleaming white teeth and confidence. I imagined being a figure of benevolent forgiveness when the man — the interloper — looked ashamed as he apologised and shook my hand. Conjuring up a vision of the reality I wanted was the first step to success.

The man pointed a finger at my chest and said, 'You're lying. George Lucas doesn't have a son named Nick. He doesn't have a British son.'

'Wow. Guess I'll have to break the news to him.' I tried to keep my voice light and wry to defuse the situation.

'George is from California. He's always lived in California. His son wouldn't be British.'

I sighed. 'Why do you think most of the *Star Wars* films were shot in England? Dad wanted to spend time with me.'

I should have known better than to choose someone like George. He's a cult figure, an icon. There are lots of obsessed fans who know his biography, who could probably recite his personal details as well as the man's true family could. It's a well-known and universally accepted fact that sci-fi enthusiasts are masters of trivia. They know things about fictional characters that their creators have probably forgotten so they're certainly going to know a few basic particulars about their real-world heroes, George Lucas included. I'd made a mistake, perhaps, in choosing a sci-fi legend, but I couldn't regret it. I, too, wanted to share in that *Star Wars* magic.

My patrons were looking decidedly uncomfortable and that would not do. I like the world to function smoothly, easily. I like everything to be joyful and light. I'm a purveyor of happiness, for goodness' sake — it's how we see the world.

'You're not related to George Lucas,' insisted the man.

'Aren't I? And how exactly do you know that?'

'I've read his biography on the Web.'

And just like that I was saved. I laughed. I could see an easy way out. Not foolproof, but it cast aspersions on his credibility. 'And you believe everything you read on the Internet?' I was happy enough to use the Net for my own research as a purveyor, but I knew it wasn't the perfect tool. 'You think each and every single fan site has all the facts? That they're completely, one hundred per cent accurate?' I turned to Tracy and Joe and rolled my eyes. They smiled nervously.

The man flushed. 'Of course not. But you're not his son.'

To be honest, George Lucas doesn't have a son of my age — or not that I'm aware of. When I first came up with this idea, I was only going to pretend to be a son or a brother if that particular celeb had a son or a brother of roughly the right age, but I soon realised that this didn't really matter. I was never going to impersonate an actual person. And I never did. I always claimed to be someone who doesn't exist. I told everyone I couldn't talk about my other family members as my mother or father, sister or brother, whatever celebrity I was claiming for my own, didn't want their other relations discussed. That way I was saved from having to be up to date on all the gossip, and I didn't need to worry about coming across fans who'd know all sorts of facts and statistics of which I'd be blissfully ignorant until they told me.

All I had to do was tailor my story to fit the celebrity's known life history. It usually did the trick.

I shrugged. A true relative doesn't care if someone doesn't believe him, so neither does a purveyor of happiness. 'Think whatever you want,' I said.

'Then prove it,' said the man. 'Show me your driver's licence, Mr Lucas.'

And then it hit me. There wasn't a graceful way out. I had no driver's license to show him. Not in the name I was claiming as my own. I had no rule to cover this situation. I couldn't start spluttering about a stolen wallet — that would make me look decidedly shifty, maybe even guilty. It was getting messy and uncomfortable and I didn't like it. My patrons didn't like it. I didn't care about convincing the drunk — belligerent sod, how dare he question me? — but Joe and Tracy were looking uneasy. I didn't want them to start doubting me now.

'Look,' I said, trying to be reasonable, 'I'd show you, but then you'd say that Lucas is a common surname and you still wouldn't believe me. We're trying to have a nice, quiet meal here. I don't have to prove anything to you. Please just apologise to Tracy for disturbing her evening and return to your own friends.'

'You're a liar,' he said.

One of the waiters approached our table. 'Is there a problem here?' he asked.

'He's lying,' slurred the man, pointing accusingly at me. 'He's not George Lucas's son. He can't be George Lucas's son.'

The waiter had taken in the situation: he apologised to me and to Tracy and Joe and escorted the man from the restaurant. But it had been a close call. Mean, determined doubters breed doubt. They spoil everything.

Gradually, laughing uneasily and ignoring the unpleasantness, we got back on track. I let Joe and Tracy talk about their dreams of starring as Jedi Knights. (Yes, starring. They'd settle for being extras, but everyone always wants to star.) But the evening had been ruined. After the meal was over I made my excuses and retired for the night.

The next day was better and I was back to being adored. The rest of Seattle seemed to love me.

And I deserve a halo for not abusing my position of power. I wouldn't accept a single bribe to let anyone be in a George Lucas film. (Meals don't count: patrons can tell the tale of how they once dined with the Son of George and that's payment enough for some food and drink.) Assertions of *potential* visitations by the famous relative are allowed — it's good to give the patrons some hope and excitement for the future, hope keeps the world going, hope makes life spicy and interesting — but nothing concrete. I never make promises I can't keep. I always say I'll try, I'll see what I can do, perhaps, maybe, one day. But you never let them pay you for a part in a movie that doesn't exist. A purveyor of happiness is not immoral.

ONE ROMANTIC EVENING
NEAR CHICAGO

The first time I saw Emma Johnston it had all the elements of a romantic evening: a full moon and the stars provided the illumination, a nearly deserted shoreline on a sandy beach the setting, soft breezes ruffled the air, which was warm without being sticky. Emma was in a long white dress better suited for a candlelit meal than a beach. She clutched her shoes, strappy high-heeled sandals, in one hand with a small handbag and she was barefoot, gazing out across the lapping waves.

I'd been heading towards the water's edge, having arrived at this new destination only an hour or so before. I was at a resort not far from Chicago on the shores of Lake Michigan, posing as the Son of Robert Redford, but I knew that word hadn't had time to spread. I was there, at the beach, for myself, wanting to greet the water as I always do, whether it's an ocean, a tiny inland lake or even a stream.

When I saw the woman in white (I didn't know her name was Emma then, of course), I stopped and stared at her. I was only yards away, but I didn't want to startle her. She seemed almost otherworldly. Her hair was a riot of wild, golden blonde ringlets partly pinned up on her head, the rest tumbling down her back. I was wondering whether to go to her or head back and leave her in peace, when she turned and began to walk, following the shoreline, the hem of her dress trailing in the lake.

I saw her face for two full seconds.

Wide green eyes shimmered with tears. Wet tracks ran down her cheeks. She was like a fairy queen, like Michelle Pfeiffer's Titania in *A Midsummer Night's Dream*. She was a vision.

And she was sad.

'I'm sorry, but are you okay?' I asked gently, my voice low and sympathetic.

She stopped walking, hesitated, then looked at me. 'I'm here for my anniversary. Can't you tell?'

Ah. She was married. My eyes flicked to her hands, spotted a ring — a massive diamond — on the appropriate finger. I was disappointed.

She saw my glance. 'I'm pathetic, aren't I?' More tears streamed down her face. 'It's over. It's all over.' She wiped away the tears with the back of her hand, twisted off the ring, then raised her arm to throw it into Lake Michigan.

I ran to her side, reached out and closed my hand around hers. 'You don't want to do that,' I said. 'You'll regret it later. You must have some good memories to go with that ring.'

'No. They've all been spoilt. He's ruined them, the bastard. He's ruined everything.'

'Then keep the ring so you can sell it. Donate it to a charity. Or give it to someone your husband — '

'Soon-to-be-ex-husband.'

'Someone he despises.'

She lowered her arm and took a deep breath. 'You're right. I'm too emotional to make any decisions at the moment.'

'Do you have any children?' I asked. 'You could save it and give it to them.'

Her eyes filled with tears again and she started to sob. I felt like the world's biggest idiot. 'No,' she said, shoulders shaking, 'I don't have any children. He told me he'd never have kids. That was part of the deal from the beginning. I thought I could change his mind but he was adamant. No kids. That's what he said.' She looked up at me, her green eyes wet and wide. 'And now he's having a baby. But not with me.'

Her sobs grew louder and I pulled her into

my arms. She froze for a second, and then she clung to me. I let her cry. I ran my hands up and down her back, soothing, comforting. I did not mouth smooth platitudes. I did not tell her that everything was going to be all right. I just held her and let her cry out her grief, her frustration, her humiliation.

There would be no mingling in the hotel bar that night, no searching for patrons, but I didn't mind. She needed me. And I wanted to help her. I wanted to make her happy again. Or at least see a glimmer of the happiness she might find in the future. I would not let her be alone with her grief.

After a time her sobs quieted, but still she clung to me. 'I'm sorry,' she murmured, into my chest. 'I don't even know you. I'm so sorry.'

She made to pull away, but I held her close. 'Hush,' I said. 'Don't worry. We'll introduce ourselves and then you will know me. I'm Nick.'

She lifted her head and looked up at me. 'And I'm Emma.'

I felt cruel asking, but I knew she needed to talk about it so it wouldn't fester inside of her. 'He told you here? Tonight?'

'Yes. The bastard.' She took a deep breath. 'Let's walk. I want to walk.'

So we strolled hand in hand along the water's edge.

'This was supposed to be our second honeymoon,' she said. 'We live nearby so it wasn't particularly exotic, but he's just started a new practice. Bill's a plastic surgeon.'

Bill. I hated him already.

'He said he didn't want to travel in case he was needed. In case of emergencies. But I know now that he just didn't want to be too far away from *her*.' She wiped her face, trying to get rid of the traces of tears. 'We planned on spending a week here, to celebrate our tenth anniversary. I've wasted ten years of my life on that bastard.'

Emma had been married for ten years? But I'd thought she was my age. Technically she could have been married very young, but I guessed that she must be older than I was.

Emma gripped my hand. 'We didn't even drive here together because he said he had to work. And then he was two hours late and I was already dressed for dinner. He broke the news as soon as he arrived. His twenty-three-year-old mistress is pregnant with his baby and they're now engaged. The bastard's proposed to her and he's still married to me. Isn't that bigamy? That should be bigamy. He should be thrown into prison for what he's done.'

'Yes, he should.' I squeezed her hand.

She flashed me a sad smile, and then her lips started to tremble. 'He's having a baby with her.'

'How old is he?' I had to say something to distract her. I wanted to keep her focused on the facts. I didn't want her to blame herself.

'The bastard is forty-four. And his whore is only twenty-three. The bitch. The same age I was when I married him. Bastard. Bastard. Bastard.'

I was surprised that Emma was thirty-three. She looked like she was still in her twenties. Hearing that she wasn't made her seem more grown up, more responsible somehow.

We spent the rest of the night together. At times she cried and I held her, at others she wanted to talk and we walked or sat, always holding hands. She told me the whole sorry tale and I hated her husband. I despised him. If I'd had the power to ruin his life I would have done it without a second thought. As the hours passed the air grew colder and I wished I had a jacket to slip over Emma's shoulders, but I wasn't wearing one, so I just stayed close, letting my heat warm her. She cried and sobbed and wondered why. By the time the sunrise glimmered across the waters to the east, she hadn't shed any tears for at least forty-five minutes. She was sad. She was hurt. She was angry.

I decided that Emma was going to be my week's work, that I would do whatever I could to help her feel better about herself, that I would make her realise how desirable and lovely she truly was. She was beautiful and intelligent and interesting. Bill must have been crazy.

We watched the sun as it rose, arms around each other's waist, squinting into the glare. Emma sighed and rested her head against my shoulder. A moment later she pulled away and said, 'I have something for you.' She opened her handbag and withdrew a small, brightly wrapped parcel, ribbons cascading down the sides. She ripped off the gift tag and crumpled it in her hand. Emma pulled back her arm to throw the tag into the lake, but then she hesitated and sighed. She said, 'I can't litter. I won't let that bastard reduce me to a person who deliberately litters.' She dropped it into her handbag and stared at the present in her hand. 'I want you to have this.'

'No,' I said. 'I can't.'

'I want you to have it.'

'Really, that's very kind, but I couldn't.'

Emma pressed the parcel into my hand. 'I want you to.'

'But — '

'Yes.' Emma looked into my eyes. 'Today is my tenth anniversary. I bought this gift for my soon-to-be-ex-husband. We were supposed to have dinner last night. I was planning on giving this to him as the clock struck midnight. The bastard.'

'But — '

'I want you to have it. I know what I'm doing.' She gave me a sad little smile. 'I am thinking clearly, I can assure you. More clearly than I've obviously been thinking for some time. Bill would hate that I'm giving away his present. You're the one who suggested I go that route, Nick, when you stopped me throwing my ring into the lake. You're not getting out of this one.'

I tried again. 'But — '

'And, anyway, it's not just about revenge. You deserve it more than he does. It would make me happy knowing you have it.'

Happy. The one word that meant I couldn't refuse outright. When I'd first spoken to her, I'd been filled with the desire to make her happy. I knew I hadn't succeeded, but she had to be feeling a tiny bit better.

I gazed down at the present, not knowing

the proper reaction to this situation. I knew that as a working man I should be telling myself that I damn well deserved the gift, as a reward for selling my particular brand of happiness, but I hadn't been working. I'd seen someone in need and I'd gone to her aid. I didn't need a reward. I didn't deserve one.

'Please,' said Emma. 'Do you want to start me crying again? I would be glad to know it has a good home.'

'Okay.' I tore off the paper, slowly, carefully, and opened the box. I could scarcely credit what my eyes were telling me. But it was true. Emma had given me a shiny, brand new, very expensive Rolex.

I didn't know what to say. I stared at it for a long moment, lusting for it the way a teenager craves his first girl. Then I looked at Emma. She was staring at me expectantly. 'Emma, I can't accept this.'

'Yes, you can.' She took the watch out of the box and held it up, showing me the back. 'See. It's not even engraved. Bill — the bastard — never wanted anything engraved. Now I can see why. He must have known for quite some time he was going to dump me. Mistresses don't normally get pregnant on the first night of indiscretion. And a married man wouldn't propose if there had been no history between them, would he?'

'He doesn't deserve you.'

Emma stared down at the watch, then visibly pulled herself together. 'Give me your arm.' She fastened the Rolex on to my left wrist. 'There,' she said, adjusting it. 'It looks perfect. It suits you.'

It did suit me. It does suit me.

'Thank you,' I said.

'No. Thank you. Thank you for being with me and for spending the whole night on the beach listening to a stranger's sorrows.'

I kissed her forehead and pulled her into my arms, hugging her. Emma's body fitted perfectly into mine, moulding itself to all the right places. There was nothing deliberately sexual about it, but we were definitely a match.

We spent the week together. I hardly bothered associating with the other guests, though once the hotel staff had spread the gossip about my father's identity I couldn't avoid it completely.

I almost wish it had been true. If Robert Redford had been my father I could have hung around Emma for months. I could have rubbed Bill Johnston's nose in that fact. I could have made him and his mistress rue that they'd never be friends with the Son of Robert Redford, and that they'd never even get to meet the man himself, while Emma was treated almost like his daughter-in-law. That's what I would have done if I could.

But I couldn't. I was just a nobody.

AND THEN THERE WERE
MORE ADVENTURES

It was an emotional roller-coaster of a week with Emma and I was sad to leave, guilty even, that I could skip off to happier times while she was stuck dealing with the fallout. I wanted to stay longer, but the power of the Rules was still strong and I knew that it was time. I had to leave. The risk of discovery was too high. I had to flit from place to place and person to person. That's what I'd agreed with myself when I'd volunteered for the job.

After Emma I went from here to there, I was charming and witty and everyone loved me. I had two and a half more months of purveying and it was fun: I was the Brother of Tom Hanks, the Brother of Russell Crowe, the Son of Harrison Ford. I went to Memphis, Virginia Beach, Cape Cod.

I drove across America and I loved sitting behind the wheels of those big automobiles. I stopped at bookshops and lingered among the celebrity biographies to pick up titbits to spice up my conversation. I used the Internet in malls and hotels to do my basic research, looking up the life histories of my favourite stars so that my stories would be plausible.

That was my life until a few short days ago.

But then I met Holly and broke the Rules and everything's different now.

INTRODUCTIONS AT
BOUNTY-HUNTING SCHOOL

The atmosphere hasn't changed during my moments of inattention and speculation about the path that brought me here. We're still in that crazed movie sequence with that same ex-Marine instructor. No matter how much I tell myself I should have done things differently, that I didn't have to end up here, it won't change anything. Maybe I could have been more persuasive. I should have convinced Holly to stay away, but we're here now and this bounty-hunting business won't disappear because I want it to. Ted isn't suddenly going to stop talking, shake our hands, wish us luck and send us on to Vegas for a week's gambling. (How I wish he would.)

No. Things don't work like that. This isn't a nightmare from which I can wake up. This is a bounty-hunting training school for tourists. A *City Slickers*-type vacation for those who've moved beyond the dude ranch. This is a place for the secretly violent to live out their dark fantasies. Apart from Holly, Ted's the only one here doing a job. The rest of us have signed up voluntarily for the course. We've all paid to be here and Ted isn't going to send us away. He wants his money.

The others have come for a week of stress-relief away from their jobs and normal lives. But I don't think they've thought this through. Don't they know we're all going to die? I mean, hello, sit back and look around this classroom. We're all lunatics.

I glance at Holly. She's sitting forward, taking in every word Ted says, and I know, in that instant, that she wishes she could be taking notes, that she sees this as a great week, that she *wants* to be here.

And then I think, So who's the crazy one? Her? Or me?

It's not that I'm a coward. It's just that I think I'm the only one here who's taking this seriously, the only one without tunnel vision. My blinkers have been taken off and I can see the wider picture. And it doesn't look good. Or maybe I *am* a coward. All I know is that I'm here and I'm not going to sulk or keep pointing out how stupid this whole situation is. When it comes down to it, nobody made me sign up for it. Holly didn't ask me to come: I insisted on accompanying her.

I catch the name Schwarzenegger and smile automatically, gracious as a good

Relative of the Rich and Famous should be, focusing on Ted as I realise he's been talking about Arnie. I haven't caught a single word other than the name, but it doesn't matter, it's not as if I need to know exactly what Ted's been saying. It'll have been the normal flattery stuff. I've heard it all before. It's always the same. 'Ooh, I love your father', women say. Men don't use the love word, but they might as well: you can see the glow of obsessive adoration in their eyes.

(I mean, come on, what red-blooded male wouldn't want Arnie for a father? I know I would. Sorry, Dad, no offence, I know you'll understand. Anyway, my father probably wishes he had Arnie for a son. What man wouldn't prefer being able to say, 'That's my boy,' when talking about Arnie rather than having to settle for me?)

And just knowing someone who's related to Arnie — well, okay, me, but it still counts, everyone in this room thinks we're related — gives men like Ted instant hero-status in the eyes of all their acquaintances, co-workers and students. The others are likely reassured that this is a high-class operation. For otherwise Arnie's son wouldn't be here, would he?

It won't occur to them to question my ancestry. They accept that I am the Son of

Arnie. To them it is fact. Once Ted was convinced, and he wanted to believe, he so much wanted to believe, I knew it'd be easy.

'Thanks. I appreciate hearing that,' I say, smiling, acknowledging Ted's comments of praise and enthusiasm for my father, for me, for our whole family. 'Dad will be glad to know he has such a large following in the Marines.'

Now that Ted's said my name and we've all shared in his anecdote about Arnie, now that everyone in this room knows my identity, they'll all have accorded me friend status. I'll be thought of as their pal, their buddy, one of the gang. People always feel they know my 'father'. They feel they know me — by some process of celluloid osmosis, I guess — but I can't complain, it's always been to my benefit. Instant rapport and instant affection is what I always receive and it makes everything so much easier.

My newest companions usually wage a mini-war among themselves for who gets to spend the most time with me. Will my new comrades fight for the privilege of dying beside me?

Ted finishes his welcome to the Son of Arnie, then, before he moves on to the next bounty-hunting pupil, adds, 'But remember, Nick, I'm not going to go easy on you just because you're Arnie's boy. He wouldn't thank me and you wouldn't thank me. There can be no special treatment. You're all beginners and you all need to learn.'

He doesn't wait for a response, he's already turning to Holly and introducing her without giving me time to speak again, and I'm glad. No doubt I would have laughed and come out with some crawly comment about giving my father a few tips when it was over, and the less I talk about Arnie in front of Holly the better. I won't be able to avoid the subject completely, but I can try to tone it down.

Once Holly's smiled at the others, Ted carries on with the introductions. He points to the next soon-to-be-dead trainee. 'This is Kevin,' says Ted.

Kevin looks about thirty. He's bearded, severely overweight, and is dressed in head-to-toe camo (the brown desert version to fit in with the Arizona landscape). Even his boots are made of camouflaged fabric. He's sweating slightly and squirming in his seat like a boy in kindergarten who's about to wet his pants with excitement. Is he suffering from a deluded case of *Die Hard*-wannabe syndrome? My guess is he's here to fulfil some male fantasy, or make up for the lack of macho adventure — or girlfriend — in his life.

If this were a movie we'd need a first sacrifice to satisfy the audience's bloodlust. Kevin could fill that role. He's friendly but looks ill-prepared for the task ahead. The viewers would feel sorry for him when he received the death blow, but it wouldn't break their hearts. I wouldn't be too confident about all of this if I were Kevin.

'Veronica,' says Ted, indicating the next would-be bounty-hunter. She's seated next to Kevin, but it's obvious they're not together.

Veronica's about thirty-five and reminds me of Linda Hamilton in *Terminator 2*. She has that lean, mean, fighting-machine aura about her, and she's fairly attractive in the same driven way. I'm only hoping that gleam in Veronica's eye is not of derangement and that there's a straight forward reason as to why she's on this course. (I can't think of one offhand. It's unlikely she's a reporter like Holly. I doubt a place like this could survive for long if the majority of the student body was made up of journalists. It just wouldn't be a viable business model.)

The remaining male pupil is in his early twenties, with the pale, thin look of a hacker or bookworm. Ted doesn't try to hide the snigger in his voice as he says, 'This is Byron.'

Byron's been doodling on a pad, but he looks up when he hears his name and gives us all a little wave. 'Hi,' he says. He catches my eye and smiles. (Have I collected another fan?)

Ted is staring at him. 'Byron? What kind of name is that?' says Ted. 'What father would name his child after a goddamn poet? What sort of man would let his wife name his son after a goddamn poet? No, don't tell us, we can guess.' Ted's lips curl into a sneer. 'You'd better understand that I don't want any funny business here.' He gives Byron a long, hard look, then turns and surveys us as a group.

That's it. Five students. One instructor.

I have to convince Holly that this is not a good idea.

THE WELCOME IS OVER AND NOW IT'S TIME FOR WORK, PLEASE SIGN ON THE DOTTED LINE AND YOUR SOUL IS MINE

Ted stands at the front of the classroom, his hands on his hips as he studies us one by one, holding our eyes for six or seven long seconds that feel like hours. Finally he speaks. 'For the next five days you are mine,' he says. 'Think of me as God. You'll do what I say when I say it. Is that understood?'

'Yes, sir,' shout Kevin and Veronica, military cadets in the making.

Ted frowns. 'What was that? I can't hear you.'

'Yes, sir,' we all say.

I feel stupid, but there's nothing I can do. I can't abandon Holly with these lunatics. I can't let her become a bounty-hunter on her own. She needs me. She might not know it, but she does. I won't desert her.

I fiddle with my Rolex, shifting in my seat. 'We'll have two days of training,' says Ted.

'Two days?' I blurt out before I realise I've

128

spoken. What happened to the five days of Ted being God? Perhaps I should have read the brochure before I told Holly I'd come.

'Yes, Schwarzenegger, two days.'

I can see the delight in Ted's eyes as he says the name.

'I'm glad to hear you were listening.' Ted flashes me a fleeting smile. 'During our training time the professional bounty-hunters on the staff will track down our chosen targets. Then it will be up to us to apprehend them in the following days. And we're talking about genuine, authentic criminals, we're not pretending here. This is for real.' Ted's arms drop to his sides and he strides towards the door, taking large, manly steps that somehow convey a sense of power and danger without being swaggering. 'Now stand up, everyone, and come with me. It's time for our first lesson.'

And, instantly, right then, I think of another item for the Rules.

Rule 31: Do not go on a bounty-hunt. It's that simple. Do not go.

A MORNING ON THE
FIRING RANGE

We follow Ted through the training compound. Holly's face is as excited and alive as Kevin's and Veronica's. Byron, trailing at the back, is the only one who looks as unenthusiastic as I feel. Ted leads us directly to the firing range — for wouldn't you know? — the first essential skill a bounty-hunter needs is deadly accuracy with a gun.

'Not,' Ted tells us, 'that a bounty-hunter wants to kill his prey, but he needs to be able to shoot to kill if the situation demands it.'

By prey Ted means a man, or more rarely a woman, on the run from the law. And being a criminal in America, the prey will have guns. Technically, of course, they might not all be criminals. Some might have been falsely accused, *The Fugitive*-style characters. But Ted's logic goes that if you're innocent you're not going to flee from the law, are you? Either way, it doesn't matter when you're standing in my shoes. If they're desperate enough to go on the run they will have guns.

Lots and lots of guns. Better guns, no

doubt, than the ones we'll be using. Their guns might look the same as ours, but Sod's Law demands that they'll be specially modified to hold more ammunition, giving them the advantage in every shootout. And if that wasn't enough, they probably won't bother to use the safeties. Or, if they do, they'll have some new high-tech safety device that'll release a second or two faster than ours. And that's if we can even find ours. Let's not forget that we're all tourists and we don't know how to use guns properly.

Vacationers, holidaymakers, adventurers, travellers, a modern breed of sightseer, call us what you will: ultimately, we're here for a fun new experience because we're bored with standing behind the safety rail on the rim of the Grand Canyon and appreciating the view.

Or the others are. Holly and I are only pretending to be the same as them. But as we are ordinary citizens, like the others, our motivation doesn't matter. We'll be just as crap.

I don't know whether to be thankful or sad that we've only got two days. Glad because there's less time to suffer the humiliations of training and finding out exactly how pathetic we are. Or sad because after these two days it'll all be over and we'll be dead.

Hell, maybe we deserve to die. Maybe

people as stupid as we are shouldn't be allowed to live. Survival of the fittest and all that. Real bounty-hunters will hear of our deaths and roll their eyes at the idea that amateurs like us ever thought we could do their job in the first place.

But I digress. Ted is still speaking and I must never forget that this might be one of those times where the hero and one or two others survive. Surely all those movies where people live despite impossible odds means that it's possible.

'This isn't the Wild West of old,' says Ted. 'There are no wanted-dead-or-alive posters. They're always wanted alive. Dead is only acceptable if you're protecting your own life in self-defence. So keep that in mind. I'm not training you to be Rambo.' Ted glances my way, quickly adding, 'Or one of Arnold Schwarzenegger's characters.'

Everyone looks at me and I attempt a half-sheepish smile because it's expected, part of my job. It's part of the Nick Schwarzenegger persona. But I don't feel like smiling. I glance at Holly, and she winks. I know that she's soaking all this up, that she's desperate to get back to her room and make some notes, that all she can see is the article she's going to write. I, on the other hand, sorry specimen of masculine bravery that I am, see bullets and pain and vast quantities of blood.

'I'm training you to become bounty-hunters.' Ted's eyes roam our faces. 'Now, some of you may be interested in this as a new career and see this as a trial run to find out if you're suitable.'

Veronica nods.

She wants to do this for a living?

'While others of you,' says Ted, 'just wanted an action vacation, and as the so-called thrills of whitewater rafting don't do it for you any more you came here. And that's fine, but while you're with me I'm going to treat you all the same. To go on a bounty hunt you need to become bounty-hunters. And bounty-hunters you will become. I'm not going to go easy on you because you're paying customers. My job is to train you, and that includes ignoring any bruises or blisters you might complain about.'

Bruises and blisters? What happened to the luxury part of the vacation? That must be the rooms.

While I'm trying to imagine what horrible exercises Ted is planning to put us through that'll cause bruises and blisters, he unlocks a box at the side of the room and withdraws a gun.

'Byron, can you tell us what this is?' Ted asks, brandishing the gun in the air.

Wait a second, I've got it. It's a pistol. I've seen them on TV.

'A Colt?' says Byron, uncertainly.

Kevin waves his hand excitedly in the air, straining, eager.

'Yes, it is a Colt,' says Ted, ignoring Kevin. 'Anyone else?'

Veronica responds instantly. 'It's a Colt .45 with a six-round box mag and an effective range of one hundred and sixty-four feet.'

'Good.' Ted smiles at her, then turns to the rest of us, his warmth fading. 'That means six shots.'

(If we have six shots our prey will have eight. Sod's Law is real.)

'Remember, our aim is to bring in the crims alive.' Ted glances at Veronica.

I don't like the way he glances at Veronica. Does he know something I don't?

'If you need more than six shots,' says Ted, to the group again, not just to Veronica, 'you might as well throw down your gun and start praying that your relatives know where you want to be buried. Remember that these crims are just that: criminals. You're not being paid enough to die.'

Thanks for clearing that up, Ted. But haven't you forgotten that we're not being paid anything at the moment, that we are, in fact, paying you for this vacation experience?

We're shown how to load the guns, how to aim, and how to fire.

After my first three shots — not bad for the first three shots of my life, but not good enough for a man who needs to be able to protect himself and his woman — I notice a ringing in my ears and ask Ted for some earplugs. He just laughs. 'No earplugs,' he says. 'Normally you'd wear ear protectors for target practice, but you have to get used to the sound of gunfire. I don't want you disorientated by all that unexpected noise when we go in for real. You won't be wearing earplugs during combat.'

Combat?

But already Ted's moving down the line to yell at Kevin for blowing away gun-smoke and reading too many dime-novel Westerns.

Holly fires again, then glances at me, eyes shining. 'And you were thinking of going surfing before you decided to come here.' She raises her gun back to the firing position, and lets off two shots in quick succession. One bullet goes wild. The other hits the edge of my target. Holly laughs. 'Told you I'd show you a good time.'

I smile, trying to keep my voice light-hearted and free of the doom I'm feeling inside. 'That's what you promised.'

She blows me a kiss. Then we turn back to

the task at hand as Ted starts to walk our way. We spend the next three hours on the firing range.

Veronica's so good she could represent her country in the Olympics, but the rest of us, well, let's just hope the crims don't put up a fight.

AND WITH THIS LITTLE BADGE YOU TOO CAN BE A BOUNTY-HUNTER (THE BADGE MAKES IT OFFICIAL)

After our mediocrity is proven once and for all on the firing range, and I'm forced to admit that I'll never be as cool and competent as John Cusack in *Grosse Pointe Blank*, Ted leads us towards the cafeteria for a short lunch break.

I pull Holly aside, letting the others pass so that we're able to lag behind and not be overheard. What I want to say is that this whole idea is insane, that we shouldn't be here, that it shouldn't be legal to offer bounty-hunting for tourists, that we should leave it to the professionals, but I don't. I decide it's not a good idea to tell the woman I'm crazy about that she's mad. For that's how she'd take it. Her editor didn't force-feed her the project: she thought of it herself and she's proud of that.

If I start telling her it's all rather loopy she'll be offended and tell me that I don't have to stay if I don't want to. And I want to stay. If I leave I know I'll come back to my senses and the power of the Rules will reassert itself and I'll never see her again. I would throw away her number in a moment of madness, when I was being strong.

'What is it?' Holly asks, pulling me out of my reverie. 'We have to keep up with the others. I don't want to miss anything.'

No, she wouldn't. She wants all the background details and comments to spice up her article.

I have to tell her who I am. I want her to know. But when can I do it? When can I tell her who I'm not?

Not now. Not yet. But I *will* tell her. One day. Soon.

'I don't think we'll be ready to go on the bounty hunt,' I whisper, not wanting anyone but Holly to hear. Wouldn't do for the Son of Arnie to be thought timid. Son of Arnie equals Big Man. Son of Arnie strong like father. That's how they all think of me. Ha.

Holly smiles, pressing close, her voice a low murmur. 'I know. We won't be ready. Isn't it fabulous?'

Ah, yes. The story. The reason we're here. I can see that convincing her to leave without the full juicy saga is going to take some work. I postpone the frontal attack and decide on a strategic retreat. 'We have to be careful,' I say, still whispering. 'My dad would kill me if he knew where I was. This is dangerous.'

If anything her smile widens. 'It is. My editor's going to love this.' She presses a brief kiss on my lips. 'Come on, let's catch up with the others. We don't want to be left behind.'

We hurry forward and soon we're back with the group.

Where Ted leads we follow.

The cafeteria reminds me of a school lunch hall, but instead of children's drawings and notices about the latest drama production on the walls there are wanted posters and advertisements for horrible weaponry and all kinds of bullets.

There's one long table in the middle of the room and it's laid with six place settings. Lucky Ted, guess he eats with us. There's no sign of the food yet, but delicious smells of onions, peppers, meat and cheese are wafting in, and I'd say we're being given the Tex-Mex food Arizona does so well. My stomach rumbles and I'm suddenly ravenous.

'You'll each find a starter kit on your chair,' says Ted. 'Go ahead and open it before the food's brought in.'

'Oh, boy.' Kevin rushes forward like a child at Christmas, a huge smile on his face, his misery at being such a lousy shot — he was the worst of us all — instantly forgotten.

Byron is just behind him, looking very young, and I have to wonder at his reason for being here. The rest of us follow more slowly, but even I feel a strange eagerness to see what kind of gear they're giving us.

Each starter kit contains: one pair of handcuffs with key, pepper spray, ammunition, a shoulder holster, an official-looking badge that says Recovery Agent and a pair of leg-irons.

Holly picks up her badge. 'Recovery Agent?' she asks.

Ted snorts. 'The sorry-ass politically correct assholes who help finance this place make us use those badges, but I don't like it. We're bounty-hunters. 'Recovery agents' makes us sound like we're in the FBI or the CIA, and I'm sure as hell not a spook.'

'Yeah, you're right,' says Kevin. 'I wouldn't want to go on a recovery agent trip. It sounds as if you're going to the scene of a plane crash.'

'Or towing away illegally parked cars,' says Holly.

'Exactly.' Kevin turns to Holly. 'And what sort of vacation would that be? You'd never think a recovery-agent vacation had guns.'

Veronica's nodding. 'And Nick's dad certainly wouldn't do a movie playing a recovery agent. It's wimpy.' A wistful note

140

creeps into her voice. 'He'd make a great bounty-hunter, though.'

I laugh. (It's expected.) 'I'll tell him you said that.'

Kevin picks up the leg-irons. 'Wow, these are heavier than I expected. They can cause a lot of damage if you hit someone on the head with them. Especially if you get lucky and get them from behind.'

'And how would you know that?' asks Holly, with a flirtatious laugh. 'I hope you don't make a habit of hitting people over the head.'

Kevin flushes and sets down the leg irons. 'No, I've never seen any before. Not in real life. I'm a gamer.'

'A gamer?'

'A role-player,' Kevin clarifies. 'I don't need a board or a computer, just my imagination.'

'You mean you play Dungeons & Dragons?' asks Veronica, an eyebrow raised in disbelief. 'I thought that was just for kids. I could understand if Byron here was still playing, he's young enough, but you've gotta be in your thirties, Kevin. Don't you think you should grow up? Or is that why you're here? To acquire a new hobby.'

Great. Now Veronica's describing bounty-hunting as if it's no different from stamp-collecting. It gets worse and worse.

Byron clears his throat, then hesitates, flushing. 'I'm not that young,' he says. 'I'm in college. I'm studying to be a writer.'

'It's not just for kids,' says Kevin, ignoring Byron. 'It's great escapism, like reading or going to the movies, but with group interaction and the need to use your mind. You have to be creative.' Kevin glances at me. 'You should try it, Nick. You'd like it. Your father would too. It's so much fun I'd recommend it to everyone. And adults appreciate it more. We know it's only make-believe. We can separate game violence from reality.'

And then it hits me with a sinking feeling. Even with his head-to-toe-I'm-ready-for-the-jungle outfit, I'd really hoped Kevin wasn't here to re-enact some dark fantasy, but now I think he probably signed up for this course because he's tired of slaying dragons and goblins with rolls of his dice and his imaginary sword and wants to try it for real. But I wonder where his gaming buddies are. It troubles me that they're not here. I'd rather have a group of them laughing, planning and joking about what's going to happen than just Kevin, alone. A group outing would be jolly. Kevin on his own is ominous.

I decide to ask him. I have to know. 'What about your gaming friends? Where are they?'

Kevin shrugs. 'They're spoilsports. They didn't want to come. They said that the whole point of gaming is to become someone different from yourself. You can excel at anything — guns, picking pockets, martial arts, whatever. Guess they were afraid they'd suck at those kind of things in real life.'

'This isn't a game,' says Ted.

'I know. That's why I'm here. I wanted to do something as me.' Kevin's face is animated. He's clearly in his element. 'Gaming is not just wizards and magic, Veronica,' he says, responding to her earlier comment. 'There are lots of different worlds to play in. My latest campaign is set in the near future. I play a cop. That's how I know about leg-irons. The technology is much better than today's, but sometimes you get involved in hand-to-hand combat and my character uses leg irons as a weapon. It's really cool.'

I notice that Holly's following the conversation carefully, watching faces for reactions as well as listening to the words.

'Leg-irons aren't a good weapon,' says Veronica. 'They're too bulky for a good swing.'

Kevin's smile fades and he shrugs. 'It works well in the game.'

'That's because it's a game,' says Ted.

143

'And, anyway,' I say, recalling what he'd said earlier when he'd first spotted the leg-irons, 'if you're a cop, why are you going around hitting people from behind? Aren't you supposed to be the good guy?'

'Oh, yeah, I am, but the world's in chaos and gangs roam the cities so we're always getting into fights.' Kevin's smiling again.

Tick. Kevin's happy. Another point to me. Shame I don't get performance-related pay. Purveyors aren't expected to work in the face of danger so I deserve a fortune for continuing my task in a situation like this.

'And on that note,' says Ted, 'let's get back to earth. We're here to capture real criminals, not to play games and use pretend weaponry. So please, people, stick to your guns and bullets. Don't go copying Kevin here and use your leg-irons to try to subdue the crims. I guarantee it won't work.'

'It does in the game.'

Ted ignores Kevin. 'When you return to your rooms at the end of the day you'll find the rest of your gear: black boots, black trousers, black shirt, black belt, black hat, black jacket, black backpack.'

Black, black, black. I take it they're planning to go in at night. (It'd probably be desert camos if we were going in during the day.) Are we forming an insertion team? Is

144

that what he's trying to tell us?

'And a black flak vest,' says Ted. 'If anything doesn't fit let me know and we'll change it.'

Hold on. Flak vest? If I query this, he'll tell me it's only a precautionary measure, to protect us from all those bullets in the unlikely event of a firefight. It wouldn't be good for business if the customers started dying. I know I should be comforted by the thought that it will increase our chances of survival, but knowing that the bounty-hunting school deems it necessary for us to wear flak vests only reinforces my uneasiness. I wonder how many students they've lost.

'I've heard black is the new pink,' says Byron, with a nervous chuckle.

'What about the guns?' asks Kevin. 'When do we get those?'

(Ted didn't let us keep the pistols we used at the firing range: he put them back in their locker.)

'I'll pass them out when it's time to go on the hunt.'

The hunt, Ted says. Like it's a treat.

THE MISSION PLAN

After lunch Ted takes us back into the classroom and tapes two large photographs to the wall: police mugshots of two men. No doubt they're the nastiest, meanest-looking criminals around so that we tourists feel we're getting our money's worth.

'Take a good look,' says Ted. 'You need to be able to identify them instantly. We don't want any mistakes.'

Like we're going to be calm enough to double-check we've got the right man. Is Ted under the delusion that we're not the old-time circus freak show we appear to be? That we're competent? We'll be lucky not to shoot ourselves in the feet, let alone worry about the identity of whoever we're trying to apprehend. We probably wouldn't even notice if it was a woman until it was too late. That, Ted, is the level of our proficiency. Completely non-existent.

But I allow nothing of my thoughts to show on my face. For I am the great Nick Schwarzenegger. I am not allowed an attitude problem. I am a purveyor of happiness and my job is to be charming, not to spoil this experience for everyone else. And, okay, I admit it, most of all I don't want Holly to think I'm a wanker.

Ted taps the photo on the left. 'This is Karl Wright.'

Karl has scraggly dark brown hair and a goatee. He's tall, well over six feet and not skinny. His eyes are glaring, full of hate and viciousness. He looks exactly like the kind of man you'd cross the street to avoid. He's certainly not someone you want to meet when you're on the wrong side of his big chance for freedom.

'Karl,' says Ted, 'was first arrested for arson when he was twelve, but he was let off as nothing could be proven. He was arrested again at thirteen and then at fourteen, and ended up serving three years in a juvy. Since his release ten years ago he's been suspected in numerous burglary and arson attacks, but the police were never able to make the charges stick. Then, last month, he was involved in an armed robbery on a liquor store.'

Great. Contestant number one is a pyromaniac and an armed robber. A psycho who's good with guns and takes what he wants when he wants it.

Ted taps the other photo. 'This is his accomplice.'

The second criminal has very short, dirty-blond hair, a crew-cut that's grown out ever-so-slightly, and half of his face is covered in a day's stubble, the other half smooth, as if he was interrupted while shaving. He's not as big as Karl and would look less intimidating, but there's something in his pale blue eyes and his smirk that's as scary as Karl's stare of hatred. The man's just been arrested and he doesn't care.

Ted continues, 'Luke Russell used to hold a job as a regular car mechanic. He broke his leg in a motorcycle accident and had to take some time off. When he was well enough to go back to work they'd given the job to someone else. Now Luke here didn't want to leave his hometown of Tucson, but he just couldn't find a job. And you can guess what happened next, can't you?' Ted nods. 'That's right. He met Karl Wright.'

'Is this sob story supposed to make us feel all sympathetic and soft and mushy towards Russell?' asks Veronica. 'If it is it's not working. A criminal's a criminal's a criminal. I don't care if a crim used to be a priest and could have become a saint. If he's turned, he's turned, and he's just like the rest of them.'

Ted smiles. 'Well, that's good to hear, honey. I wouldn't want to think a couple of bail-jumpers could win your sympathy.'

Although Luke Russell scares the shit out of me, I feel a little sorry for him. Maybe all he ever wanted was to be a car mechanic and when his dream was destroyed he just couldn't cope. I know all about the death of dreams.

'So how did they meet?' asks Holly, playing with a strand of her hair, twirling it round a finger. She's lapping up the background details.

'Luke and Karl met in a bar, ended up on the same side in a fight, and then became partners in crime. They did pretty low-key stuff for a while, stealing cars, that sort of thing, or at least that's what we suspect. Then in Phoenix they held up a liquor store. They beat up the owner pretty bad, but he survived and was able to identify them.'

'And those scum-suckers got bail?' asks Veronica.

Ted nods. 'Yep. As they'd never been convicted, except Wright as a juvenile and that doesn't count, they weren't deemed a risk to society with all that innocent-until-proven-guilty-in-a-trial crap that protects professional criminals such as them. They were allowed bail. Which, of course, they immediately jumped.'

Are we bounty-hunting trainees considered

a risk to society? I rather think we will be a danger to the public when we're let loose on the world. Why aren't people worried about us? They should be.

'When was this?' asks Holly. She watches Ted, wide-eyed, hanging on his every word.

'They didn't show up for a mandatory meeting with our bail-bond officer yesterday morning.'

'Bail-bond officer?' Holly's voice is soft and sweet, seemingly interested, seemingly innocent. 'What's that?' She knows this. She's done her background research. She's only asking to see how Ted will define it.

Ted frowns at her. 'Something anyone who wants to be a bounty-hunter should know.' He turns to the group. 'Who can tell Holly what a bail-bond officer is?'

Kevin raises his hand and waves it back and forth eagerly.

'Okay, Kevin,' says Ted. 'Go ahead and tell us.'

Kevin launches straight into his explanation. 'When accused criminals don't have enough money for bail, they can go to a bail-bond officer and get the necessary funds — for a fee, of course. They have to sign a contract saying they won't run and that, if they do, they agree to be hunted and brought back. That's where we bounty-hunters come in. We're the ones who find and apprehend the bail-jumpers.'

'Thank you, Kevin,' says Ted. 'Keep in mind that what Kevin means by an accused criminal is someone who's been arrested and charged and who hasn't been tried in court yet. And, yes, these suspects have to agree that they'll be chased down like dogs if they run. They consent to being shot at and injured, even killed, if this becomes necessary to haul them back. And it's all about money. If the bail-jumper isn't found, the bail-bond officer loses the money he's generously allowed them for bail.'

I make a mental note not to sign a contract saying I can be hunted down like an animal at any point in my life. Always read the small print: that's a new motto for me to live by. I take a surreptitious peek at my Rolex, wondering how many hours are left before dinner. As always, the Rolex brings thoughts of Emma. I wonder how she's doing and if she's divorced yet. I hope she's coping. I hope she's happy.

'As soon as someone jumps bail, the bail-bond officer turns to us,' says Ted, looking at each of his students, making sure we're paying attention. 'And when we bring 'em in, the bail-bond officer gets his money back, we get a percentage for our work and everybody's happy.' Ted smiles. 'I should point out that you all waived your portion of the reward when you signed up for this course.'

'Isn't this dangerous?' I ask. Surely someone else can see this. I can't be the only one. Would I be the first character in a horror movie to realise that something was wrong? That the strange noises in the house weren't just a nasty coincidence? Would I be the only one to think exploring the deserted cellar on one's own was a bad idea and that maybe we should just get the hell out while we still could?

'Son,' says Ted, 'if you wanted a non-dangerous vacation you should have gone to Disneyland. Your father could have told you that. He knows what these things are like. But don't you worry, Nick. I won't let anything happen to Arnie's boy.'

Oh, thanks, Ted, I feel so much better. Your words have reassured me. Not.

'What about the rest of us?' asks Byron.

Ted stares at him, then at everyone individually, wanting his message to sink in. 'This is for real, people, not some fancy gimmick for you rich city folk. Veronica knows I mean business. These are criminals, genuine lawbreakers, true bad guys, not actors.'

'But where are they?' asks Holly. She flashes her eyes at Ted with that sexy look she has that turns a man's middle to mush. She must be trying to lull him into a false sense of security so he'll tell her more than he should, so that he'll never suspect she's a journalist. 'They could be anywhere in the country. Or they could be in Mexico — we're not very far from the border.'

'That's right,' says Kevin. 'I signed up for this weeks ago. How'd you know they'd be on the run if they're real criminals?'

'Wright and Russell aren't the only bail-jumpers out there,' says Ted. 'There are dozens of them, but they are our best and closest targets. And, if we're lucky, they'll be sticking together and then we'll get two crims in one sweep. My people are out searching for them even as we're sitting here wasting our training time. Don't worry, we'll find them. They won't get away.'

'They'd better not,' says Veronica.

'They won't, honey. We won't let them.' Ted turns to the group. 'And when we catch them, you all get a fancy certificate for your wall.'

That tourist thing again. Glad to see Ted remembers we're not professionals.

SO THIS IS WHERE THE BRUISES
AND BLISTERS KICK IN

We spend the afternoon learning techniques for recapturing the crims. Ted makes us take out our handcuffs and stand in a circle.

Kevin, like a stag in rutting season, makes a beeline for Veronica. 'Do you want to be partners?' he asks her, smiling. 'I promise to go easy on you.'

Ted frowns. 'I'm the one who assigns the work. You leave Veronica alone and come here, Kevin. You can be my assistant.'

'Really?' Kevin glows, unable to believe his luck.

He should have listened to his instincts. It wasn't luck that brought him to Ted's side. At least not good luck. Oh, Kevin assists Ted all right. He becomes the experimental test subject we practice on.

Our handcuffing lesson can be summed up in four words: we throw Kevin around. We throw him to the ground, we toss him across the circle, we throw him again and again and again, and occasionally we wrench his arms behind his back and handcuff him. I can't really see the point of this exercise, it's not as if we'll be standing in a circle playing hot potato when we ambush — Ted's word, not mine — the crims, but we have fun. (Everyone but Kevin has fun that is.) There's nothing so bonding and group-forming as having a common enemy and, according to Ted, for today that enemy is Kevin.

After an hour Ted calls a halt to the handcuffing. 'Okay, people. That's enough for now. Let's move on to leg-iron techniques.' He picks up a set of shackles. 'Kevin, come here. I need your help.'

'No,' says Kevin. 'It's someone else's turn. I need a chance to practise too.'

Ted's face loses every trace of warmth. 'Do you want to be a bounty-hunter, Kevin?'

'Yes,' he whispers.

'Then you do what I tell you to do when I tell you to do it. I thought that was understood. It's no good you saying, 'Yes, sir,' in the morning then complaining in the afternoon. I don't want Nick here telling his father we run a ramshackle organisation. Is that clear?'

'Yes, sir.' Kevin steps forward. Or, rather, limps. He's looking a bit stiff and sore. The first — and, dare I hope, only — victim of Ted's promised bruises.

Ted addresses the group. 'By the time you

get out the leg-irons the crim should already be subdued.' He unlocks the shackles, then snaps them shut. 'And by subdued I mean handcuffed, shot, unconscious or whatever. You won't be able to put these on if the crim is up and fighting and his hands are free. Veronica, honey, you handcuff Kevin again.'

Veronica's face lights up with a magnificent Julia Roberts smile that declares her eagerness, and steps into the centre of the circle. Before Kevin can back away, she's grabbed his arms, wrenched them behind his back brutally and, just like that, the cuffs are on. 'Don't worry, I'm going easy on you,' she says.

Holly winces. I catch hold of her hand and give it a tiny squeeze to show that I understand, that I'm not heartless, that, after all, I am here because of her and not because I wanted to come.

'Ow. That hurt. Be careful,' says Kevin. He tries to shrug his shoulders and stretch his arms a little, but he can't move without flinching, and that tells us he's in pain. 'You should be a cop.'

Veronica snorts. 'I was.'

'You were?' asks Byron, studying her in surprise.

'Really?' Holly's eyes are wide, friendly, interested.

Frowning, Veronica nods. 'Until last month. Bastard lawyers made them fire me. Said I was too rough for some poor little criminals. Not my fault they didn't get enough calcium as children and their bones weren't strong.'

'I could really like you, honey,' says Ted. He gives her a big smile, then returns to teacher-mode. 'Now, there are two ways you can do this. If the criminal is calm you can just put them on his legs like so.' He bends down and snaps the leg-irons on to Kevin's ankles, then immediately takes them off, setting them casually to one side. 'But,' says Ted, 'usually the crim'll still be fighting, kicking and squirming if he's conscious, so what you have to do is this.'

Ted punches Kevin in the stomach, then grabs him and throws him to the floor while he's still gasping for breath. The shackles are back on Kevin's ankles before we have time to do anything but blink.

Ted stands, leaving Kevin on the floor. 'Now that's how you might have to do it out in the field, but I don't want you practising that way in here 'cause Kevin might get hurt, and we need every hand we've got when we go in.'

Kevin might get hurt? What about the past hour and a half?

157

'Kevin,' says Ted, 'stay there. Everyone else just practise putting the leg-irons on and off him and you'll know how they work if it does get rough. Once we're done here, we'll head outside and I'll show you the correct way to use pepper spray.'

Kevin's cheeks, flushed pink with exertion, pale, and he looks as if he'd swoon if he weren't already on the floor.

Ted continues, 'In the Marines they make you take it in the face just so you know what it's like, but I don't want any of you pansies — Kevin, Byron — out of action 'cause your eyes won't stop streaming.'

ROOMS MADE FOR LOVERS (EXACTLY HOW MANY COUPLES DO THEY GET HERE ANYWAY?)

After Ted judges us competent at leg-ironing and pepper-spraying, we're given an hour off to rest and clean up before dinner.

Holly leads me by the hand to her room.

But I can't be alone with Holly in her room. What if she wants to have sex?

I can't have sex with Holly.

No, I'm not crazy. I'm not stupid. I *want* to have sex with gorgeous, wonderful Holly. But I can't.

I have to think up an excuse, some reason why I can't go to her room, why I have to make a phone call or sort through my luggage or something. But my mind is frozen. My tongue, normally so glib, with lies lined up and ready, is silent. I say nothing as Holly leads me to her room.

I'll have to think up some reason why I can't stay. It'll be a lame excuse, but I have to do something to get away. I have to.

What's happened to me? I'm trying to get

out of having sex with a beautiful woman. I deserve to be shot.

But I won't do it. I have some principles. I will not have sex with Holly while she thinks I'm the son of Arnold Schwarzenegger. It hasn't bothered me with other women that maybe they slept with me because of what they thought my name was, but that was okay back then, when I was a purveyor of happiness. I gave them pleasure. I made them happy. I know that I did. But things are different now. I can't do this to Holly. I *won't* do this to Holly. She'd never forgive me.

(It's not so strange that we haven't been to bed together yet. We've only known each other a few days. The kisses have been passionate and the hands have been roving, but that's it. I know I go on and on about how mad I am for her, yet it's only the beginning. And I will not ruin it by listening to the advice of runaway hormones. I will not sleep with her while she thinks I'm Nick Schwarzenegger.)

Holly unlocks the door to her room and we step in. The door closes behind us with a thud.

We're alone in Holly's room.

Suddenly I feel very hot and a sweat breaks out on my forehead. I force myself to drop her hand and step away to study the décor although there are hundreds of things I'd rather be doing with her, and none includes any physical distance between us.

'This is really some place,' I say, making my voice light-hearted as I gesture round the room. 'Reminds me of an over-the-top movie set.'

I saw it earlier after we'd checked in, when I met her here so we could go to Ted's introductory talk together, but it still makes me blink. Someone must have gone insane one Valentine's Day and decided that pink, fluffy and lots of hearts tied in well with the masculine theme of this trip.

Holly smiles. 'It's great, isn't it?'

My face must show the horror I'm feeling at the idea that she likes it because she bursts out laughing.

'Great for my article,' she says.

'You can tell them all about the honeymooners who come here for a romantic getaway of sex and bloodshed,' I say. (My room is decorated in red and gold and has a distinct harem feel to it so there's obviously some sort of theme going on here.)

'Or the rich men who bring their mistresses.' Holly nods at her very ominous-looking black SWAT-team insertion clothing laid out on the sofa, as Ted had promised earlier. 'I doubt many wives would want to come along on this kind of trip. Sneaky husbands could invite them in the safe knowledge that they'd say no, and that would leave them free to take their mistresses.'

How cynical she is. Poor thing needs a bit of my tender care to make the world seem a happier place.

I continue studying the room, not daring to look her in the eye, scared of what I might see, terrified of my own reaction. 'The Jacuzzi and the vibrating bed are the giveaways.'

'It wouldn't be my first choice for a romantic break,' she says. Then, suddenly, she is pressing herself to me, rubbing against me like a kitten.

I want to hold her tight and kiss her until she's trembling with desire, but I merely raise an eyebrow and concentrate on maintaining a conversation. I can't let lust control me. 'It wouldn't?' I say, struggling to sound calm and relaxed, trying to ignore the feel of Holly's gorgeous, sexy body. 'But I thought that's why we were here. I'd assumed all this work business was merely an excuse to lure me on an extended holiday after our time at the resort in Phoenix was over.' I'm joking, of course. Unfortunately I know all too well that she takes her work very seriously.

'I never said business trips couldn't be fun. A girl expects a few perks with the job.'

She kisses me.

I kiss her back — how could I resist? — but I know that distraction is in order. I can't let her keep thinking along these lines. A kiss leads to roving hands, roving hands lead to carnal thoughts, carnal thoughts lead to action, and action would lead to doom and disaster. What will I say if she asks me to stay the night? Or, worse, to go to bed right now?

How can I say no without offending her and ruining my chances of a future together? I can hardly claim to be a born-again Christian who doesn't believe in sex before marriage. What would I say? Sex is evil? It wouldn't come out right. I don't have the lingo. My most recent exposure to religion was *Dogma* and I'm not convinced that that was very accurate. And, besides, Holly already knows I'm not exactly holy. (It's pretty obvious even without knowledge of the purveyor-of-happiness factor.)

She'd assume I was rejecting her. She'd get angry and think I was a tease. No, she couldn't believe there was such a thing as a male tease. She'd think I was weird. And, believe me, girls like Holly — recall that Liz Hurley thing again — don't go for weird.

But we're still kissing. While I'm thinking that I shouldn't be kissing her, that I can't let it move on to something else, I'm still kissing her. I like kissing Holly.

I have to stop.

I break away abruptly, pulling my lips from hers and my body from her embrace. For a second Holly looks confused, then her face colours slowly.

I take a shaky breath, smile, pull her close and kiss her forehead. 'It's nearly time for dinner,' I say. 'We don't want Ted marching down the corridor to summon us if we're late.' I'm hoping that comes across right.

Holly smiles. 'We can't have Ted's most famous pupil disappoint him.'

She's teasing me and I know then that I'm forgiven for ending our passionate clinch the way I did. 'When this is over,' I say, 'I'm taking you somewhere special.'

'But this is special.' Holly's eyes twinkle as she grins at me. 'You can hardly get anywhere more unique.'

'Then I'll take you to a place where luxury means pampering twenty-four hours a day and not just when you're sleeping in a comfy bed at night.'

She makes a face. 'I don't want to go to another five-star resort. I'm fed up with resorts. I've been to so many this year.'

'Then we'll go to my house and you can help me with the interior design.'

164

'I'd like that,' says Holly.

What the hell am I saying? I have no house. I have nowhere. I was renting the flat in Wimbledon and my half's been lost to Richard's young blonde nightie-wearer. My stuff — my clothes, my guitar, my entire DVD and CD collections, everything — is stored in my parents' loft. I'm not supposed to lie to Holly any more than necessary to keep this Schwarzenegger thing going. I didn't have to mention a house.

I must be losing it.

Calm. Deep breaths. No, liars can't take deep breaths to reassure themselves. Deep breaths give a liar away.

Now that I've said it, I'll try to take advantage of it. If I can coax her away from here I can tell her the truth, and the sooner I tell her the truth the less I'll have to lie to her. I don't like deceiving Holly.

'Let's leave,' I say. 'We can pack and be out of here in under an hour.'

'Oh, Nick, don't tempt me. You know I'd like nothing better than to run away with you, but I can't. My editor would kill me.'

'So? You're a freelance, you've got plenty of editors.'

'I can't. This is my big break. A chance for some groundbreaking journalism. No more travel pieces. No more cosy features on women's fashion. No more endless wandering from hotel to hotel. I want to do biting exposés. I want something I can sink my teeth into.'

'But we don't need to go on the hunt, do we? You can just write about the training and say how appalling it is that partially trained tourists are allowed to do this. Surely there's enough there for a piece.'

'I have to go on the hunt. I can't write about how dangerous it all is if I'm not there to see it at firsthand. You don't have to stay if you don't want to, but I do.'

I cup her chin, look down into her eyes. I give in. If she's staying, I'm staying. And I did want my time in America to be an adventure. This certainly qualifies for that. 'Of course I'm going to stay with you. I only thought it'd be more fun for us to be on our own. Call me selfish, if you want, but I just want to be alone with you.' And once this is over, when we're on our own, when we're far, far away from here, I can tell her the truth.

Holly relaxes and her eyes shine. 'I really am glad you're here. Thanks for coming.'

'You're welcome.'

'It's going better than I expected. This room, Ted our instructor, the other pupils, the training, the danger, the whole concept of the vacation, everything. It's fantastic. My article's going to be fabulous. Just think how scathing I can be about it all. And Kevin has great comic potential — I could use that, humour is always good. And Byron — he's so sweet, he could add some human interest to the piece. Shame I promised I wouldn't mention you, but I can see how the publicity might be negative for Arnie. But Veronica, wow, she's perfect. I can't wait to look up her records. Sounds like she was fired for brutality. There's so much here for me to use.'

I smile at her joy. I don't have the heart to point out that we might all die. 'As long as you're not hoping something goes wrong,' I say.

Her face freezes. 'But I am. Aren't I awful? Half of me has been longing for catastrophe because it would make a better story.'

'You're not awful,' I say. And to convince her I kiss her, and that leads us right back to where we were before. Shit. I'd managed to distract her, I'd managed to distract myself, but now my hormones are fighting for control again. I'd like nothing better than to sweep her off her feet and carry her to that big pink bed that's just waiting to be used.

Briefly I consider confessing it all, right now, so that it's out of the way, so that when an opportunity like this next presents itself, I'll be able to take advantage of it without a guilty heart. I'd tell her this very second if I could. I'm ready to face her accusations. And her disappointment. But I can't. Not here.

She'll probably loathe me when she hears the truth, though I'm hoping that'll only be temporary. But I can't tell her at the bounty-hunting school: it's not safe. She'd be distracted. I'd be distracted. It wouldn't be good for either of us. We need our wits about us while we're here.

And not only Holly would hate me. Ted would hate me, and the others would too. I'd become a social outcast, and I'd be forced to take Kevin's place when the next time comes for punch-bag practice. I don't want to be the one they all despise. I don't want to be the one sent in at the front as disposable cannon-fodder.

Okay, okay, I admit it: I'm one of those people who like to be liked. That might be considered a personality flaw, but it's not a bad one. And my decision isn't only based on the fact that I don't want everyone to hate me: it wouldn't be safe for them to know. And how could I look out for Holly if she made sure she stayed as far away from me as possible?

No, I can't tell her today. But I will tell her, once we're out of here.

If we live.

But now I've accepted that we'll be going on the hunt, I'm going to try for a more positive attitude. I don't think telling myself that we're going to die all the time is doing my psyche any good. Though if we *are* going to die, maybe I should just give in and take Holly to bed right now.

No, don't think like that. Mustn't think like that. We'll make it. Ted's promised to look out for us, hasn't he?

We're still kissing and I'm enjoying it, I'd be lying to myself if I said I wasn't, but it has to stop right now.

A minute later, two, three, four, I'm losing track of time, I pull away, not out of her arms, just enough to end the kiss and glance at my Rolex. 'It's nearly time to eat,' I say. And that's not a lie. I'm trying to be good.

Is that disappointment I see on Holly's face? I'd like to think so.

I know what I have to do. I'll be charming and entertaining at dinner. I'll regale the others with stories of my father, with tales of the adventures Arnie and I have had together. They'll ask all sorts of questions and the hours will pass and we'll be sent to bed. We'll be told to get straight to sleep for an early start and then it'll be too late and I'll be safe for one more day. There can be no more kissing tonight. I don't know how much

169

longer I can resist.

And as I'm being good and noble, as I've made my decision to keep my hands to myself, as I'm just about ready to head for the door, Holly pulls me to the bed.

'I want you,' she murmurs against my throat. 'I want you now. I can't wait till after dinner.'

I have no will left to resist her as she pushes me down on the bed and straddles me. Holly unbuttons her blouse and I am lost. It's as if my hands belong to someone else, they're not listening to my brain: they reach up and touch her.

Soon her clothes are gone, my clothes are gone, and at last I'm inside her. It's wrong, I know it's wrong, but it's too late to turn back. The deed is done — the deed is happening.

Her legs are wrapped around me and it feels good. It feels so good.

There's a knock at the door. We ignore it.

There's another knock, louder this time. 'Hey, Holly, is Nick in there?' It's Kevin.

I thrust deeper into Holly. Her nails dig into my shoulders.

Kevin knocks again. 'Hey, Holly, are you there? Ted sent me to find you and Nick. It's time for dinner.'

I'm close, so close, and Holly's there too, with me, teetering on the edge.

We hear a scratching at the door and a fumbling at the handle, but it's locked. Kevin can't get in.

'Hey, guys?' calls Kevin. 'You in there?'

There's a slight banging on the door, as if a body is pressing against it, trying to peer through the peephole. We ignore the sounds. We ignore Kevin. Holly cries out, screaming my name.

'Guys?' There's another rattle at the door. 'Hey, guys? It's time to eat.'

Holly moans, again and again.

'Holly? Nick?' says Kevin. 'Can you hear me? I know you're in there.'

A second passes, then another. Holly smiles, kisses the tip of my nose, then turns her head towards the door. She calls out, 'We'll be there in a few minutes, Kevin. You tell Ted to go ahead and start without us.'

'Okay, but don't be too long. I think Ted wants to discuss plans with us over dinner.'

'Goodbye, Kevin,' I say.

'I'm leaving, I'm leaving. See you soon.'

And there's silence.

We wait a moment, listening, but Kevin does not speak again. My lips cover Holly's. We're already late, what's another half-hour or so?

DAY TWO:
THINGS AREN'T LOOKING GOOD

I'd like to say I wake up bright-eyed and eager for the experiences the new day will bring, but that's a lie. I had enough of my temporary buddies last night to make me want the morning off. During the enforced team-building dinner, stories about Arnold Schwarzenegger, my dear old dad, were the highlight. I told them about the time he rescued a drowning child from a local swimming pool, how he dived into the deep end, plucked the toddler from the water and saved that little boy's life. I said that my dad was always doing things like that, helping out wherever and however he could. With a fond smile I described the stray dog he'd found and brought home, and how it turned out to be part wolf and was vicious with strangers but acted like a lap dog whenever my dad was near.

Over dessert I moved on to things Arnie and I had done together, satisfying their urge to hear as many humanising personal details as possible. I told the usual story about losing my mother when I was four years old and how I grew up in England at my grandparents' house. I shared memories of the month Arnie and I spent on horseback in the Serengeti, camping out in tents in the middle of the savannah. They were wide-eyed when I recounted the day we were chased by lions. I told them that Arnie's favourite exercise is bench pressing, that his favourite colour is blue, that he loves eating steak and pizza but sweet and sour chicken is his absolute favourite dish in the world, though apple pie comes a close second. I said he was a world-class yachtsman and that he was considering writing a novel about a young bodybuilder who's trying to make it in Hollywood.

I made up story after story and they still couldn't get enough. They wanted more, more, more.

After dinner, Ted got back to business and I was glad. I'd felt strange regurgitating the same old tales in front of Holly. They no longer seemed so innocent and harmless with her listening.

Ted led us through possible scenarios for capturing the crims. We were taught the basics of swarming a house where they'd holed up, ambushing a car along a deserted road, ambushing a car along a busy road, and attacking a gas station or supermarket in which they'd taken refuge. Most of these demonstrations seemed to consist of poor Kevin — dressed up for dinner in a clean T-shirt, the slogan 'How about it, Baby?' plastered across his chest — standing in as the house or the car or the crims or whatever, and Ted circling round and pouncing whenever he was ready to attack.

It was all highly amusing for the rest of us, of course, particularly after the beer started flowing, but I could have done with a night away from the gang. I know that originally it had been my plan to stay with them, to remain in public so that I wouldn't have to rebuff Holly and hurt her feelings, but that was no longer an issue. We'd had sex, so I didn't have to avoid her any longer. In fact, I wanted the evening and Ted's lessons to end so that we could return to her bed and practise some more of that horizontal getting-to-know-you-better stuff. Spending the whole day and then the whole evening with the other would-be bounty-hunters was not my idea of a good time.

The highlight was bidding the others goodnight and heading back to Holly's room, leaving Ted and Veronica looking cosy over a pitcher of beer. Kevin was giving Byron some manly advice, explaining the advantages of using brain and not brawn to attract women.

Holly and I were up for hours, and when I say up, I mean up. We were just starting to drift off to sleep when a banging sound started coming from Veronica's room next door. It took me a second to realise that the noise was the rhythmic slamming of the headboard against the wall. Holly gave me a wide smile and listened for a moment, then she started kissing me, and it was another hour or two before we had a chance for some shut-eye.

But the night is over and it's morning now. And I'm not feeling too guilty. The sex was great. I enjoyed it. Holly enjoyed it. There's nothing wrong with that. It might make things a little trickier when I confess, but it's too late for second thoughts. What's done is done. It's just a shame there's a whole day's training to get through before we can go to bed again.

Once we're showered and dressed we join the others for a bite to eat in the cafeteria. We were unable to resist a last-minute shag so we're late — again — but no one comments. Ted and Veronica are flashing secret smiles at one another, and he's looking rather smug. Byron is quietly eating his breakfast. Kevin's wearing a 'Size Does Matter' T-shirt. I like to think he's declaring his partiality for big women rather than the obvious. Size and Kevin are not what I want to think about. Kevin seems oblivious to the whole flirtation thing and is quizzing Ted about the day's activities between huge bites of food.

'My body is a temple,' says Kevin, over and over, when Ted keeps turning away to talk privately with Veronica. He chuckles at his own joke every time he makes it, shovelling forkful after forkful of sausage and bacon into his mouth. 'I only eat things that taste good.' He smacks his lips. 'If you were an ancient Greek leaving gifts to your gods, you'd only leave treats and succulent foods, you wouldn't worry about all those nasty, healthy vegetables. Cholesterol wouldn't even factor into the equation. Even if they'd known what it was.' He chortles, snorting, nudging Byron. 'Get it? That's why my body's a temple.'

Byron gives him a weak smile. 'Yeah, right. Okay.'

I decline to comment, and Holly gives me a knowing look.

When breakfast is over we're taught the rudiments of first aid. It had the potential to be really good, but we have to swap partners and I'm stuck with giving Kevin the kiss of life. Let's just say the scent of all the onions he'd had in the omelette that followed the sausage isn't helping. Holly is paired with

Byron, and Veronica is with Ted. I really think Ted should have had a bit more consideration for his number-one pupil (i.e., me). The Son of Arnie should not have to give Kevin mouth-to-mouth resuscitation, unless it's a true emergency. I think the sex has gone to Ted's brain. He's not paying me the attention I deserve.

'That's right, Byron,' says Ted, as Byron puts his lips to Holly's. 'We'll make a man of you yet.' Ted smiles at me, then turns back to Byron. 'Blow, son, don't kiss her — I don't want Nick getting mad at me. Don't be afraid of her. She's pretty but she won't bite. Just keep practising. You need to get comfortable around a woman. I think it's about time you lost your virginity. Don't you?'

Byron flushes a deep red. 'But — '

'Just kidding, son. Just kidding.'

At last we're able to choose our own partners and it's much more fun working with Holly. The time flies by.

After the first aid lesson when I'm thinking we've been given just enough knowledge to make us dangerous if we ever come across anything complicated — for we'll be under the mistaken belief that we know what we're doing — Ted takes us through more target practice and handcuffing lessons.

'Right, you'll do,' says Ted, after two hours

of sweating and a few more bruises for Kevin. 'Go back to your rooms, clean up and try on your uniforms. Then assemble in the cafeteria for inspection. Don't forget to bring the rest of your equipment with you. I want to go over everything again.' Ted puts his hands on his hips and watches us. 'You have six minutes.'

DO THE CLOTHES MAKE THE MAN?
(LET'S HOPE THEY GIVE US THAT
SWAT-TEAM EDGE)

For speed, Holly and I split up and each head to our own rooms to change, mostly because that's where our clothes are. The red and gold colour scheme in mine makes me blink: it's easy to forget that beyond those plain corridors are rooms designed to be a rich man's fantasyland.

The door shuts behind me and I turn the lock, then strip off my own clothes, leaving them in a pile on the floor. I slide on the black combat socks, the black trousers, and as I'm slipping the black shirt over my head I catch a glimpse of my Rolex. It's not exactly insertion-team gear, but I love it.

I pull my shirt into place and stare at my wrist.

I don't want to take off my Rolex. It reminds me of Emma.

A WEEK WITH EMMA

Other than buying the *Big Issue*, giving a few coins here and there to the homeless and sponsoring endangered rhinos in Africa through the WWF, helping Emma Johnston that moonlit night on the shores of Lake Michigan could be classified as the first genuinely unselfish act of my life. It was certainly the most generous I'd ever been to a stranger.

And it wasn't just a half-hearted gesture. I truly wanted to help her. It was noble and pure — or at least it started out that way.

It's been over two months since I saw her. Things are different now from what they were when I was the happy-go-lucky Son of Robert Redford. I wonder how she's doing. Is she still getting divorced? She'd better be, for her sake. I don't know how long it takes, but Bill the Bastard will probably try to push it through fast so he can marry his pregnant mistress before she gives birth. I hope this means he's forced to give Emma a much bigger financial settlement than he would if he wasn't pressed for time.

I know she'd be fine without his money — she comes from a wealthy Chicago family — but he owes her. He owes her big-time. She deserves something for putting up with him all those years.

Dear, sweet, wonderful Emma.

At breakfast that first morning, after we'd spent the whole night talking by the lake, Emma found out who I was, who my father was. It was inevitable. I'd known it would happen at some point — but I didn't think of it when Emma and I went to the breakfast room. If I had I would have ordered us a basket of food and taken it down to the beach so we could eat on our own, avoiding other people to delay the revelation of my 'identity'.

As soon as we entered the restaurant it started. Startled glances and beaming smiles were sent our way from every corner of the room. And not because we'd obviously been up all night and were still dressed in the clothes of the evening before: Emma in her long white dress, me in the trousers and shirt in which I'd arrived at the resort. No, those looks of adulation and joy had a more familiar origin.

'I really admire your father,' said the man who showed us to a table by the window. '*Butch Cassidy and the Sundance Kid* is one of the greatest movies of all time.'

'Thanks,' I said, smiling, gracious as always, accepting part of the credit for myself, as if talent passes through the blood of the generations and was partially mine by right of birth. 'I'll tell him you said so. He's always had a soft spot for it.'

Emma stared at me curiously, but she held her tongue until we were seated and left on our own with the menus. 'Who's your father?'

I shrugged as if I was used to the question, which by then I was. My mouth opened and, for the first time, I felt like a cheap fraud. I wished I could just be an ordinary bloke for her. She didn't need the complications that my name-of-the-week saga would bring. But I'd already decided my fate when I'd checked into the hotel so there was no going back. She was obviously going to find out in the next minute or two anyway.

'Come on,' said Emma. 'It can't be that bad. He couldn't have been one of the real outlaws behind the story. Maybe your great-grandfather but not your father. Tell me.' Her lips almost curved into a smile.

'He's Robert Redford.'

'Robert Redford?' An angry pink flush swept up her neck and face. If anything, it made her look more beautiful, less fairy-like perhaps, but it suited her, and I couldn't suppress a flicker of longing. 'The Robert

Redford?' she asked.

I nodded. 'Yes.'

'Wow.' Emma sat back in her chair and studied my face. She was clearly mortified. Flush followed flush across her cheeks as she recalled the details of the previous night: how she'd cried in my arms, told me her life story, confessed her husband's treachery.

I leant across the table and took her hand. 'It doesn't matter,' I said. 'I'm still the same person I was before.'

Emma opened her mouth to say something, but before she could speak, a waitress came over to our table. 'I'm sorry to bother you,' she said, 'but I just had to tell you how much your father's movies have meant to me over the years.'

That opened the floodgates. Every waiter and waitress in the room found some reason to pass near our table and pause, sharing in a bit of that Robert Redford magic.

'I loved *The Horse Whisperer*.'

'Your father did a great job directing *A River Runs Through It*. That movie got me hooked on fly-fishing, no pun intended.'

'I was thinking of entering the Sundance Film Festival in a year or two. Do you know anyone who's looking to finance an independent picture?'

'Did you get to meet Demi Moore when he

was making *Indecent Proposal*?'

'It must have been amazing for him to work with Paul Newman.'

'Oh, you poor thing. Susannah on the front desk told me all about your mother. It must have been awful for you to lose her when you were so young and grow up without really remembering her. And your poor, poor father, letting his little boy be raised in England so you could feel close to your mother. Honouring her last wishes and letting you spend the school year with her parents was so generous of him. Such a sacrifice. No wonder his acting has always had such poignancy. What suffering he must have gone through. I can understand why he doesn't like to talk about it.'

'What's your father working on now?'

When our food arrived they left us alone, but stares and smiles were still directed our way, and not just by the hotel staff: the other guests were looking excited too. Yet no one bothered us during the meal.

Emma toyed with her food. She was still flushed and she glanced out of the window, then back at me. 'Are you here on your own? I didn't even think to ask last night. You must think I'm so inconsiderate going on and on about my problems and not even thinking about you.'

'Don't be silly. You know I was glad to be with you. And I am here on my own so you needn't worry that you're taking me away from anyone.'

'But you're Robert Redford's son.'

'So?'

'If you're here alone you must have come to get away from it all and I'm just ruining your vacation.' Emma looked so sad and fragile as she sat there, across from me, humiliated, heartbroken, despairing.

'Hush. You're not ruining anything.' I smiled at her. 'I'm a lucky man. Not everyone in this room can say he spent the entire night with a beautiful woman. And, anyway, you've seen what it's like. I can't get away from it. Not once people find out about my father. I'd much rather spend my time with you than just socialising with his fans.'

And so, with much persuasion on my part, I managed to convince her that even the Son of Robert Redford was not above comforting a damsel in distress. I was chatty and charming, not wanting to give her time to dwell on the circumstances that had brought us together or my paternity. We knew almost nothing about one another. She'd learnt my name — which was fake. I knew about the state of her marriage, the faithlessness of her soon-to-be-ex-husband, and that she lived nearby. And that was all. It was only logical that we share our life stories, but I had an aversion to regaling her with tales of the good times I'd had with my supposed father, the adventures I'd had on the fringes of Hollywood.

I didn't want to talk about any real-world facts over breakfast: it might have reminded her of last night's events and interfered with her momentary peace of mind. And I want to avoid all references to Tinseltown. Instead I started on my other pet subject: music.

It was amazing. She was amazing. Not to be sexist or anything, but normally women know nothing about the finer details surrounding music. My mates and I would say — have said — that their brains just aren't geared up to appreciate the whole experience properly. To be fair, some women can play instruments, some can sing and some are in bands. They can hum along and even recognise songs on the radio. Many are very talented, Madonna, Sheryl Crow and P.J. Harvey, for example. But in our cocky heads we understand that it is men's knowledge of music trivia that makes our enjoyment of music superior. We may not like all the latest trends but, by God, we keep up with them. We can criticise anything and sound like we know what the hell we're talking about. And usually we do.

It probably says a lot about me and the kind of women I tend to go out with, but I'd never before met a woman who loved music the way I did. Without hesitation Emma agreed that Prodigy's best album was *Music for the Jilted Generation*, despite some differing opinions in the press. She knew that Sinead O'Connor had sung on Peter Gabriel's *Us*, that Billy Corgan allegedly played most of the guitar and bass on *Siamese Dreams*, and that *Full Moon Fever* was recorded in Tom Petty's garage. It's not what you might expect of a woman who looked like a fairy queen and who'd played the violin for twenty-two years, but she was as aware of the wider musical world as any of my mates. She knew which seventies rock bands had retired and which were still going. A woman who'd been to three Jethro Tull gigs was a woman to steal a man's heart.

As soon as our plates had been cleared away and we were drinking coffee, the Robert Redford fans started their progression past our table again.

'I love your father.'

'Your eyes make me shiver — they're just like *his*.'

And on and on and on. Emma flushed

again, but her cheeks weren't as pink as before. She was clearly getting used to the idea. And, really, what was befriending the Son of Robert compared to being told by your husband of ten years that he'd made another woman pregnant and had already asked her to marry him? Nothing.

'Breakfast is my treat,' I told Emma, in a lull, when we were temporarily alone, both wanting to go to our rooms and get some sleep.

'No, I want to get it.'

'You can't refuse without hurting my feelings. You wouldn't let me say no to the Rolex. I won't let you say no to me now.'

She smiled, but her eyes were sad. 'Okay, you win, but I get to treat you to dinner.'

'Fine,' I said. 'Then lunch is mine.'

I wasn't behaving as a purveyor of happiness should when he's on the job, but this wasn't work. Yes, I was staying at the resort under my usual false pretences, but I wasn't going to be searching for any patrons. I'd already decided to devote all my time to Emma. She needed me.

Our waitress came over, refilled our coffee cups, and I asked for the bill. 'Oh, no, Mr Redford, it's on the house. Compliments of the hotel.' She beamed at Emma and me. 'You folks have a great day.'

I gave Emma an embarrassed smile as the waitress walked away. 'I get a lot of that,' I said.

A few minutes later we went our separate ways, to freshen up and rest, but I made Emma promise to meet me for lunch. I didn't want her to spend too much time on her own. I ordered a picnic with all the trimmings and we ate it on a secluded stretch of the beach out of sight of the hotel. I wanted Emma to relax and she couldn't have done that with constant reminders of the Son-of-Robert factor.

During lunch she wanted to talk about the Bastard, but after that we hardly spoke of him again. She didn't want to think about him and I *certainly* didn't. I wanted us to be able to relax and enjoy ourselves.

It was a wonderful week, even better than when I was in Florida being Goldie Hawn's brother. Perhaps it wouldn't make as a good a story to tell my friends back home, but it was more meaningful than frolicking with beach babes. And if I wanted the week to sound impressive, all I'd have to do was describe Emma and reveal how she'd given me a Rolex after our first night together. Sure, I could make it sound sordid and dirty, but I wouldn't. I could never do that to Emma. I liked her. I really, truly liked her.

We spent nearly every moment together including the nights, not having sex but holding one another as we slept. Occasionally she'd look weepy, but gradually the teary eyes faded and she became angry. And I was glad. I wanted her to hate him. She should hate him.

Emma and I became friends. Yes, she needed me, she wanted someone's shoulder to cry on, arms to hold her close when she was sad, but she could have phoned her mother, her sister or any of her friends. She didn't have to rely on a man she'd just met. Maybe for her, like me, it was a magical time, apart from real-life, separate, special, a wonderland all of our own.

On the third day, we were determined to have fun and not only to spite the Bastard. We decided to go boating. Emma was going to take me sailing, but it was such a warm day that she changed her mind and decided it was time I learnt to windsurf. 'I'll teach you,' she said, and ran down the beach to reserve a couple of boards.

I set off after her, chasing her, and soon we were giggling and snorting, cavorting like schoolkids, throwing sand at each other until I scooped her up like a groom carrying his bride over the threshold on their wedding day. I raced towards the water. She kicked and struggled, but I wouldn't put her down and I ran into the lake with Emma in my arms. The water was cold but I ploughed right in and dived under, soaking us both. I released her and we both came up for air.

Her wet hair shone a deep gold. She gave me a sultry look and swam close. I stared into her eyes. And then she splashed me with a great sweep of her arms, shrieking with laughter as she swam away. I chased her again and caught up with her, tugging gently on her ankle to pull her back to my side. I tickled her. She squirmed and wiggled and then, before I knew what was happening, I was kissing her and she was kissing me back. Passionately. Senselessly.

I knew that she was married. I knew that, and I knew that single men were not supposed to kiss married women and that married women were not supposed to kiss men who weren't their husbands. But Emma wasn't really married any longer. Not really. Only technically. And that was just a matter of time.

We kissed and kissed and kissed. She was in my arms and her arms were around me. Our bodies were pressed together and I longed to untie her bikini top and slide down her bikini bottoms and plunge into her, right there in the water, but I couldn't. There were people around.

So we kissed and I nibbled her neck, and then, by unspoken consent, we left the water, holding hands as we ran back to the hotel and to her room. The bridal suite.

We made love in the bed she was supposed to have shared with her husband. We made love all that afternoon and evening, ordering room service for dinner, napping once just after midnight, then carrying on through the rest of the long night. It was a sexual marathon of pure bliss.

I could lie to myself and claim that I was being selfless. That I was only there to help Emma. That she needed me to make her feel beautiful and sexy and good about herself, but it wasn't like that. Thoughts of selflessness didn't enter my mind. I wanted to sleep with her.

We gazed into one another's eyes as we made love. Hers were the deep green of emeralds and I lost myself in them. The night went on for ever and time did stand still.

Emma was —

There's a loud knock at the door and my mind snaps back to the present. I don't have time to daydream. I have to remember that this bounty-hunting thing isn't a game. I can't let thoughts of the past distract me. I pull the sleeve of my shirt down, over my wrist. I leave my Rolex on.

As I head for the door, I realise it's probably Holly. Oops. I was supposed to meet her in her room. She must have given up waiting and come to fetch me. I open the door to find her standing there in her black combat clothes, as stunning as ever.

Holly looks me up and down. 'Ooh, aren't you yummy?' she says, stepping close and giving me a lingering kiss. Then she pulls away and slips past me into my room. 'Much as I'd like to try out the springs in your bed, we don't have time.'

I close the door. 'Are you sure?'

'Sorry, sexy, but I don't want to miss a second of Ted's teaching.' She points at my feet. 'Get your boots on.'

PHOTOSHOOT

When Holly and I arrive the others are already there. Veronica stands in front of a huge wanted poster, posing with a handgun, looking hard and menacing as Ted snaps half a dozen photos of her in her bounty-hunting outfit.

'Come on, honey,' says Ted. 'Let me see you move.'

It's bizarre. It's like a scene from some strange dream where nothing makes sense, but there it doesn't have to because it's a dream, and the reality that we're actually tourists, that we're here on holiday, strikes home. Ted's taking souvenir photos so we'll all have something to take away and keep on our desks.

I can't let him take any pictures of me. I never allow myself to be photographed when I'm working. Even at the beginning, at the planning stage, when I was drawing up the Rules, I knew that snapshots were a no-no. It's doubly important to avoid them in a situation like this.

Veronica whirls and points the gun at

Kevin. She stares down the barrel, as if she's about to shoot him.

Ted's flash goes off once, twice, three times.

'Hey, don't use up all the film,' says Kevin. 'I want some photos too.'

Ted takes one more shot of Veronica. 'Great job,' he tells her. She gives him a sultry smile. 'Kevin, you can go next.'

Kevin dashes across the room to stand in front of the wanted poster as Veronica moves away. 'Give me the gun, Veronica,' he says, holding out his hand. 'It's my turn now.'

Veronica rolls her eyes and ignores him. She hands the gun to Ted and he instantly holsters it.

'But I want to use the gun, too,' says Kevin.

'No, not the gun, Kevin.' Ted stares hard at him. 'It's not a toy. It's a dangerous weapon.'

'But she — '

'Veronica knows what she's doing. Use the leg-irons if you need a prop. We all know how much you like those.'

'But I — '

'You don't want to look just like everyone else, do you?' asks Ted.

'I guess not.' Kevin doesn't sound convinced, but he fumbles around in his bag and finally withdraws the leg-irons. He holds them up to the camera, trying to look tough.

Ted snaps one picture. 'Next.'

'That'll be me,' says Holly. She looks excited: these photos will make a great addition to her article.

'But you only took one,' says Kevin. 'What if I had my eyes closed? I need a good photo. I want to get a few copies and hang them up in my office.'

'In your office?' asks Holly. 'What do you do?'

'I'm a dentist.'

'A dentist?' Veronica laughs. 'And here I was thinking you reminded me of the first slime-sucking informer I ever interrogated.'

Kevin pales, but before he can work up the nerve to ask her what happened to that informer, Ted says, 'Well, Mr Dentist, move aside. It's Holly's turn.'

'But you took lots of Veronica. It's not fair.'

Ted just stares at Kevin until Kevin's shoulders slump and he moves out of the way. Holly flashes him a look of sympathy as she takes his place. Ted snaps half a dozen photos of Holly, then a few of Byron. He allows them to pose with the gun.

When he's finished with the others Ted turns to me. 'Your turn,' he says.

'Oh, no, I couldn't.' My tone is regretful. 'I can't have my photo taken. I never have my photo taken.'

'But you look great,' says Byron. 'The uniform suits you.'

'It does.' Veronica nods. 'You take after your father.'

Maybe I look so tough and convincing as the Son of Arnie that the bounty, a.k.a. the crims, will take one glance at me and, fearing for their lives, hold up their hands and surrender. I'd like that.

'I can't have photos taken,' I say. 'The press would have a field day if they got hold of a picture like that.'

Ted frowns. 'I'm not going to give it to a goddamn reporter, son. This is a souvenir, a memento so you can remember your trip. It's included in the price. It's part of the package.'

'I know you wouldn't give it to them,' I say. It's important to reassure people you don't mean that they personally would do such a thing. You need to create an us-versus-them situation. 'But what if someone finds out I'm here? Or that I was here? They could break in and steal the negatives.'

'We run a tight ship on this ranch,' says Ted. 'No reporter's getting in here.'

I avoid looking at Holly, but she doesn't seem concerned. 'Nick's right,' she says. 'They'd use it to embarrass Arnie.'

'Sorry.' I keep my voice disappointed, my

expression resigned. 'I'd like a photo, I really would, but I can't afford to do anything that'll reflect badly on my father. A photo like that could be used out of context.'

Ted nods slowly. 'I hadn't thought of it that way. Very thoughtful of you, son. It can't be easy having a movie star for a father. But he'd be real proud of you.' He slaps me on the back. 'Now, stand aside, Nick. You can just watch. We can't be taking a photo that could be used against Arnie. I won't stand for it.'

And they buy it. Ted takes a few group photos of everyone but me. Then it's over and the danger has passed.

I'd like to say I'm cunning. I used to think so once, but now I'm not so sure. If I were cunning I'd come up with a legitimate way to get us out of this whole bounty-hunting business. But I won't be able to convince Holly to leave for genuine reasons. The only way out I can see is to fake an illness or injury so severe she wouldn't be able to leave me. It's no good. Either the doctors would rumble me and say there was nothing wrong with me, or when I told her the truth about my identity, she'd tie two and two together and realise I had faked the illness too. And then she'd never forgive me, for not only would I have lied to her twice, I'd have ruined her big break.

There's no way out. I'm going on the bounty-hunt. We're all going on the bounty-hunt.

But just think of the tales I'll be able to tell my mates when it's all over and I'm back in London. I could skip over the Arnie factor and the story would still be exciting. Now all I have to do is live through the next few days and I'll have the memories I wanted of vivid, sparkling, adventurous times.

THE TIME IS UPON US

We're still in our black combat gear (Ted wants us to get used to our uniforms so we'll feel comfortable when the time comes), in the middle of another handcuffing lesson, when the call comes in to tell us that Karl Wright and Luke Russell have been located. 'They're holed up in a house in the desert,' says Ted, a smile on his lips, looking nearly as happy as he did when he introduced me to the group as the Son of Arnold Schwarzenegger.

'You've found them?' Byron whispers.

'Of course we found them, son. That's our job. And yours is to bring them in. Alive, if possible.'

'But how did you track them down?' asks Holly.

Ted's lips compress. His smile is gone, all trace obliterated so totally it might never have been there. His joy at the coming carnage is probably subdued by the realisation that he's not leading soldiers, that he has to settle for us. 'We'll go over all that after we've accomplished our mission. We're making our move now, people. There's no time to waste.'

I feel sick.

'Cool,' says Veronica, a huge grin on her face.

And just like that Ted's eyes regain their sparkle. Ted and Veronica share a long look. Aw, how sweet. Has he finally found his soulmate? Someone equally in love with death, bloodshed and violence?

A second later Kevin mimics Veronica, repeating, 'Cool.' Then, louder, 'That's really cool.'

Finally I find my voice. 'Now?' I ask, trying to ignore Veronica and Kevin, not wanting to see the psychotic looks of death-lust on their faces. 'But what about the rest of our training?' Surely we need the extra three hours that were scheduled for this afternoon and evening. We haven't even completed two full days. We're not ready.

'Sorry, son, there's no time for more training,' says Ted. 'The crims aren't far from here and they might make a run for the border at any time. And once they're in Mexico they'll be in police hands, not ours.'

Holly looks both nervous and excited. Well, she should be nervous. She knows this is dangerous, that's why she chose to write an article about it. Why can't she see that we're about to die? She should be regretting the impulse that sent her here. She should be thinking of ways to back out.

Maybe it was a good thing I ignored my conscience and slept with Holly. I should be thankful I lived long enough to get the chance.

Ted glances round the group, judging correctly that some of us are terrified. 'Don't worry. You won't be going in alone. I'll be there to keep an eye on you and lead the way, and we'll have another operative at the scene too.' He glances at his watch. 'Now, I want you to go back to your rooms and double-check to make sure you've got all of your equipment. I'll get the guns and we'll meet back here in ten minutes.'

'Yes, sir,' says Veronica. She strides from the room.

The rest of us look uncertainly at each other.

Ted sighs like a man who's about to run out of patience. 'Don't you worry about getting those clothes dirty, you've paid for them, you get to keep them. And, for God's sake, carry your flak vests. I'll tell you when to put them on.'

PREPARATIONS FOR MASS SUICIDE (IS THIS HOW LEMMINGS FEEL WHEN THAT LAST RUN IS ABOUT TO START?)

I go back to my room and make certain that I'm leaving nothing behind to incriminate me. Once I'm satisfied that my luggage is filled only with clothes and harmless mementoes of my trip, I open the safe by punching in the code I set when I arrived. I pull out the money-belt I'd locked away yesterday and fasten it round my waist under my shirt. (Sorry, Ted, I know it's non-regulation.) Inside it I've hidden my passport, driving licence and all the documents pertaining to my real identity, along with a not insignificant amount of cash to be used in emergency.

There's no way I'm leaving any ID here at the training school where it might be spotted and my real name discovered.

The only time I want anyone seeing the name Nick Reed is when my corpse is searched. At least that way my parents will be informed and won't have to wonder for too long why the postcards have dried up. (Needless to say, they don't know that I'm training to be a bounty-hunter.)

What I need to worry about is getting injured. Dead is bad, but at least I wouldn't have to go through any tortuous confrontations over my identity. Getting injured or becoming unconscious is the real concern. Then someone might be tending my wounds and find my money-belt and discover that I'm not who I say I am. Or they might, horror of horrors, need to see my medical insurance, and that, of course, is in my real name.

I can't let anyone learn that I'm not Arnie's son. Not now. If I survive I must keep myself awake and lucid. I have to prevent my money-belt being discovered. That's my first priority, after keeping Holly safe from harm.

Stay alive and remain conscious.

I adjust the straps of my holster and glance in the mirror. I look like an extra in a low-budget film.

There's a knock on my door. 'Just a second,' I call double-checking the safe, reassuring myself that it's empty. I glance at the Rolex on my wrist, knowing I should lock it away so it doesn't get damaged, but I want to keep it with me. Out of habit I relock the safe even though there's nothing in it. I pull my sleeve down over my watch so Ted won't see it and tell me off for wearing one whose hands can be seen in the dark. Then I open the door.

Holly enters, looking as sexy in her combat clothes as she's looked all day. Liz Hurley in military mode. Sultry, tough, sensational. Kinky. My mouth waters. I want to kiss her and drag her to my bed. I feel the urge. But there's no time. Anyway, she'd probably refuse me if I offered her a quick shag, Austin Powers style. She's one focused babe. Holly wants that career. She wants hardship and toil. Maybe she needs her head examined. I know I do. If we survive the next few hours, perhaps we could see a psychiatrist together. We might get couple's discount.

'Are you ready?' asks Holly. She sounds tense and I'm thankful she has the sense to be anxious.

I decide it's worth one last effort. 'You sure you want to do this?'

'No.' She smiles and shrugs. 'But I'm going to.'

And there we have it. If Holly's going on the hunt, so am I.

FRIENDS WHO SLAY TOGETHER, STAY TOGETHER, OR SO VERONICA THOUGHT BEFORE SHE WAS FIRED

'Have you ever killed anyone?' asks Kevin, two hours into what Ted tells us is a four-hour journey by car.

(Or, in our case, mini-van, people carrier, or whatever you want to call the one vehicle you would never think to take on a covert operation like this one. No rugged Jeep or 4×4 festooned with spotlights, nothing military or capable of giving chase across the countryside: we tourists require comfort. And, strange as it sounds, it makes everything a little less sinister, more like an excursion on a package holiday, and relaxes us in a way a military-style vehicle wouldn't. But maybe that's the point: Ted doesn't want us all jittery and panicked before we even begin.)

'Are you talking to me?' asks Byron, in some surprise. He's sitting beside Kevin in the back.

Holly and I are in the middle row of seats, holding hands, and Veronica's up front with

Ted, who, of course, is driving.

'I'm asking everyone,' says Kevin, 'but mostly Veronica and Ted. They're the ones most likely to have killed people.'

'Yeah, I've killed men before,' says Veronica, turning to glare at Kevin. 'And you know what? You remind me of the last one. Something about your eyes being too close together. I shot him right in the chest and the bullet must have hit his aorta 'cause blood went everywhere like a great big geyser.'

There's a long pause, then Byron asks, 'How long were you a cop?'

'Eleven glorious years.'

Kevin jumps right in now that Veronica has turned her attention to Byron. 'What about you, Ted, have you ever killed anyone?'

'I'm a career soldier, son. What do you think?'

Kevin's persistent, I'll give him that, although there's something about his line of questioning and his tone of voice, excited rather than nervous, that makes me glad I'm not one of his co-workers. Statistics always say that dentists are more prone to depression and suicide than any other professionals. Add that to Kevin's presence here on this course and I would not be reassured if I worked with him. If Kevin snaps he might want to take a few people with him.

'I've only ever killed people in games,' says Kevin. 'I know I've got a good imagination, but it's not the same when you're sitting at a table eating tortilla chips and drinking beer.'

'I could never hurt anyone like that,' says Byron. 'I'm a pacifist at heart. I couldn't kill an animal. Or even a fish. I'm a vegetarian. If I got lost in the wilderness I'd probably starve to death.'

'Then why the hell did you come on my course?' asks Ted.

Byron flushes. 'My dad made me. He sent me here to experience what he calls the real world. To make a man of me, he said. No offence, Ted, everyone, I know you all want to be here, but I don't think this is the real world. For some of you it could be, but not for me. I wouldn't last more than ten minutes if I tried to do this on my own.'

None of us would, Byron.

Byron continues, 'My dad thinks I should have outgrown spending all my time with books, but he doesn't understand. I'm not a jock like him. I'm more like my mother, God rest her soul, an intellectual. And I'm trying to be a poet.'

'Just like your namesake?' asks Holly. She smooths her hair, tucking the loose strands behind her ears. I wonder if she should tie it back to keep it out of the way, but maybe

208

she's trying to remain glamorous in case Ted surprises us with any more photo-opportunities.

'Exactly.' Byron nods eagerly. 'I strive to be like Lord Byron, though obviously my poems aren't as good as his. I write in a modern style, but I like to think I get my inspiration from him and his contemporaries.'

Kevin's shaking his head. 'You should have tried role-playing first,' he says. 'The game would have let you see if you enjoyed fighting in imaginary battles or not, and if you hadn't liked that you'd have known you wouldn't like it for real. You need an adventuring spirit for something like this.' He turns to me eagerly. 'You know, Nick, I've always wanted to meet someone involved with Hollywood. I've got a theory that role-playing would be great training for actors. You really have to get into your character's head and use lots of improvisation as there's no script.'

For a second I wonder if I should try it. I've always wanted to be an actor. And then I remember that I'm too old and that I've given up those dreams. I may be taking a year or so out to play at being a purveyor of happiness, but in reality I'm nothing more than a salesman. That's what I've always been and it's what I'm doing now, even if I'm selling happiness rather than insurance. It's what I'll always be. I'm a salesman. I'll never be an actor. I'll never be a rock star. It's too late for me.

'We could start some kind of school,' says Kevin. 'With your connections and my knowledge we'd be sure to succeed. Imagine all the pupils we'd get. All those young people desperate for stardom. They'd sign up for a course run by Arnold Schwarzenegger's son, you bet they would.'

Byron's looking excited too. 'And I could write the scenes. Not the lines, of course, that's up to the students, but I could come up with the situations. My teachers always said I had a fertile imagination. It'd be fantastic.'

I give them a polite, uncommitted smile and let the dialogue flow over me. I've no inclination to participate in the conversation. I just want to sit here and hold Holly's hand. I'd like to stroke her face and kiss her too, but I know this isn't the time or the place, and for now I'm content just to sit here with her. If we were on our own, I'd tell her the truth. I'd tell her my name. I'd tell her I've been lying. But we're not alone and it would wreck her concentration. I can't have her distracted and distraught when we try to capture the bail jumpers.

When it's over — if we survive — I'll tell her. I want her to know the real me. I want her to like the real me. But I'm still me, it doesn't matter what I call myself. If I was well read I could recite Juliet's balcony scene where she declares her love for Romeo in spite of his name, but I don't know the lines. Only something about roses and smells, and I don't think it would come out right.

Holly squeezes my hand and I turn to look at her face. She's pale but her eyes are bright. I kiss her forehead. 'Are you scared?' I ask her.

'A little.'

We're talking in low voices, but Byron must have overheard us because he remarks, 'My father says you're not a real man until you feel true fear and overcome it.'

'I've got to go to the bathroom,' says Kevin.

Ted sighs. 'Again?'

'Yes, sir. Sorry, sir,' says Kevin. 'I've got a small bladder, sir. It's genetic, sir, nothing I can do about it.'

'Fine I'll stop at the next gas station. I'm sure all you boys and girls need a potty-break.'

'And can we get some coffee and doughnuts?' asks Kevin. 'I'm hungry.'

Ted is unhappy at the reminder that we're all tourists and not the Marines he'd prefer to have along on this mission. 'I really don't think — '

I interrupt him: 'Actually, I could do with a snack.' Strange but true. I don't know whether it's the thought of comfort food or if my mind is trying to trick my body into delaying the inevitable, but either way I want something.

'Me, too,' says Holly, perking up.

Veronica laughs, a deep, throaty sound. 'It'll be just like old times. Sugar highs to compete with the adrenaline rush. I think we need it, Ted.'

'You're right. We need whatever help we can get.' Ted's shoulders don't slump but he looks resigned. Like a man who's past his prime and knows it.

Aw, poor Ted. I'd feel sorry for him if he weren't leading us all to our doom.

ARRIVAL AND PREPARATIONS FOR ATTACK (DO NOT TRY THIS AT HOME)

The small print at the bottom of the disclaimer says that the company is not responsible for loss of life, limbs or sight. It is not intended as discouragement from attending the bounty-hunting training school, as it is only handed out at check-in, when you've already committed yourself and would feel a coward for backing out.

We decide to eat in the car rather than waste time, so we stock up on all sorts of snacks and junk food to keep us going on the rest of the journey. When we're settled back in our seats, Ted hands out photos of the two crims and tells us to study them again. 'I don't want you shooting the wrong targets,' he says, as we set off across the desert.

Targets. Ted means people. He doesn't want us shooting innocent bystanders or men who bear an unfortunate resemblance to our two bail-jumpers. Like we'll really be calm enough to tell in the dark or in a firefight or in any other circumstance but a line-up.

Ted must have done this before, and his students must have survived or he wouldn't be allowed to do this again. Would he?

Once we've studied the photos for ten minutes, munching on snacks, Kevin breaks the silence. 'We've gotta sing,' he says. 'I always sing on road trips.'

Byron smiles. 'Yeah, let's sing. It'll be like summer camp.'

'Ninety-nine bottles of beer on the wall,' sings Kevin.

Byron joins in and they're singing in unison. 'Ninety-nine bottles of beer. You take — '

'Shut the fuck up,' says Ted.

Instant silence, and he didn't even need to yell.

'That's better.' Ted's hands unclench from the steering-wheel. 'You sit in the back and practise being quiet. Consider it a much-needed lesson. We need silence and stealth for this mission to succeed. Use this time to practise. You can eat, but you can't talk.'

The rest of the journey passes in relative harmony with Holly snuggled close to my side, resting her head on my shoulder, and Kevin sulking in the back. Night falls, and we can no longer see the harshness of the terrain. We drive and drive and drive. What in

England would be a trip half-way across the country is merely a short hop in Arizona.

At last Ted pulls off the highway on to a back road and we all sit up, alert now, knowing we're almost there. Ted keeps driving. He turns left, then right, then left again. He seems to know where he's going without needing to consult a map. I'd like to think it's because this is all a set-up, that these aren't real criminals, that this is just a house they use for all their bounty-hunting training trips, but I know that's not true. This is for real. And, as Ted says, it's not a theme park. It's not a movie either. Arnie's not going to burst on to the scene at the last second to save us.

Twenty minutes later Ted slows, turns off the lights and drives thirty yards down a rutted track before he stops and kills the engine. We sit in silence for a moment, letting our senses adjust.

Shit, shit, shit. This isn't right. We shouldn't be here. Bet Holly wishes she'd changed her mind now. She should have listened to me when I suggested leaving.

Somewhere — somewhere within walking distance — wait two nasty criminals determined not to go to prison, and it's our responsibility to apprehend them and bring them in. This is not a good idea.

Ted turns round and studies us. 'You keep your mouths shut.' His voice is low. We must be close. 'This is no time for singing or whining or asking questions. You need to do exactly what I tell you to do. Nod if that's clear.'

We all nod.

'Wait until I've finished speaking. Then you can move. First, open your doors quietly and do not, I repeat, *do not* slam them shut. Put on your flask vests, load your guns and slip your packs on to your backs. On the count of three. One. Two. Three.'

We open our doors, climb out of the vehicle and do as instructed. The moon is nearly full and stars fill the night sky so it's very bright and I can see well enough to follow Ted's directions. As I'm loading my gun with shaking hands there's a sudden movement behind us.

My heart leaps in my chest. Thump, thump, thump. That's right, Heart, beat while you still can.

A man, dressed in black, materialises next to Ted.

They're here. They've found us. Holly fumbles with her box of ammunition and the clips spill from her trembling fingers, scattering in a wide arc at her feet. She grabs my arm, half hiding behind me.

Kevin's flak vest lands on the ground with a thud.

A pungent odour hits the air as a stream of urine runs down his leg.

'Took you long enough,' whispers Ted.

He's talking to the man in black. The man in black is one of us. He's on our side. I let out the breath I didn't realise I'd been holding and feel my heart slow to a more normal rate.

The man in black glances at Kevin and I see his teeth flash white in the darkness as he smiles. 'Sure is a strong whiff of fear in this bunch, Ted.'

'That's Kevin stinking up the place.' Ted turns to us and says, in his low whisper, 'This is Donnie. As you should have guessed by now, he's our lookout man.'

'Hi, y'all,' says Donnie, his whisper a bit too loud for my liking. He's still grinning. He's clearly enjoying seeing the yellow-bellied tourists quaking with fear.

'Get your gear ready,' says Ted. 'When you're finished we'll follow Donnie to the house. And, Kevin, stay at the back.'

QUIET AS A HERD OF
CHARGING ELEPHANTS

And so it is upon us. It's time for me to pay for breaking the Rules. Time for me to suffer and even out the score for my months of fun as a purveyor of happiness. The world needs redress. Balance.

I hold Holly's cold hand in mine as we walk, crunching, coughing, scratching, breathing, the noise of us all making me tense. They'll hear us coming. They'll know we're here. We'll give them just enough warning to prepare their barricades and guns but not enough to escape and save us having to attack.

It's going to be a *Tombstone* showdown and when the smoke clears most of us'll be dead or dying. (See? I said 'most'. Not 'all'. Remember: survival is possible. So I'll keep telling myself.)

Suddenly Donnie halts and Ted holds up his hand for silence. We can see a lone one-storey house. It seems well hidden, the sort of place you'd have to know about to find. Was that the crims' mistake? Does this house belong to someone they know and is that how the training school found them? Ted said he'd tell us once the mission is over. But it doesn't matter how it happened. The crims were found, we're here, and the only thing of importance is our survival.

Curtains cover every window, preventing us seeing inside, but the interior lights are on, making the house glow in a cheerful, friendly way, like a lighthouse welcoming weary fishermen home from a long day at sea. But it's only an illusion: there's nothing friendly waiting for us.

There's no car parked out front. For an instant I hope that the crims have already left and that this house is merely a decoy, but then I notice, behind the largest curtain in what I assume to be the living room, the flickering blue glow of a television. They could have left it on, but I know in the pit of my stomach that they're here, that Donnie made certain of it. They probably parked their car at the rear of the house. The only thing to do is cross our fingers that the crims are watching television and that it's on so loud it covers the noise of our arrival, letting us take them by surprise. If I'm going to dream, I might as well imagine a scenario that'll let us emerge victorious.

I tug on my left sleeve, pulling it lower,

making sure my Rolex is covered. Ted draws his gun and indicates that we should do the same. My heart flutters, seems to miss a beat, then races to its own staccato rhythm, thundering in my chest. I hope no one here has a weak constitution or we might be summoning an ambulance sooner than expected.

Holding the pistol in my hand is like having a security blanket. It's how clutching a torch when you're alone in the woods at night makes you feel better, safer.

But there's a problem. Only Ted, Donnie and Veronica know what they're doing with a gun. The rest of us are amateurs, civilians, tourists. We don't stand a chance. Hell, our shots'll probably ricochet off the walls and then some of us bounty-hunters will fall, succumbing to friendly fire as our own bullets hit us in the back.

This is not a good situation.

We're all going to die. And there's nothing I can do about it unless I want to run off into the night and leave Holly here, or hit her over the head and carry her unconscious body into the desert where we'll probably stumble over a rattlesnake nest and be bitten to death anyway. And if that didn't happen she'd wake up and hate me for ruining her chance to expose this insane vocation for what it is. The only thing I can do is try to keep Holly and myself alive. Stay near the back and let those who can hit what they're aiming at go first. Remember: survival is possible.

And those who do make it through the next twenty minutes will have an amazing tale to tell for the rest of their lives. I blink, freeze for a second as it hits me that I'm having the adventure I craved. I'm living an exciting life. This is what I wanted. My lips turn up at the corners so that I'm almost smiling. I wouldn't call this fun, but no one could say it was boring. It's certainly not living life on a scale of grey. After this I cannot go to my deathbed saying that I've never lived.

Donnie waits for Ted to give us our instructions as we study the house. Ted and Veronica exchange tight, excited smiles, then Ted points at Byron and Kevin and indicates that they should follow Donnie. Kevin looks like he's about to protest at the group being divided, or at having to go with Donnie and Byron, but he holds his tongue. Donnie leads them round towards the rear of the house where I'm guessing there must be a back door. Ah, yes, that's right, I'd nearly forgotten, Ted and Donnie are aiming to catch the bail-jumpers. They're trying to accomplish more than just survival here. It's not only about giving the tourists their money's worth. This is a working holiday.

I know that's why we've been split into two groups, but all I can think about is how our numbers have been whittled down before we've even begun.

(As a working holiday I'd rate this way below the purveying kind, more on a par with gutting fish on some trawler for fifteen hours a day in the middle of the Pacific Ocean while you're green with seasickness. That's a fair equivalent of the experience. Miserable to live through but — with a bit of exaggeration — good to talk about afterwards.)

Ted, Veronica, Holly and I are left for the assault on the front door.

'Try not to kill the crims,' Ted whispers, 'but if they shoot first do whatever it takes to subdue them. Understood?'

We glance at one another, then nod, Holly and I nervously. Holly's hands are shaking, but she says nothing.

Ted leads us towards the front door. My hand tightens involuntarily on my gun when we enter the area lit by the porchlight, and I'm poised, ready and waiting for shots to ring out, half expecting the crims to be keeping a lookout.

We're all going to be shot to bits and if we don't die from shock we'll bleed to death long before help can arrive. We're in the middle of nowhere. There's no convenient A&E around the corner to save us. We are so stupid. *I am so stupid.* Did I really think I wanted my year in America to be an Adventure? My life in Wimbledon wasn't that bad.

Finally we stop in front of the door. Ted holds up his hand and silently counts one, two on his fingers. I'm confused by thoughts of *Lethal Weapon.* Does Ted mean *on* three? Or on the beat after three?

On three Ted kicks the door, the wood splinters around the lock and it's open. He's obviously done this before. Maybe it's a Marine thing, being good at going in first, but Ted rushes inside, hardly bothering to check that we're following. Fools that we are, we're drawn after him. Even I am. And it's not just because I won't let Holly go without me. I can feel the blood coursing through my veins, the adrenaline pumping, the excitement making me want to participate — or, at least, observe.

Ted leads us straight towards the room with the television. He shouts, 'Bounty-hunters. Put your hands in the air. We have you surrounded.' Pressing himself against the wall, he peeks into the room. Two shots come through the doorway and strike the far wall.

Guess that's our answer. There will be no surrender.

Veronica is next to Ted, poised, waiting, ready for action. Holly and I stand further back in the hallway, not knowing what to do.

But Ted isn't about to let us miss out on the action. 'Storm the room when I do,' he whispers.

What?

Before I have time to question the logic of this insane idea, Ted is off, once again leading the way forward. He runs into the room, firing his gun. Veronica is right behind him, and then, like mindless puppets on a string, Holly and I follow.

The room, as suspected, is a living room and the television is still on, playing to itself now. Time seems to be moving in slow motion and I'm able to note that *Eraser* is on the screen and that Arnie is clutching a big fuck-off gun. Go on, Dad, I want to shout. (It's okay, he's the good guy.)

And then I have the urge to laugh, but I don't. I know it wouldn't come out right, that the others would think I'm cracking up under the stress, but it is funny. Poetic justice for a liar like me to have the man I've claimed as my father witness my execution from a TV screen. Not that he'd actually see it and be able to testify in a court of law, of course. But his presence is thick. I wonder how long it'll be before the others notice. Or if they'll notice. It's probably only me, the man with the guilty conscience, who has the time to note such trivialities as what's on the television when I should be concentrating on dodging bullets.

This can't be real. This can't be happening. Arnie can't be on TV during a bounty-hunt. This must be a dream.

But it feels so real. It sounds so real. It's no dream. This is happening. Shit.

I can see a man half hiding behind the sofa and I realise that it's Luke Russell. The crew-cut, blond, blue-eyed one. The crim who looks like he just doesn't care. Or that's how he looked in his photo. Luke looks like he cares at the moment — a whole lot, in fact. It's just a shame that what he cares about is killing us.

Bullets are flying overhead and Holly pulls me down beside her. We huddle behind a solid, reclining armchair. Insufficient cover but better than nothing. It's deafening. That's the one thing that stands out clearly. It's all movement and noise and I wish this was a movie. Then the camera would focus on the action I'm supposed to see, rather than leaving me in a state of confusion where I don't know what's happening and I don't know where to look. I need a director to direct my gaze.

My ears are ringing.

Holly peeks over the top of the chair and fires her gun. Once, twice, three times. Bang, bang, bang, right next to me, before she ducks down to safety.

Just when I'm starting to wonder if I should be doing something more than hiding, I see my hand clutching my gun. It's not a prop. It's a real weapon, with bullets and everything. I'm holding the gun and I know that my fingerprints are all over it. I can't risk a shot. I certainly can't shoot anyone, not even to protect myself. Here I am, using a false identity and running around the country playing cops and robbers, and I'm not even American. The courts would crucify me. Whatever licence Ted is using for us has me listed as Nick Schwarzenegger. Great. The jury would really believe an upstanding guy like me when I said it was self-defence, wouldn't they?

I don't know where Ted and Veronica are, but I don't want to lift my head and look. Then there's more gunfire and Donnie is in the room, gun blazing. Out of the corner of my eye I see Byron run past and dart behind another chair, hiding, not firing, cowering like I'm doing.

Kevin is right behind him, but he takes three or four lumbering steps into the room and freezes only a few feet from where I'm crouching. He's standing there like a great big target. He's so close to me. So close to safety.

The sound of gunfire seems to fade a little and I become aware of the overwhelming smell of Kevin, and it's not just the stench of urine. It's the scent of fear.

'Kevin,' I shout. But he doesn't seem to hear me.

Holly turns, glances beyond me and yells, 'Kevin, get down.'

He doesn't move. He doesn't react. He does nothing.

And before I have a chance to think about what I'm doing, before I have a chance to talk myself out of it — I've always said I'm no hero, I'm a selfish bastard when it comes down to it — I stand up, dash the short distance to Kevin's side and start hauling him to safety. He's dragging his feet and I wish I'd just rugby-tackled him to the floor rather than trying to move him, but it's too late for that.

I'm starting to glow inside, my chest swelling with saintliness. I can almost feel the halo appearing above me and wings sprouting from my back when something hits me on the head and it goes black.

NOISE AND CONFUSION

There's something I should be doing, something I should be remembering. I hear sounds, voices. Was that a shout? The words seem strange, foreign. I nearly understand. I'm straining. I almost grasp it. Wait. No, it's gone. I sink back down into the peace and calm of the darkness.

COLD HARD CASH
(EVEN PURVEYORS OF HAPPINESS CAN'T SURVIVE SOLELY ON FREE DINNERS AND FREE LODGING)

Gasp, shock, horror, yes, I know, but you can't survive on free food and free rooms alone. You need money for those incidental things. And you can never tell when you're going to fail. You'd better have some spare cash ready in case you have to pick up the bill, because the last thing you want is the cops on the scene looking into your story and discovering you've been scamming lots of freebies, that you've been doing it for months and you're not even who you say you are. Believe me, you want to avoid detection.

If there's one thing I've learnt from my months as a purveyor of happiness, it's that luxurious hotels have a seemingly unending supply of women's perfume on hand to give away to important guests. (And no matter how wealthy, not every visitor is important enough to receive a thank-you present.) If the Relative I've chosen for a particular visit is a woman, I can guarantee that, at the end of my stay, I'll be given a wrapped gift. 'Just a little something for your sister,' they'll say, or for my mother, depending on who I'm being at the time. They'll hand it to me as I'm checking out, but I never open it until later, when I've left the hotel behind. Nine times out of ten it'll be perfume.

But I was never discouraged. Perfume was perfect. The Rules told me to exchange all unwanted gifts for money, and perfume was always easy to offload. Jewellery and other expensive presents were trickier to return — too many questions, awkward to find shops that stocked that particular item, nearly impossible to get that much cash handed over without a receipt — so normally I just kept them. And it wasn't solely due to sheer greedy lust for the finer things in life. The son of a Hollywood star should be able to afford expensive luxury goods. It's an image thing. It added to my plausibility, after all.

I could have ditched the perfume, of course, and not bothered, but that would have defeated the whole purpose of the thing. If I wasn't exchanging my little gifts for cash I would have had to use my own money, and what's the point of that?

Santa Fe. (Great place, great food, great weather.) My hotel gave me a gigantic bottle of Chanel No. 5 as a thank-you present for being such a lovely guest, assuming a classic wouldn't be the wrong way to go. Although they didn't come right out and say it this time, I knew they had given it to me to give to my mother, a.k.a. Jane Fonda. It's as if they were trying to bribe her into coming to stay. The cheek of them. But I didn't mind: it's what I counted on to keep me going.

(Thanks, Mr and Mrs Williams, for settling my bill, that was really so very kind of you. And, yes, I'll be certain to tell my mother what a fabulous place Vermont is and how your house — a mansion, of course — would be a perfect setting for a film. Or a visit if we're in the area. Not that I can guarantee that she will stop by, of course, but I know you understand that she's a very busy woman.)

I normally like to get rid of perfume as soon as possible and pocket the cash, but I judged that Santa Fe was a little too small for that. I didn't want to bump into anyone who could recognise me as the Son of Jane, so I drove on to Albuquerque and stopped at the most expensive shopping mall there. I went straight to the perfume counter of the largest department store.

It was midweek and quiet. The salesgirl looked about twenty and she seemed very, very bored.

'I'd like to return this perfume I bought,' I said to her.

'Do you have a receipt?'

'No, I'm sorry. I can't find it.'

'I can't give you a refund without a receipt.'

'Oh, that's too bad.' I checked the time, making sure she saw my Rolex. Wealth means trust and believability in a situation like that. Doesn't it? 'My brother said his wife is really sick of receiving perfume. I was hoping to return this and get her something else.'

Never mind the flaw in my logic. I was hoping the salesgirl wouldn't have time to wonder why a man with a Rolex would worry about getting his money back instead of just buying a second present to go along with the first.

Now, I could have dropped a name or two while I was trying to exchange the Chanel for cash. I could have pretended to be the brother of Antonio Banderas, claiming the perfume was originally purchased for Melanie Griffith. I could have spun some elaborate tale of our being half-brothers with a father twice widowed in his youth, my mother being English and Antonio's Spanish, but it seemed too far-fetched and much too complicated.

Lying to the woman at the perfume counter was so unnecessary. I didn't want to lie for the sake of lying. Perhaps hearing that I was related to Antonio Banderas would have made her happy but it wasn't necessary. I had to believe that I was persuasive and charming enough to succeed on my own. And this was the USA: the customer is always right in the end.

Normally I succeeded. Sometimes I just needed more patience. And persistence. If you're annoying enough they'll often give you the cash just to get rid of you. (I only went for annoying after charm had failed.) If the salesperson was fierce and uncooperative, I always demanded to see a manager, and if that didn't work, there were always other shops. Someone, somewhere would usually oblige me.

My success rate was never a hundred per cent. I'll admit that freely. I'm not invincible. I'm not a superhero. Sorry, Holly, sorry, Ted, I know you're counting on the Son of Arnie to have been born for combat, and I hate to disappoint you, but I'm just a bloke who wants to have a good time and spread some cheer in the world. Sort of like St Nick.

UNCONSCIOUS AND UNAWARE

My mind is whirling, my thoughts confused. I hear noise, loud noise, and I want to open my eyes and see what's happening, but I have no strength. I can't move. Is this oblivion? Am I dying? I wonder if I should panic, but I don't. Everything seems hazy, distant, unimportant, and then it all fades away until nothing remains.

WALKING WITH EMMA

Emma and I walked for hours, holding hands, strolling by the water and in the woods, venturing deep into the resort's gardens. Our favourite discovery was not a plant, or a view of sailboats drifting across the deep blue water. It wasn't even the gnarled oak that reminded me of Sherwood Forest. Our favourite discovery was a sign: Warning — sprinklers may come on at any time.

Bold black letters on a stark white background, it was positioned beside one of the carefully landscaped 'nature trails' as if it was a minefield.

'Sprinklers? What sprinklers?' I said, coming to a halt, peering at the grass and flowerbeds.

'They're probably buried underground,' said Emma. 'But what I want to know is why we're being warned.'

Yeah, what happened if you ventured off the path? Were the hidden sprinklers weight-sensitive? Did you get wet and melt like the Wicked Witch of the West if a drop touched your skin? Had some deranged gardener got fed up with the careless feet that trampled his seedlings into the ground and switched the water supply to an acidic substance that dissolved human flesh but strangely hurt no plants?

'Maybe there's a psychotic gardener who loves his grass and lilies just a little too much,' I said.

'And he'll do anything for the perfect lawn.'

Just then there was a noise, and as if by magic, dozens of small sprinkler heads rose out of the ground. They began to spray water into the air.

'Run,' cried Emma, starting to laugh. 'Run.'

Hand in hand, we sprinted through the spray but by the time we reached the shelter of the trees we were soaked. We laughed for what felt like hours, until we were holding our stomachs like we were thirteen years old again and life was full of surprises.

EMMA?

But I can't hear Emma laughing now. I'm not laughing either. Where am I? I try and concentrate, I try to move, but pain explodes inside my head and I am lost.

HOW TO PREPARE FOR THE NEXT SUCCESSFUL STINT AS A PURVEYOR OF HAPPINESS

Every move, every new location means starting from scratch. All those friends you've made and the fans you've met are gone and you've no one left to rely on but yourself. All those waitresses and bartenders you went out of your way to charm are nothing but a memory. Every time you move on you're starting over, with a fresh, clean slate and only your charisma and your experience to draw upon.

No purveyor of happiness who aspires to be worth his weight in diamonds — one's weight in gold isn't enough, these days, not when we're all so greedy and fast becoming used to five-star luxury — would ever consider turning up at a new locale without first preparing the way.

Here's what you do: once you've decided on what city or region you want to visit (often determined by the car you've chosen from your current driveaway scheme), you stop at any suburban mall or shopping area and head to a bookstore. Find the travel section and a guide about your intended destination and look up the area's luxury hotels and resorts.

It's not just that you're fast becoming a snob, it's that you have to stay at these kinds of places: you won't find suitable patrons to support you for more than a beer or a meal in tourist-class accommodation. That's the way it works and you have to adjust. It's one of the pleasures of the job.

Keep in mind that you don't have to buy the book: you can just look up the information you need and jot down the appropriate phone numbers. Though, obviously, if you're that way inclined and you like guidebooks you can buy it, then stop and sightsee — although not while you're on duty: there won't be time. Sure, you might get lucky and be taken by yacht or helicopter to see the Florida Keys, but you're not a tourist, you're a purveyor. Your job is to make your patrons happy with your presence. If they want to go sightseeing (a few do) you can tag along, but otherwise you have to be at the hotel or the resort to socialise. How else do you expect to find someone to pay your bills if you're not around?

If you're into scenic beauty or doing the tourist trail, make sure you do it on your downtime, when you're travelling across the country, when you're in your drive-away car and using your own name. Then you can do whatever you like. That's the whole point of this gig: you're free to work when you want to work and to rest when you want to rest.

Never pick a chain hotel. You want a privately owned one so that when you call it you speak to a person who works there and not some telephone operator half-way across the country in a central reservation centre. This is important: the person you speak to on the telephone is your first point of contact. You need them to spread the news of your arrival. Remember that Hollywood is a magic word.

And it makes your life so much easier when you use a relative with a unique name.

Rule 32: Choose a celebrity with a recognisable surname. This is not a hard and fast rule and can be broken in certain situations if it's done carefully — i.e. George Lucas: everyone recognises the surname Lucas when you casually throw in a reference to Luke Skywalker. But it's a lot easier to get started with strangers if you say your name is Tarantino rather than Jones. For Tommy Lee Jones, of course: we all love him as an actor, but there's no lightning speed recognition of his surname on its own.

And you should phone only a day or two before your arrival. Yes, sometimes your desired hotel will be full, but you can usually find somewhere luxurious to stay so long as it isn't a holiday weekend. It's important that the excitement of your intended visit builds in momentum, so that by the time you turn up everyone on the staff is expecting you.

Oooh, Leonardo DiCaprio's brother. Will he look anything like him?

Oh, my, Sean Connery's son. Is he as charming as his father?

And do remember that people are interested in the brothers and sons of the stars. Every move you make will be watched. It's essential to behave sensibly — but that doesn't mean you have to be dull. You can have a good time. You can certainly sleep around — that's normal, even expected for someone like you. You can get drunk in the hotel bar. You can get drunk at parties. But you can't get so wasted you start throwing bar stools around or starting fights. You're not a rock star, you're a Relative. You must not get involved in group orgies or games of strip poker, no matter how tempting the invitations. You can't do anything that would interest the tabloids. Feeding the celebrity gossip chain is not part of your job. And it's not fair on the celebs and their real families.

241

You must keep that in mind.

If you do get carried away and participate in some juicy saga of three, four or even five in a bed, enjoy it while it lasts, for you must leave as soon as it's over. You can't stick around to allow word to spread. There can be no repeat performance. You can't be there when the photographers show up. The press will catch you out if they're alerted to your presence. They will not hesitate to label you a liar.

You can be the life and soul of the party, but you mustn't go too far. People notice what you do. It's the nearest they're ever likely to get to a Hollywood star. It's their one chance of a brush with fame. Give them good memories.

And remember to follow Rule 18 and be a good tipper. Even when you're given free drinks you should tip. Hotel employees are responsible for laying the foundations for your visit. They deserve to be rewarded.

I always tip well.

Wait. What am I talking about? Tipping? Avoiding scandal? Making reservations? But I'm not preparing the next leg of my journey. What's happening? Where am I?

HOLLY, HOLLY, HOLLY

I know there's something I should be remembering, some little fact that's niggling at my mind, and then it hits me. Emma. No, not Emma. She's gone. I had to say goodbye to her. I had to leave. The Rules made me leave. It's Holly. I've met Holly. My very own gorgeous, adorable Liz Hurley. Holly.

HOW LONG DID YOU SAY YOU'VE BEEN LEADING TOURISTS INTO ACTION, TED? (OH, YES, THAT'S RIGHT, YOU DIDN'T SAY, DID YOU?)

I become aware of two things: I'm not dead and I'm lying on the floor. More precisely, I'm lying on the floor, handcuffed. I blink, trying to concentrate.

Everything's muzzy, murky, dim, and I can't remember why I'm here. I don't know what's happening. Why am I lying on the floor? A stab of fear hits me. I could be suffering from brain damage like that chap in *Memento*. I know who I am, I remember taking voluntary redundancy and flying to America. My long-term memory seems fine, but what if my short-term memory has been permanently damaged? What if I'm doomed to that terrible half life of tattoos, notes and betrayals? I don't think I could cope with that. I'm not tough enough.

But wait. I can remember the bounty-hunting school. I can remember the attack.

Did we lose?

Of course we lost. I'm handcuffed. Ted wouldn't handcuff the Son of Arnie.

I blink again, but my vision swims and I can't see anything. Gradually I realise that people are talking and that I can hear them.

'He could be bleeding to death while you're just standing there doing nothing.' It's a woman's voice and it's close. In fact, it's right next to me. It's Holly. She's alive. She made it. I want to smile but my facial muscles don't seem to be co-operating. Holly continues, 'I'm going to see how he's doing, so please don't shoot me.'

Holly, sit down, I want to say. Holly, don't be brave. Holly, be careful. I open my mouth and try to speak but only a groan emerges.

'Looks like Pretty Boy's awake.' That voice I don't know. One of the crims, I guess.

My eyes flutter and I concentrate. Focus, Nick. Focus. I groan again as the bright lights ram into my brain, and it's only then, as I twitch my neck in a reflex action away from the glare shining down into my eyes, that I feel the pain at the back of my head. The agony is so intense I wish I could pass out.

Something hit me. Someone hit me from behind. That's so unsporting.

But what can you expect on a bounty-hunt? I'm lucky I wasn't shot. At least, I don't think I was shot. I panic. I could have been shot. Holly might be talking about me. My life's blood could be seeping away into the floor as I lie here, wasting my last few moments wondering what the hell happened. I force my mind to do a quick body scan. I don't feel injured apart from my head, and if that had been a gunshot wound surely I'd be dead. No. I've not been shot. I blink again and gradually relax.

'Nick.' It's Holly and she's leaning over me.

She looks unhurt and I try to smile at her. 'Hi there,' I say.

'Hi.' There are tears in her eyes.

'Oh, please,' says that unidentified male voice again. I look up, away from Holly, and see a man standing over us. A large man with scraggly dark brown hair and a goatee. I recognise him from his mugshot: it's Karl Wright. And he's holding a gun. Some kind of pistol. Why am I not surprised? 'Go check out the other man and see if he's still alive,' says Karl. 'If I have to put up with any love talk I'll fucking puke and have to shoot someone to make myself feel better.'

Holly hesitates.

Karl waves his gun at her. 'Move, beautiful.'

She obeys him, and as she stands awkwardly I see that she's handcuffed too.

She walks away and I struggle to sit up, wanting to know what's going on. I look around the room.

Kevin is sprawled on the floor beside me, face down, hands shackled behind him. He's drooling, in the midst of a *Twelve Monkeys* dribble-fest as a puddle of saliva grows beneath his open mouth. His trousers are still wet so I judge I haven't been out that long. Byron is huddled in the corner, his handcuffed arms loosely draped over his knees, trying to take up as little space as possible. Veronica and Ted are wearing leg-irons as well as handcuffs and I wonder how the crims subdued them. I can see blood trickling down Ted's temple but otherwise he looks okay, and Veronica is glaring at Karl with pure hatred in her eyes so I guess she's not injured too badly. Our bounty-hunting packs and guns are heaped in a pile at the side of the room, as far away from Ted and Veronica as possible.

How the hell did the two crims overpower us all?

Holly crosses the room, and as I watch her it's only then that I notice Donnie, blood pooling beneath him, unconscious on the floor. Luke Russell stands over him. Luke doesn't look so scary now that he's not shooting at us.

I frown. Something's missing. The television. My eyes dart across the room, seeking the comfort of Arnie's face in *Eraser*, but the screen is shattered, destroyed by a stray bullet. Arnie's gone. He's not my father, I know that, but I can't help but think his disappearance is a bad omen. I shiver.

How did the two crims manage to subdue Ted, Veronica and Donnie? The rest of us were negligible, but surely those three were more than competent. Donnie was taken out by a bullet, I can guess that much, but what happened to Ted and Veronica?

Welcome to the profession of bounty-hunting. We searched, we hunted, we found. Well, the training school searched, hunted and found the crims, but we did as we were told and moved in and attacked as good trainee bounty-hunters should. We got those first steps right. We're just not very good at the recovery bit.

I can see why Ted's not too keen on the recovery-agent title. Difficult to call yourself a recovery agent when you don't recover things.

So much for my days as an action man. I'm glad I didn't try to become a professional mercenary. I can see that it wouldn't have worked out. I would have failed. Just like I'd failed as a bounty-hunter. I'm not cut out for this physical work. I need a stunt man to do the tough moves.

'Donnie needs a hospital,' says Holly. 'He's lost a lot of blood.'

'You mean he's not dead yet?' Karl laughs harshly. 'Guess it's my lucky day.'

'What about Kevin?' I ask.

'Scumbag fainted,' says Veronica.

If the crims — I'd better start thinking of Karl and Luke by their names in case I blurt out the wrong thing and make them angry — are logical they'll want to escape and leave us all alive. They won't want to murder us: that would be stupid. The police already know what they look like and have their fingerprints on file. Running from the law after a shootout with bounty-hunters is one thing, but murdering seven of us would get them on a most-wanted list. Then it wouldn't be incompetents like us chasing them, it'd be professionals. The police and the FBI would hunt them down like dogs because they were wanted felons, not because they had signed some contract to get their bail money. I have to hope Karl and Luke are clever enough to realise that.

(Please, God, look after Donnie. Don't let him bleed to death.)

'What are you going to do with us?' I ask.

'What should we do with you?' Karl studies

my face, looking uncannily like a man examining an ant in the split second before he's going to squash it with one stomp of his foot.

'You'll get a big reward if you let us go,' says Byron.

'A reward?' Luke looks interested.

Byron clears his throat. 'My dad's rich. He'll pay you a lot of money to release us.'

'Donnie really needs a hospital,' says Holly.

Karl shrugs. 'Tough shit.'

'But you don't want him to die,' I say, attempting to reason with him, guessing that Karl's the leader of the two. 'You don't really want to kill any of us. There'd be a huge manhunt. With police and everything.'

'We can kill you if we want to kill you,' says Karl. And he doesn't look as if it matters to him either way.

Byron gasps. 'You can't kill him. He's — '

'I'm as rich as Byron's father,' I say, interrupting. I glare at Byron. I don't want Karl and Luke finding out about Arnie. Who knows what they'd do if they become aware of that little gem? 'Why don't you just leave us here in our handcuffs and you can make your escape? We won't be stopping you.'

Luke hesitates. 'I sure do like the sound of that reward money.'

Ted stares at me, ignoring the crims, and

just when I think he's about to start reciting his name, rank and serial number, that or plead for my forgiveness, he sighs. Ted turns to address Karl, his face expressionless. 'If I don't make a report in five minutes the police will automatically be called in.' Ted glances at me again. It must really rankle that he hasn't protected the Son of Arnie like he said he would. 'The police will arrive in exactly thirty-one minutes. If you're here they will capture you. Shootout or no shootout. You have time to leave, I suggest you do so.'

Ted is telling the crims to run? For a second I wonder if the bump on my head has affected my hearing, but then I realise that he is doing what he can to keep me safe. He doesn't want me involved in a siege situation.

'Let's get out of here,' says Luke. 'I don't want to go to prison. I *can't* go to prison.'

Karl thinks for a moment, eyes scanning the room and its unlucky occupants. 'Okay, we'll leave, but we're taking hostages.'

Hostages?

'We don't need hostages,' says Luke.

'Yes, we do,' says Karl. 'We're taking hostages.' He stares at Luke until Luke shrugs in agreement.

I go cold. What about Holly? I can't let them take Holly.

'Take me,' I say. If they take me they might

leave Holly here in safety. That's all that matters now. This is why I came along: to protect Holly. This is my moment, my destiny, the reason I was drawn to her, the reason I came on this insane bounty-hunt even though I knew I shouldn't. I can save her. I want to save her. I will save her.

Karl shrugs. 'Okay.'

'And me,' says Holly.

What the hell is she doing? Can't she see I'm protecting her? No article is worth this.

'You?' asks Karl. 'Why should I take you, beautiful?'

Beautiful. He called Holly beautiful. He had called her that before, but it didn't register then, when I was still woozy.

'Nick's my fiancé.' Holly doesn't blush at the lie. 'I don't want to be separated from him.'

Karl raises his eyebrow. 'And where's your ring?'

'It was too big,' she says, quick as quick can be. 'It's being resized.' She gives him a dazzling smile. 'We only got engaged last week.'

'No, take me,' says Ted. 'Leave the couple here.'

'What *is* this? Who the fuck are you people? Fucking Good Samaritans?' Karl shakes his head. 'You're bleeding. You're a liability,' he tells Ted. 'I'm not taking you.'

'If we have to take hostages let's take the couple,' says Luke. 'They'll be easier to control if they're worried about each other.'

'Fine. And him.' Karl points at Byron. 'He can be our whipping boy if the lovebirds don't do as we ask.'

'You don't want the woman,' I say. 'You don't want Byron. Just take me.'

They ignore me.

I have to tell them. I have no other choice. I have it in me to save Holly, to save them all. I will perform this one noble act and no one else will have to die.

'Really, you don't need anyone else,' I say. 'I'm Nick — '

'Shut up.' Karl sticks his gun in my face. 'Shut the fuck up.'

I freeze. I'm too late. But if they hear I'm Arnie's son they'll know they won't need any other hostage but me.

'But,' I whisper, hoping he won't shoot me, 'I'm — '

Karl backhands me across the face and thrusts the barrel of his gun closer, so it's pressing against my cheek. 'Open your mouth again and I'll blow your fucking head off. But first I'll blow off the head of your fucking fiancée so the last thing you ever see is her brains splattered on the wall.'

I remain silent. I do nothing. I say nothing. I'm a coward. I know that I'm a coward, but I can't risk him shooting Holly.

A few minutes later, having searched all the packs, taken anything of use (including the weapons and ammo), Luke smashes Ted's and Donnie's phones. Karl keeps his gun pressed against my face. I do not speak, I do not move, but I tell myself that I will be ready when the time comes to save the others.

'You two,' says Luke, speaking to Holly and Byron. 'Come on.' He ushers them from the room.

Karl, keeping the pistol to my cheek, grabs hold of my arm and twists me round so that we're both looking at Ted. 'So long, soldier boy.' Karl laughs. 'Maybe it's time you got a real job.'

He forces me from the room. A gun against my face is a big motivator and there's no way to resist. My eyes meet Ted's and I try to smile at him to show him I have no hard feelings. And, curiously, I don't. What's happened has happened and there's no need to apportion blame. I was never under any illusion that this was going to go off without a hitch.

Luke, Byron and Holly are waiting in the hall. Karl, keeping his gun pressed against my face and his finger on the trigger, waves Luke on, and then the crims take us outside and force us into the back seat of a pickup truck parked at the rear of the house.

And just like that it's happened. We're hostages.

AND THEN THERE WERE THREE

Once we're all crammed into the pickup, Karl drives off. It's pretty unpleasant. The handcuffs are tight around our wrists and the flak vests make us bulkier than normal, worsening an already crowded situation. As the miles pass I shift slightly and take Holly's hand in mine. It must be about midnight. Awkwardly I flick aside the edge of my black sleeve to check my Rolex, suddenly worried that I might have broken it during the attack. But it seems to be in one piece and the hands say it's twelve eighteen.

If I could read the stars I'd know which direction we're headed in, but I can't see the few constellations I do know, and even if I could I doubt it would help me. The closest I've ever come to studying the physics of the universe was a one-day astrology seminar I attended with my ex-girlfriend Georgina when I was still trying to impress her with my New Man tendencies.

So here we are in the middle of the Arizona desert. We've been kidnapped by criminals on the run who are desperate to avoid recapture.

And one of them has already called my Holly beautiful. That's bad. But it could be worse.

Being dead is worse than this. Other things are too. Being burnt alive at the stake. Being beheaded by an axe that's so dull it requires seventeen strokes before your head is finally severed from your body. Karl and Luke being the bad guys in *Deliverance*, just waiting for the right opportunity to rape and kill us. There are worse things than this.

Holly, hostage and ex-trainee bounty-hunter, looks pale in the moonlight, but her voice is composed when she speaks. 'Do you mind telling us why you've taken us hostage?'

Karl's at the wheel, but he doesn't glance away from the road to answer. 'For human shields.'

I was afraid he'd say that. He's seen too many movies or watched too much news. He knows the villains' lingo.

Holly's obviously thinking ahead and gathering information for her story. Bet she'll be commissioned to write a series of articles now. I can see the headlines: HOW I WAS KIDNAPPED WITH ARNOLD SCHWARZENEGGER'S SON. OR BOUNTY-HUNTERS FAIL TO STOP CRIMINALS TAKING TOURISTS HOSTAGE. OR EVEN ON THE RUN WITH THE SON OF ARNIE. AND LATER, NOT ARNIE'S SON.

NICK'S A FRAUD. ARNOLD: I HAVE NO BRITISH SON.

Holly will become a celebrity. For a time. All the major publications and television networks, desperate for an inside look at her story, will wine and dine her. She'll be offered book deals and possibly a film deal. It really could be her big break, but not in the way she's expecting, for the truth here, my truth, just makes this whole thing juicier.

Byron could use it to his advantage too. He could write poems about being a hostage with me. He'd get a publishing deal.

And me? I'll be the lowest of the low. I'll be hissed and booed wherever I go and I'll have to flee back home to the UK once the US government finally decides, after months of investigation, that I haven't done anything illegal. Technically. My bills were always paid. Or is there some law saying you can't receive gifts from people who think you're someone else? Maybe this whole pretending-to-be-someone-else thing is illegal. I don't know. All I do know is that that's not the worst of my troubles right now.

The good news is that I guess I was wrong: we aren't all going to die. We haven't all died and things are now looking maybe seventy-thirty in favour of death for we three bounty-hunters who remain. That means thirty — seventy in favour of life. Better odds than I'd have given us before.

And the others are all alive. They survived the hunt. Bravo for them. Well done, you lot. (Well, everyone apart from Donnie. I can't say for sure about him.)

Maybe Kevin had it right all along: maybe it's best to be the least-popular person. Byron's too sweet to hate, Veronica too scary, Holly too sexy, and I was the Son of Arnie, so that left Kevin to take bottom position in our group ranking. But Kevin's free and out of harm's way now, isn't it? He's safe — so what if he's stinking of urine, it's his own, and a shower and a fresh set of clothes will soon change that. Perhaps I should have rugby-tackled Kevin to the floor when he was frozen during Ted's ill-fated assault. Then I too would have smelled of Kevin's pee and the crims wouldn't have wanted me along.

But they still would have taken Holly as a hostage and then where would I be? The crims wouldn't have let me come if I was reeking like Kevin, so we're back to where we are. I am where I should be. And at least I don't stink of Kevin's urine. That's one thing I am glad about.

Luke twists to look at us. His head turns on his neck, his body shifts in his seat, his hand raises, the pistol pointing at us — at me.

He searches our faces one by one, as if we're offensive pools of vomit and he's the one saddled with cleaning up the mess. Or perhaps he's just curious.

I stare at the gun, images of blood, death and splattered brains filling my mind.

I can't keep away from the movie imagery. Perhaps it's my way of dealing with a reality so bizarre, or it says something psychologically about me other than the obvious that I go to the cinema a lot. Maybe there is a real-life psychiatric condition that refers to this. It could be a form of neurosis or something, this tendency to interpret the everyday — and the not so everyday — based on movie scenes. Or it could just be the comparisons I'm after, an easy way to categorise life's events.

I should be thinking, How the fuck do I get out of this? But, right then, as I'm staring at the gun barrel, as we're driving down that lonesome highway, I'm hit by the Muse.

I'm going to write a book. A Hollywood Guide to Life. One of those self-help books, a spiritual guide type thing, but based on wisdom and anecdotes gained from films. Then I could do a sequel covering British cinema, European cinema, world cinema. It'd be great. I can see a real market there. Everybody loves movies. I could spend my days watching films with Barry Norman. And just think of the new editions I could bring out. I could write updates every year. I could be rich. Bestseller lists here I come.

But I digress. Gun. On top of headrest. Pointing towards the back seat. As vehicle drives along road.

Gee whiz, what movie could I be thinking of?

I force myself to tear my eyes away from the pistol and tell myself not to look at it again. I meet Luke's gaze and I try to smile, all friendly like, but I'm afraid the twitching of my lips is more like a grimace. 'Hey, have you seen *Pulp Fiction*?' I ask. I lose the smile and let my expression return to neutral.

'Huh?' Luke looks confused.

Guess he doesn't see the world through Hollywood-hued spectacles. He's going to need a copy of my book.

'*Pulp Fiction*,' I say again, pressing on. 'You know, Quentin Tarantino.'

'Course I've seen it,' Luke says slowly, evidently wondering where I'm going, but not worried: after all, he is the man with the gun. And I'm the one in the handcuffs.

Karl cocks his head to the side and I can tell that he's listening too. Byron and Holly are watching me. Everyone's wondering why I'm talking when I should be minding my own business. But I can't be silent. Talking is the one thing I'm good at. 'Salesman-charm', my father calls it, but bullshitting is nearer the truth.

'Well,' I say, mostly to Luke, but including everyone, especially Karl, 'You know that scene where John Travolta and Samuel L. Jackson are driving along after they raided that apartment and took that guy prisoner? And John Travolta's character is holding his gun and turns round to look in the back seat? Then the car goes over a bump or his finger slips or whatever, and the gun goes off and he blows that guy's head apart?'

'Yeah, that was really funny,' says Karl, chuckling.

'Sick, but I wasn't the only one laughing. All those fucking yuppies with their safe jobs, expensive cars and big houses thought it was pretty damn funny too.'

'It was a great scene,' I agree, 'but don't you think we should learn from that and you should move your gun, Luke?'

Luke's eyes narrow and he glares at me, but then he glances at his pistol and starts to laugh. 'Oh, man, oh, man, oh, man. Bet you're wetting your pants right now.' He's laughing with the hysteria of a man on the edge. And he doesn't move the gun.

'No, he's so cool,' says Byron. 'Or he

wouldn't be thinking about a movie.'

Luke's gun is still pointing into the back seat.

Even if the road is as smooth as silk a sneeze could cause that trigger to be squeezed just as easily. Slain by some snot and a tickle in the throat. Where's the dignity in that?

'Do you think you could move your gun?' I ask. 'You don't want to kill us by accident, do you? And we are handcuffed — it's not as if we can go anywhere or do anything.'

Luke frowns. He leaves his gun where it is. 'You called me Luke and we haven't been properly introduced.'

Holly smiles, all friendliness and charm. 'That's Nick, I'm Holly and this is Byron,' she says.

'Fucking bounty-hunters,' says Karl. 'I hate bounty-hunters.'

'But we're not really bounty-hunters, we're tourists,' blurts out Byron. 'My father made me go on the training course for my vacation, he thought it'd be good for me.'

Karl snorts but doesn't say anything.

'And what about you?' Luke asks me. 'What's your sorry excuse?'

'He came with me,' says Holly, before I have a chance to speak. 'I want to write a screenplay about bounty-hunters and thought

I should see what it's like at first hand.'

'Well, heck, pretty lady, why didn't you say so?' says Karl. 'How 'bout I just shoot your fiancé in the chest? Then you'll have a whole fucking lot more to write about.'

Byron's face pales. 'You can't shoot him. He's Nick Schwarzenegger.'

'Byron,' I say, but it's too late.

'He's Arnold Schwarzenegger's son,' continues Byron. 'You have to know that. You can't kill Nick.'

Shit. Fuck. Disaster. They're not going to believe him, or if they do believe him the truth will come out somehow and I'll be doomed. We'll all be doomed. They'll kill us in vengeance for my daring to take Arnie's name in vain.

'Arnold Schwarzenegger's son?' asks Karl, slowing the truck as he turns and looks at me.

'Yes,' I say. To deny it would be pointless. Now that it's out I'll have to try to use it to keep us all alive.

'Arnie's son?' Luke shifts the gun so it's not pointing into the back seat. He studies me, searching for the resemblance.

The identity documents in my money-belt suddenly feel hot and large, like they've doubled in size. At any moment Luke will glance down and see the newly bulging outline underneath my flak vest and discover that my name is not Schwarzenegger.

Maybe I should just confess it all now and let them shoot me here in this truck. At least it would end the torment of wondering when the truth will blow up in my face and I'd get the pleasure — admittedly short-lived — of re-enacting a classic Tarantino moment.

But I can't. I'm not suicidal — not while there's still a chance we might make it.

Karl's still staring at me. I really wish he'd turn back to watch where he's going. The road may be deserted but it's still a road. Finally he voices his judgement. 'You don't look like Arnie,' and switches his gaze to where it should be.

This is going to be the one time someone important doesn't believe me. The one time they don't accept my word.

'I take after my mother's side of the family,' I say aloud, 'but Dad and I have the same cheekbones.' I have to make them believe me. I'm good at this. I've been doing it for months. Lying is my forte.

Holly nods, agreeing with me. 'And you've a touch of Arnie about the jaw. Not identical, but the similarity's there.'

'Wow. This is fucking amazing,' says Luke, clearly into the idea. 'I'm a big fan of your dad. I love his movies.' He's still holding his gun, but it's pointed away from us now, towards the roof. He turns to Karl. 'We can't kill Arnold Schwarzenegger's son.'

Karl's watching the road, paying attention to his driving again like a good, law-abiding citizen. He shrugs. 'I still say he doesn't look like Arnie.'

'But he does,' insists Luke. 'You just haven't had time to see it. It's in the eyes. Not the colour, but the shape, the look. It's there, believe me. He's got Schwarzenegger eyes.'

'Hard and fierce,' says Byron, his tone reverential. 'Like ice. Makes him look like a warrior. Just like Arnie.'

'My point exactly. He's Arnie's boy,' says Luke.

'I don't know.' Karl frowns. 'Check his ID.'

'I don't have any on me,' I say quickly, not wanting them to search me and find my money-belt.

Stupid, stupid, stupid. What was I thinking, taking my real ID along? I should have left it behind. No, I couldn't leave it behind, but I could have found some safe place to store it before I went on the bounty-hunt with Holly. Before I even went to Ted's training school.

If my lies do come out, Holly and Byron will probably stand on the sidelines and cheer as Karl and Luke shoot me dead, then riddle my corpse with bullet holes like a road sign in the middle of nowhere in Texas. Maybe they will even ask to borrow a gun and join in. But that wouldn't save them in the end. Karl and Luke won't believe that they weren't in on it and then they'll be dead too. We'll all be dead.

Yep, a psychiatrist would have a field day with me. Lies, obsessions with movies and death. What does that say about me? That my childhood was dull? Well, I could have told you that myself. Happy but dull. That was me. That was my fucking life. Why the hell do you think I wanted to be a purveyor of happiness in the first place?

So I've got the excitement I craved and now I'm complaining. Yes, I'm moaning, grumbling and whining that, actually, no, this isn't what I meant, this is too much, it's too exciting, it's not safe and gentle, I'm not in control and there's no emergency handle to pull to stop everything whenever I want. What a mess.

And I'm not just talking about the situation. I'm talking about me. Suave, smooth-talking, lying Nick.

I should never have broken the Rules. I shouldn't have liked Holly. Okay, okay, it was impossible not to like her, but I shouldn't have stopped to talk to her. Or if I did I should have followed the Rules and known that nothing could come of it, rather than trying to form a relationship. I'd left Emma at the end of the week; I should have done the same with Holly. Why couldn't I have enjoyed Holly's company then said goodbye to her?

Holly believes that I'm the son of Arnold Schwarzenegger. When she finds out the truth she'll never trust me.

Never.

But I can't worry about any of that now. What's done is done. I have to concentrate on getting us out of here alive. And if I have to dig my hole deeper and keep on lying, that's what I'll do. I have no choice.

'We could hold Nick for ransom,' says Luke, his voice rising excitedly. 'We could demand a getaway plane and half a million bucks in cash.' He smiles like a kid seeing all his presents under the Christmas tree for the first time. 'And we could say that we'll only do the hand-over if Arnie comes in person.'

Shit. I can't let them start trying to claim ransom money from Arnie or the whole sorry tale will come out when Arnie refuses to pay and they'll shoot us all. I'm a fool.

'Don't be a fucking idiot,' says Karl. 'The police would never let Arnie anywhere near us.'

Luke's smile fades. 'Yeah, but we phone Arnie directly and tell him not to contact the police. He'll be so worried about his boy that he'll do what we say.'

'Um, Dad's actually filming in the Sahara at the moment,' I say, choosing the first isolated place that springs to mind.

Holly starts stroking my hand lightly, but I daren't glance her way. I have to keep my eyes on Karl and Luke.

'So?' Karl shrugs. 'We'd never get to meet him anyway. If we want to ransom you, he'll have people who can sort it out.'

'But I want to meet Arnie,' says Luke.

Great. Luke's a fan. I should have expected that. Everyone else is. Now he's going to try to come up with some ransom plan that will let him meet or at least speak to the man himself. Shit. Shit. Shit.

'You're not going to meet Arnie,' says Karl. 'Even if Nick is his son. And I don't like the idea of getting involved with ransom demands. We'd either have to hole up somewhere and hope the cops don't track us down, or we'd have to keep stopping to make phone calls and I don't like it. If we don't do ransom, they won't have a fucking clue where we are. No letters, no phone calls, nothing. They won't be able to set up a trap. We're just one truck. Do the words 'needle' and 'haystack' mean anything to you?'

'Well, we could always keep ransom in mind,' says Luke, 'if things go wrong.'

Karl glances at Luke. 'Okay, if we get stuck somewhere and start using them as human shields, we'll issue our ransom demands. No sense wasting a chance to make some money. But for now we'll just keep going. I'm not going to prison. I hate sharing a fucking cell. I hate being caged like a fucking animal.'

'Maybe you should just drop us off,' I say. 'You could make a quick break for the Mexican border.'

'Yeah,' says Holly. 'We'll only slow you down.'

'It's too late for that,' says Karl. 'They'll be expecting us to go to Mexico. And I hate being predictable.'

'We're not going to Mexico?' asks Holly.

'Nope.' Karl smiles. 'We're going to Canada. Largest unpatrolled free border in the world.'

'But surely there are checkpoints,' I say.

'On the roads,' says Karl. 'But you think all those prairie and mountain areas in Montana, Idaho and North Dakota are covered? No way. It'll be easy. And I'm not hiding out someplace they don't speak English.'

'But it's cold in Canada.' Luke frowns. 'I heard they have to plug their cars in all winter to keep the engines warm enough so they won't freeze up solid.'

Karl laughs. 'That's only in the mountains.

Let's just worry about getting there, then we can choose where to stay.'

'I've always wanted to go to Vancouver,' says Luke. 'But only in the summer.'

'What about us?' I ask. 'You plan on letting us go?'

'We need hostages and you're it, whether you're Arnie's son or not,' says Karl. 'If you're good maybe you'll live through this.'

'We can't kill Arnie's son,' says Luke.

Karl shrugs again. (I don't like the way he keeps shrugging.) '*If* he's Arnie's son.'

'He is,' says Byron.

'He's gotta be Arnie's son.' Luke looks at me and nods to himself. 'You take a closer look when we stop. You'll see.'

'Okay,' says Karl, 'if he's Arnie's son we won't kill him, but we've still got the other two.'

'But Holly's my fiancée,' I say, the words flowing easily. 'Dad adores her. And Byron's the son of my dad's best friend. You can't kill them. My father would be devastated.'

Karl laughs. 'But he'd thank us for sparing his boy so it'd be fair.'

Is Karl warming to the idea that I might really be Arnold Schwarzenegger's son?

'Do you think we could get his autograph?' asks Luke. 'He could write, 'To my friend Luke, thanks for looking after my boy Nick, your friend, Arnie.'' He turns to me, that eager, half adoring look in his eyes that I know so well from my months as a purveyor. 'What do you think?'

'Shut up, Luke,' says Karl. 'Arnie's not going to be giving us any autographs. You just watch the hostages while I try to get us out of here. And, you in the back, shut the fuck up too. I want some quiet time to think.'

A CHANGE OF TRANSPORT

Karl sticks to the back roads as he drives on and on. We sit in silence for an hour, but it seems much longer. I don't know if it's the stress of the situation or that I keep imagining all sorts of horrible things they could do to us, but time seems to have lost its meaning and it feels as if we've been riding in this truck for years.

We're all in our own private worlds. Karl's thinking, Luke's thinking, I'm thinking, Holly's thinking, Byron's thinking. All of us concerned with escape. The crims from the law and us from the crims. My hands keep falling asleep and I have to flex and shake my arms as best I can to retain some feeling, but I'm careful as I move not to jostle Holly or draw attention to myself.

Karl turns left, then right. He seems tense now, eager, and I have the feeling that we're not just drifting aimlessly. Karl has a destination in mind. I'm hopeful he's sticking to his stated desire to use us as human shields for protection from the police. It would be senseless to take us to cave to execute us and leave our bullet-ridden corpses for coyote food. It would be equally absurd to bury us in a *Very Bad Things* grave in the desert that's meant to hide our remains for ever. He hasn't even given his idea a chance to work yet. It would be ridiculous to change things now, wouldn't it?

Eventually we turn on to what can only be described as a two-track road, and I use the word 'road' in its loosest sense. It's rutted, it's bumpy, and its inhospitableness is amplified when we reach a metal gate barring the way forward. On the gate are three large No Trespassing signs. Clearly the owners don't want to leave it to luck or the law of averages. They want people to see their signs.

Looming just beyond the gate, at the side of the road like a half-size billboard, is another sign: 'Trespassers will be shot on sight. That means you.'

Karl stops the truck and turns off the ignition. 'You stay here and watch the prisoners,' he says to Luke.

'Where are you going?' asks Luke. He doesn't seem to mind that he hasn't been consulted about this. But I'm upset: I want Karl and Luke to discuss their plans aloud so that we can overhear and at least have some idea of what's in store for us.

'The cops'll be looking for the truck,' says

274

Karl. 'We need a new one.'

'But won't you get shot?'

Karl laughs, genuinely this time. 'I'll be careful.' He opens the door and starts to climb out, but the truck emits a shrill beeping noise to let him know he's left the headlights on. He switches them off and turns back to Luke. 'Don't let them outside. I don't want them making any noise or trying to escape. I don't care if they claim they have to pee. Don't let them out of this truck until I get back.'

Luke shrugs. 'Okay.'

He's a bit too blasé for my liking. Shouldn't Luke be more concerned about the Son of Arnie's comfort levels? I mean, handcuffed in a cramped back seat is not something to rave about to my father, now, is it? But I say nothing: a real child of Arnold Schwarzenegger would put up with the discomfort. I certainly will. I'm not about to start complaining over the lack of leg room.

Karl takes the keys and pockets them, then shuts the door. He walks round the gate, not even glancing at the signs. We're all quiet as we watch him head away from us until he's lost to the darkness of the night.

Luke gets out his gun again and waves it vaguely in the air. 'Now, you all be quiet. I don't want to have to shoot anyone. There's to be no talking and no peeing. Got that?'

We all nod.

'Good,' he says. 'Now, I won't be shooting you, Nick, I think you know that, but if you start causing trouble I'll have to shoot one of the others, even though it'd make me feel bad to hurt one of your friends. You understand me?'

I nod. What else can I do when a gun-toting lunatic on the run from the law has just told me not to talk?

'Okay,' says Luke, putting away his gun, smiling at me. 'I'll want to hear all about Arnie later, Nick, when we're on the road again, but I better do like Karl said and be quiet.'

We sit there and sit there and sit there. It's getting pretty uncomfortable with my knees jammed into the back of the seat in front of me, the three of us squashed into the space two children would find small, and I want to shift around, but I try not to move. Holly, Byron and I make eye contact and exchange short, tight smiles, trying to give each other courage. It's not much, but it helps to know that I'm not in this alone, even though the part of me that isn't selfish and scared wishes that Holly and Byron had been left behind. I hold Holly's hand.

It feels like hours later when there's

movement ahead, car headlights approaching us from beyond the warning signs. I'm thinking we're toast, that Mr No Trespassing will see us and set off the landmine he's no doubt cunningly hidden in front of the gate, which, unfortunately for us, will be directly underneath where we've parked.

Then the car stops. (I can't tell what type it is with the headlights shining straight at us.) The driver's door opens. And out climbs Karl.

I never thought I'd be happy to see him, but I am.

He unlatches the gate and swings it to the side — it's been unlocked all the time — then strides through, bold as you please. I'm half expecting shots to ring out, but there's nothing.

Luke opens his door. 'Are we ditching the truck?'

'Nope,' says Karl. 'We can't dump it here, it'd leave a trail tying us to the car.'

'Did you steal it?' asks Luke.

'Do I look like a fucking idiot? Of course I didn't steal it. We can't drive around with stolen plates. Traffic cops would pull us over. I know the people who live on this ranch and they owe me from a long time ago.'

That would explain Karl's sense of purpose

in coming here and his ignoring of the warning signs. 'That means you' obviously doesn't mean him.

Karl glances into the back seat. 'Did they behave?' he asks, as if we're children to be rewarded for good behaviour and punished for bad.

'Yep,' says Luke. 'So what're we doing with the truck?'

'We could dump it down a cliff,' says Karl, 'but that's too hit or miss. We've gotta make sure it all burns.' His eyes gleam strangely and his face glows with an unholy light. He's got the look that Jack Nicholson had in *The Shining* when he was chopping down the bathroom door with an axe. 'We'll take it away from here and set it on fire.' Karl smiles, nodding to himself.

Ah. So much for vain hopes of sanity.

I exchange glances with Holly and Byron. They're both looking pale, and Byron's eyes are wide, scared. I can only hope my expression isn't as terrified. I have to remain calm and cool. Arnie's son wouldn't panic. He would be used to his dad saving the day.

'Wish you'd gotten us another truck,' says Luke. 'It's gonna feel all weird riding in that car so low to the ground.'

'Then you drive the truck until we dump it

and I'll take the car.' Karl turns to us. 'Get out,' he says. 'I want you with me.'

I hesitate. 'Can't you just leave us here?' I ask. I'd rather take my chances with Mr No Trespassing even if he is a friend of Karl's. 'You don't really need hostages. Dump the truck on a quiet road near the Mexican border and they'll think you tried to sneak across the border on foot.'

'Please let us go,' says Holly.

Karl shakes his head. 'No way. We need hostages. They'll still be looking for us and I want some bargaining power. And having Arnie's son under our control gives us that extra edge. The cops won't do anything stupid if you're with us. Even your commando bounty-hunting buddies surrendered when I knocked you out and held a gun to your head. Now that I know who your dad is it all makes sense. That's what convinced me that you are who you say you are. Nobody wants you dead, Nick. Nobody wants to be responsible for killing Arnie's boy. And that gives us the advantage. They'll have to be more careful than they would be if Luke and I were on our own.'

As soon as Byron blurted out the name Schwarzenegger I'd known this would happen, but hearing it spoken, for ever irretractable, hits me in the gut.

The fact that I'm Arnie's son will keep us alive.

Shame that that fact is false.

Guess we'll see just how good an actor I really am.

DESTRUCTION (I DON'T LIKE THE WAY THIS MAKES HIM SMILE)

We drive for another thirty, forty, fifty minutes, putting distance between where we acquired the car and where we're going to dump the truck so there won't be an easy trail for the cops to follow. Once Karl finds a locale that's deserted enough for him, our mini-convoy stops. He parks the car, a Pontiac Grand Am, and turns off the headlights. The car is new without being brand new, so it shouldn't draw any unwanted attention unless Karl starts breaking traffic laws. It must have been some favour that Mr No Trespassing owed him.

Luke, as agreed, stops the truck about fifty feet back, switching off his headlights a second later. We're in the middle of nowhere. My stomach spasms at the thought that there's no one around to hear us scream. There are no city lights, no car lights, only the moon and the stars to illuminate the night.

I clench my fists, concentrating on keeping my emotions from my face. I don't want to infect the others with my fear. If I was really Arnie's son, I could have already talked our way out of this situation or encouraged the crims to ransom us when they were discussing it earlier. I could have assured them they'd get to meet Arnie or, at the very least, talk to him on the phone. I could have helped with the negotiations for a helicopter and a few hundred thousand dollars of getaway money to secure our release.

If I was Arnie's son.

But I'm only a purveyor of happiness, and we're not supposed to get into situations like this. I've no easy escape route. If my story starts to unravel, if I say the wrong thing or Karl and Luke grow suspicious of my claims, I can't run away. It's not simply a case of checking out of my hotel and slipping off into the night. I'm trapped. I have to give the best, most convincing performance of my life.

At least there's more room in the back seat of the car than there was in the pickup, though it's impossible to be comfortable wearing handcuffs and flak vests. The stale smells of sweat and terror are starting to seep out, making me feel hot, heavy and itchy. It's as if I've gained thirty pounds of blubber around my mid-section and have yet to learn how to adjust my normal patterns of movement, breathing and perspiration.

I'm half hoping that in his excitement to light the fire Karl will make a mistake, giving us the opportunity to escape. In his haste to see the flames flicker into life, he might leave us unattended for a vital few seconds. It's unlikely he'd leave the keys in the ignition so we could drive to freedom, but we could run. We might be handcuffed, but there's nothing stopping our legs working. And maybe, if we found somewhere to hide, if they didn't shoot us as we fled, aiming for our heads or lower bodies to avoid our flak vests and reap maximum damage, they wouldn't bother to search for us for long.

But Karl waits for Luke to reach the car before he opens his door and climbs out. 'You stay here,' Karl tells us. My eyes follow his hands as he pockets the car keys. (Damn and double damn.)

I wonder if he's done this before. And if he has, what I really want to know is: did the hostage live?

Luke is left to keep watch over us, but he does this from outside the car, wanting a clear view of the spectacle to come, while still able to keep an eye on us.

Karl takes a long, white rag from his pocket as he heads to the truck, moving as swiftly and eagerly as a hound nearing the end of a scent trail with its prey in sight. He flips open the fuel flap, unscrews the cap, and shoves one end of the rag into the petrol tank, leaving the rest to hang out. He reaches into his pocket again and pulls out something small — matches or a lighter.

I can't see his face from here, no matter how much I twist and peer, but I imagine he's smiling. He's probably gone all Jack Nicholson again, the mad light of ecstasy burning in his eyes as he holds his precious mini-fire, enthralled by its potential power to destroy.

'He's crazy,' whispers Byron.

'Yep,' says Holly.

As Karl moves the flame towards the white cloth, I experience a sudden and disorientating feeling of *déjà vu*.

It's a *Gone in 60 Seconds* car bomb. He's doing a *Gone in 60 Seconds* car bomb. I voice the thought aloud, in case the others don't see the world in my Hollywood-hued way.

Has this always been Karl's favourite technique for destroying a vehicle or has he only started using the rag-in-petrol-tank method since seeing the movie?

The old questions run through my head. Is it life imitating art or art imitating life? Have criminals become more criminally similar since the advent of crime films? Do mobsters feel they have to live up to the actions and reputations of the characters in *The Godfather*? Do heroes act more heroic, pose more heroically before tackling that lunatic spraying bullets into a crowded shopping mall, not thinking in terms of visual impact, but subconsciously altering their stance to fit the accepted heroic mould? Which came first, the movie slogan or real-world events? It's all intertwined now and not easy to separate one from the other. Movies have become part of our cultural and societal understanding and are no longer just mirrors held up to the cosmos. Cinema influences life and life influences cinema in a never-ending circle.

I'm starting to go into that pompous philosophical mode I enter into sometimes when I try and think — usually unsuccessfully — profound thoughts, but then Karl lights the rag and I'm jerked back to awareness.

Karl runs towards us. His arms are pumping and he must be sprinting, but it looks as if he's in a scene from *Chariots of Fire*, running in slow motion, Vangelis playing in the background. He glances over his shoulder, once, twice, judges the state of the blaze, puts on an extra burst of speed and comes to a sudden halt beside Luke, spinning to watch. He's judged it perfectly. With a *whoof*, the whole truck goes up in flames.

It takes longer than it does in movies, and it doesn't explode, bursting apart in one huge ball of fire and shooting shrapnel, it just burns.

We watch in silence.

My eyes almost feel as if they're glued to the truck, but I force away my gaze and watch Karl. He's smiling, running his fingers through his goatee, mesmerised by the sight before him. The junior arsonist has grown up: he now has adult needs and desires. He's not just a man on the wrong side of the law, he's a psycho. If he can't get away he's going to kill us in a fit of fury. He's going to kill us anyway. We're going to die.

The flames are still high when Karl seems to recall where he is. He looks around, sees us, then heads our way. Luke climbs into the passenger seat and Karl slides behind the wheel, starts the car and drives off. I can feel their urgency: we have to get out of here before anyone comes to investigate, before anyone sees this car and ties it to the truck.

Holly, Byron and I exchange long looks. I try to smile reassuringly. I have to be the strong one here.

But as we head away I can't help myself. I turn and watch the fire until it's lost from view. And I'm happy. I have a deep sense of satisfaction that the getaway vehicle is engulfed in flames. I'm glad it's been destroyed. The fire will cleanse the truck of fingerprints. Theirs and mine.

My prints are all over the gun I used to storm the crims' hideout, the gun that's now in the backpack sitting casually between Luke's feet in the front footwell. They'll be all over the bounty-hunting training school too, but I can hope they're smudged and unclear if the cops do dust for prints. Even if they find some and keep them on file, they'll have no name to go with them. They won't know who I am because I've never been arrested. They will know pretty quickly that I'm not Arnie's son, but they won't know my real name. My parents won't be questioned and won't have to worry that I'm in danger. They'll only find out once the hostage situation ends and I'm dead or alive, but either way the need for frantic hoping, praying, wondering, worrying will be over.

But at least the truck is gone.

I've never been a violent person. Even as a boy I never had the urge to smash, tear and destroy as much as some of the others in my class, but now I'm happy we've left behind the burning wreck of a truck. It's a freeing, invigorating feeling to destroy something you no longer want. Karl must be on a natural high, his blood surging through his veins, riding a wave of adrenaline. I can only hope that this will all be over before he comes down.

Or maybe I want him to come down now, before the cops spot us, so he's slow and lethargic, not so quick to react.

I don't know what I want.

I only know that I have to be the Son of Schwarzenegger like I've never been the Son of Anyone before. I will be the living embodiment of the Son of Arnie. It's all that's keeping us alive.

WE'VE ALWAYS WANTED TO KNOW
(TELL US MORE, MORE, MORE)

Once we're a few miles from the burning truck, the sense of urgency fades. Luke turns to me, an expectant look on his face, his blue eyes, so pale and soulless in his mugshot, now glowing with excitement. 'Tell us something about your father.' His gun, I'm pleased to note, is safely in its holster on his belt.

'Oh, I love hearing about Arnie,' says Byron, glancing at Luke and flashing him a quick, nervous smile, as he fiddles with his handcuffs. 'Nick's got such great stories.'

'He has, hasn't he?' Holly grins. 'Arnie's going to be my father-in-law and I still get a kick out of hearing about him.'

I meet Holly's lovestruck look with one of my own, noting the mischievous tilt to her lips even though she's still pale. She's playing the part of my fiancée well and that can only help us. I turn back to Luke. 'What do you want to know?' I ask him.

As Luke asks a dozen questions, I surreptitiously adjust my Rolex beneath my sleeve, more out of habit than any idea that it will bring me luck. Holly, sitting as always in the middle, is silent now, listening. The intent look in her eyes is the same as the one she had on the bounty-hunting course whenever Ted started giving us one of his mini-lectures. She's probably planning the articles she'll write if we make it through this, trying to memorise our conversations to add depth.

For the next two hours I tell outrageous lies, listing Arnie's likes and dislikes — or what I imagine they might be:- his favourite movies, his favourite roles, his favourite colour and his favourite foods. I reveal juicy titbits about his co-stars that I make up on the spur of the moment. I disclose hush-hush secrets gleaned from celebrity magazines, giving each tale a unique spin so that I'm not just quoting stuff that's already in print but seemingly sharing behind-the-scenes information that's only obtainable by those in the know. It's all perfectly believable gossip, nothing too bizarre and nothing nasty. I don't do nasty. I relate tales of minor bruises and scrapes Arnie has earned while performing his own stunts, his workout routine, anything and everything I can think of.

'And then there was the time he came across a burglar in the house,' I say. 'Dad chased him down the road and sat on him until the police arrived.'

'He loves working with James Cameron.'

'Jamie Lee Curtis is even sexier in real life. And so is Sharon Stone, if you can believe that's possible. I met her while Dad was filming *Total Recall*.'

'We always have fish and chips whenever he visits me in London. With extra salt and vinegar. He likes them just the way I do.'

'He flew all my American friends to England for my twenty-first birthday and rented the whole of Leeds Castle so we could have a week-long party.'

'No, I've never thought about being an actor. I like working behind the scenes. A lot of the big studios hire me to scout out movie locations.'

'Dad loves skydiving. And hang-gliding. He's into flying small planes too, and he's even thinking of moving on to bigger planes and learning how to fly his Lear jet, though he hasn't had any lessons yet.'

Luke is keen on stories of Arnie's bravery — people always are — so I slant my tales in that direction, learning from my audience even as they are learning from me.

'Dad broke three ribs last year when he went diving in Australia and a hammerhead shark rammed him in the chest.'

'Really?' asks Luke. 'I never heard about that.'

'Me neither,' says Karl, frowning.

'That's because it was all hushed up,' I say breezily.

Shit. I was getting carried away. I have to remember this isn't a normal purveying mission and try to control my imagination. I can't let them start getting suspicious and doubting me because my tongue is prone to a salesman's exaggeration.

'Hushed up?' asks Luke. 'You mean kept out of the news? How? I thought actors are always being followed.'

'Oh, they are,' I say, 'but Dad was diving with friends from a private yacht way off the coast of Australia. One of the other guests was a doctor so Dad didn't need to be admitted to hospital with all the interest that would have caused.'

'But why would he care?' asks Byron. 'It makes him sound so exciting.'

'Dad loves sharks. He didn't want them to be hunted and killed. Some types are already endangered. He thought the best thing to do was keep it quiet. They alerted the authorities, of course, but one of the other men said he was the one rammed. Dad thought if his name was kept out of it people wouldn't pay much attention to a non-fatal attack. And he was right.'

'I like sharks,' says Luke, smiling. 'I think

they're great. Guess that makes me just like Arnie.'

Karl snorts and glances at Luke, but he doesn't say anything.

They seem to buy it. I move on quickly. 'Did you hear about the time his hotel caught fire and he carried an unconscious porter down thirty-six flights of stairs?'

'No,' says Luke.

'Well, I was only five or six, so I guess you'd have been too young to remember.'

Luke frowns, then starts nodding. 'Now that you mention it, I think it does ring a bell.'

I continue with the stories, not wanting to let myself relax in triumph that Luke is becoming just like a normal patron and pretending he already knows all these things about my famous relative when I'm making most of it up. I'll try to stick to more normal, mundane stuff. Nothing too outlandish. Nothing that will make them stop and think.

'He loves performing his own stunts,' I say. 'He's really good at martial arts and acrobatics so he can do a lot of his own fight scenes.'

'Of course I get to go on set. Dad likes the family to watch him, except for scenes where his characters get hurt.'

Byron's soon asking questions too. Holly,

as my supposed fiancée, keeps pretty quiet. She should know all this. But she's definitely paying attention, smiling when the others smile, nodding when they're nodding, she's just as keen as the rest of them. I could almost but not quite forget that we've been kidnapped: it's like we're suddenly friends, sharing in our adoration of Big Man Schwarzenegger. (Okay, Okay, I admit it: I'm a fan too. Why else would I choose him?) Karl's the only one who's not celebrating Arnie's existence, the only one who's not asking endless questions, but he holds his tongue and I think he's listening.

I want to ask what happened during the bounty-hunt, to find out exactly what went on while I was unconscious, how long it took Ted and Veronica and the others to surrender when Karl held that gun to my head, but I don't want to spoil the mood. I don't want Karl and Luke to recall that we participated in the assault. I want us to remain buddy-buddy. I'll ask Holly tomorrow. Surely they'll allow us a few moments alone.

I keep talking about Arnie. We chat, we laugh, we joke, the atmosphere is more relaxed. But I never forget who my audience is. I can seem relaxed, I can try to act like they're friends, like we're all friends, but I must never let my guard down. I can do nothing that might give me away. I have responsibilities now, I can no longer think only of myself. Holly and Byron need me to protect them and I will not let them down. I've betrayed them once with my lies, but I will not betray them again.

It grows very late. Conversation dries up as first Byron, then Holly drifts off to sleep, followed by Luke. I know I should try to doze. But I'm too keyed up. Holly slumps against me, her head on my shoulder. I'd like to put my arms around her and hold her close, but the handcuffs prevent this.

I stare out of the window. It's dark and I'm forced to imagine the landscape. I picture the dry earth, the rocks, cacti and yuccas I've seen for the past few days. The image in my mind won't match what's outside here and now — the desert changes quickly when you bother to look — but it'll still be desert.

I've been watching the road signs so I know we're still in Arizona, heading north towards Canada.

It's a long way, over a thousand miles as the crow flies from the Mexican to the Canadian border, and longer than that by even the most direct roads, through various mountain ranges on the way. It'll be like driving from London to southern Italy, but without the checkpoints or the ferry across the Channel. It'll take us a couple of days to reach Canada. That's two whole days to rely on the kindness and cunning of the crims to keep us alive. Two whole days in which I'll be forced to keep up my pretence.

The big question is not whether I can keep lying: I know I can do that. Truth is, I'm terrified that the story of our kidnapping will make it to the media and someone will interview Arnie and he'll say I'm not his son. Then the crims will hear and so will Holly and it'll all be over.

Just like that, it'll be over with a bullet in the head. Bye-bye, life. Bye-bye, Holly.

I'd say our odds aren't good.

Or my odds aren't good. Maybe there's something I can do to save the others. When the time comes. I'll have to think about it so that I'm ready. I won't let Holly and Byron go down with me. They deserve better.

OPTIMISM:
A FUNDAMENTALL SKILL EVERY PURVEYOR OF HAPPINESS NEEDS

The hours pass, Karl's still driving and I wish he'd get tired and swap places with Luke, if only for a change. I don't like the fact that Karl's not tired. He should be spent, his energy levels burnt out. I want him to show a little human weakness.

I stare out of the window. I'm exhausted, but I still can't sleep. I find I don't want to, even though it would bring temporary oblivion. I'm afraid of what nightmares might torment me. Maybe I'd cry out the truth about my identity and give it all away.

I decide to use the time to concentrate on a possible change of profession. If I survive the next few days I'm going to need one.

I like the idea of writing a book about the Hollywood philosophy of life, but here's another idea: I could use my experiences from the past few months to pen a how-to guide. Learn from me, I could say, do not do as I have done. And never break the Rules.

Oh, sure, I have plenty of examples I could use of how to do it right, but I could also talk about my mistakes and tell a few home truths: like, don't go on bounty-hunting trips. Bounty-hunting's a bad idea. Particularly when you start under false pretences.

And my first piece of advice, even before listing the Rules — and instructing my readers to stick to them as if they were written in stone — would be about optimism. I know it'd be difficult for all those naturally cynical Brits to put into practice, but every purveyor of happiness needs a bit of optimism inside of them. For how else are you going to believe that people will accept your lies? Confidence is important, as well as charm and the ability to lie convincingly, but optimism lies behind it all.

So if I'm a purveyor of happiness, which I am, I'm supposed to be optimistic. And if I'm optimistic the first thing I should accept is that survival is possible.

I'll use this time to work on sample chapters of my how-to manual so that I'll be ready to write a book proposal when we're free. I wonder if I'll need an agent *and* a manager. And what about a publicist? Will I need one right away? Or does that come later?

Won't it be ironic if I survive this and

become famous for giving up my dreams of becoming famous?

I glance at Holly. She's still sleeping. I want to kiss her, just a quick peck on the cheek for comfort, but it might wake her so I turn my head to stare out of the window and remember.

A HOLIDAY FROM MY HOLIDAY

I needed that week with Emma to recharge my batteries. It felt wonderful to have time to be myself — even if that self was the Son of Robert — without having to hustle for free meals or gifts. I didn't worry about patrons and it was marvellous.

Emma taught me how to sail and how to windsurf. I took her canoeing and water skiing. It felt like we were on honeymoon, not that we'd only just met. We had a real connection.

I distracted her. I made her happy. I wouldn't let her think about her rat of a soon-to-be-ex-husband. As far as I was concerned, the Bastard didn't deserve to see her again, but I knew that she couldn't avoid him for ever. Most of the divorce discussions could be done through lawyers, but eventually she'd have to face him. I wanted her to feel so loved after our time together that she'd have the strength to look down her nose at the lying, cheating son-of-a-bitch and wonder what she ever saw in him. I wanted her to think of me when she thought of joy. When she thought of love.

I wanted to be the man in her life.

I wanted her like I'd never wanted a woman before. All my past relationships seemed like so many meaningless flings. Mere infatuations. The lustful encounters of someone who'd yet to grow up.

I wanted her to be mine. I wanted to be hers.

But I was a purveyor of happiness. I had a job to do. I couldn't stay. The Rules wouldn't let me stay.

I could give her one perfect week to remember, but that was all.

The Rules told me I had to leave. The Rules told me it was time.

I had no choice.

A TIME OF JOY, A TIME OF SORROW

Neither of us spoke of the future. Emma and I talked of many things but mostly of the present. Our only references to the past — other than the necessity of occasional responses by me to questions about Robert Redford from hotel guests or staff — related to our interests, our preference in music, films and books. We existed in a special place of our own making, and the outside world did not intrude. Emma and I did not even speak of my 'father' after that first breakfast together.

We were lovers. We were friends. The sexual spark raged inside us both and no matter how many times we made love it was not extinguished. But even if she'd been truly and properly married I'd have liked her. I'd have wanted to spend time with her and get to know her, though I'm sure any real husband would have spotted the lust and longing in my eyes ten miles off and barred me from her presence.

We swam, we walked hand in hand along the water's edge, we danced. I helped heal her broken heart. We left the resort only once, to see a local band. We sipped beer and shared silly smiles like teenagers discovering the strength of their raging hormones.

I felt guilty for sleeping with her, it was eating at my guts, but I couldn't stop. I didn't want to hurt her, I didn't want her to expect more from our relationship than there could be, but I didn't have the willpower to end it. I told myself that she needed me. I was the Transition Man necessary for her to reclaim her life. I could make her feel beautiful, sexy and desirable again.

Bill the Bastard must have been crazy to leave her. But his loss was my gain.

A week with Emma was not long enough, but back then the power of the Rules was strong and I had no choice but to move on, to leave her behind. I could have stayed a few more days, the Rules allowed me a maximum of two weeks in any one location, but I knew that I had to leave as scheduled. I couldn't let myself be tempted to break my pact. I was in America to explore and have grand adventures. I needed stories and excitement to keep me going in the years of plodding normality ahead. I couldn't wimp out only two and a half months into my trip. I had a minimum of a year, maybe two, depending on how well I did at purveying and how long I could stretch my money, to live life to the full.

Neither of us spoke of the future.

Emma wanted to drive me to the airport, but I wouldn't let her. I wasn't really flying back to London to visit my grandfather in hospital after he'd had a heart-attack — that was merely the excuse I gave her for leaving.

I said goodbye to her on the beach where we had first met. I kissed her, I held her close, I didn't want to go. Eventually I pulled away. Emma's eyes were swimming with tears.

She sniffed, wiped her eyes and tried to smile. 'Sorry I'm being so silly,' she said.

I cupped her cheek. 'It's been an amazing week.'

'Yes.' Emma stared into my eyes. Then she opened her bag and withdrew a business card. 'Call me sometime.'

I glanced at her card — she's an interior designer — and put it into my pocket. 'I will,' I said. 'I'd love to see you again.' Stupid, stupid tongue of mine, I should have said nothing. I shouldn't have sounded so sincere.

She rose on tiptoe and kissed me on the lips. 'I hope your grandfather's okay.'

'Thanks,' I said, pulling her closer, moulding her body to mine.

We kissed, we clung to one another.

Neither of us wanted to part. With my departure she'd have to go back to reality, and so would I.

I left Emma as I'd found her, crying on the beach.

A resort car — complimentary for Mr Redford, of course — drove me to the airport. I had to cover my trail, as if I really was flying back to England. When I entered the terminal building I was no longer the Son of Robert, I was back to being Nick Reed.

I got a drink and a burger, not feeling hungry but wanting something to fill the hollow pit in my stomach. I couldn't leave the airport immediately in case the resort driver was hanging around to pick up someone else and saw me getting into a taxi. I took Emma's business card from my pocket and stared at it for a long time. Emma Johnston. Beautiful, fabulous, fantastic Emma Johnston. I wondered what her maiden name was — I hadn't liked to ask, as I didn't want to remind her of what had happened with the Bastard.

I had to be strong. I was a purveyor of happiness. I'd known from the beginning that I'd have to make sacrifices along the way. I had to follow the Rules. It was all so simple back then. I had my philosophy and I stuck to it. I could never contact Emma again.

Once I'd finished eating I threw her card

into the rubbish bin, turned on my heel and walked away. I got as far as the doors when I told myself I was being silly, that there was no reason why I couldn't keep her card as a memento. I raced back across the airport terminal. I didn't stop to think about ketchup, mustard and leftover food, just pushed open the lid of the bin. I froze. It was gone. There was a new black bag inside and it was empty. I'd lost Emma's card for ever.

I stared down into that black bag. I couldn't believe it. Then I closed my eyes, took a deep breath, straightened my shoulders and walked away.

I was a purveyor of happiness and I had to follow the Rules.

My steps slowed and I stopped. It was only a business card. A reminder of the week. There would have been no harm in keeping it. Would there?

If I acted quickly I could track it down. I scanned the crowds, searching for a cleaner, for a man emptying the rubbish bins. No one.

I began to run down a corridor, my eyes darting this way and that. I saw a man with a bucket and a mop cleaning up a spill and I skidded to a halt, my eyes wild, my breathing unsteady. 'I threw away a card by accident,' I said, gesturing back the way I'd come. 'I need it back, but the trash has been emptied.'

'Tom's on duty today,' he said, pointing. 'He just went that way.'

'Thanks,' I said, and chased after Tom.

A minute later I was still running, then another minute passed and I wondered if I'd ever catch him. I wanted that card back. I couldn't believe I'd thrown it away.

Just then, ahead of me, I saw a man pushing a rubbish trolley. I called, 'Tom.' The man stopped, turned, looked at me curiously. 'I threw away a card by the food places,' I said, running towards him. 'I didn't mean to throw it away. I need it back.'

'Oh.' He cocked his head to one side, studying me.

I reached him and glanced into his rubbish trolley. It was empty.

'I just took the last load out to the dumpsters,' he said.

'The dumpsters?'

'Yep. And you can't go out there. It's airport personnel only.' He shrugged. 'Sorry.'

'But I need that card.'

'Even if you could go, you'd never find it.' He glanced at his watch. 'Dump trucks should be here by now. Sorry.' He turned and wheeled away his trolley. He stopped at the next bin, took out the full bag and replaced it with a fresh one.

I'd lost Emma's card for ever.

After a time I shook my head to clear away unsettling thoughts and headed for the exit.

But that business card wasn't the only thing Emma had given me. I did have something to remember her by. And I was never going to get rid of the Rolex. I'm keeping that always.

CONVERSING WITH CRIMINALS
(IT CAN'T HURT TO BE FRIENDLY)

I missed the dawn. I know I must have dozed, but I don't remember falling asleep. Holly and Byron are already awake. It makes me feel strange, vulnerable even, knowing that they've seen me with my defences down, but they're not looking at me with hate so I know I didn't blurt out any secrets in my sleep. Or spoken another woman's name with longing.

I feel guilty. I can hardly look at Holly and return her tight smile with one of my own. I spent the night dreaming of making love to Emma. It's almost as if I've been caught cheating on Holly, but I don't feel sordid. Memories of Emma could never be that.

I force myself to concentrate. I need to pay attention to the situation at hand. I can't lose myself in the past — no matter how vivid and welcoming it seems.

Karl's still behind the wheel. He must have driven all night: I would have woken if we'd stopped to change drivers. The road isn't crowded, but there are other cars around. I wonder where we are, but I decide not to ask.

I can wait until I see a sign.

I yawn and stretch as far as I can, given the circumstances. I really crave a toothbrush and a glass of water, in that order. Maybe a toilet first. 'Could we stop for a break, stretch the legs, get some coffee, find a restroom?' I ask. 'Maybe buy some toothbrushes and tooth-paste?'

'Good idea,' murmurs Byron.

'This isn't a first-grade field trip,' says Karl. 'There are no scheduled bathroom breaks.'

It's a good thing Kevin's not here, because I doubt he could have held out for so many hours. The urine would have seeped out or his bladder would have exploded under the strain. Then Karl would have stopped the car, frog-marched Kevin out of sight of the road, made him dig his own grave, and shot him dead with a *Miller's Crossing* bullet-in-the-head execution.

Luke yawns. 'I gotta go too,' he says. 'We can stop and use the side of the road.'

'What about me?' says Holly. 'You want me to squat beside the road in the middle of the desert? People will be able to see me for miles. I thought you didn't want to draw any attention to us. That's not going to make us blend in.'

I open my mouth to smooth things over, but Karl says. 'Fine. We'll stop. But don't you sass me. I don't like women who sass.'

Well, it was surprisingly easy to get him to change his mind. Maybe we'll be able to reason with him after all.

Karl continues, 'We need gas anyway, but none of you are going in on your own. And that includes the woman. If there's any nonsense we shoot him.' He points at Byron. 'Got that?'

Holly nods and slumps back in her seat. She looks frightened suddenly, and I want to hold her in my arms and comfort her. I want to make everything better, but I don't know how. I take her hand in mine, just letting her know I'm there.

Luke turns on the radio and fiddles with the dial. There's a lot of static and crackles and we can make out a few bars of music — country, rock, classical, even a burst of jazz — but the reception isn't good enough and he gives up. He sighs like a man mightily put upon, then opens the glove box and rummages inside.

'Any sign of a tape?' I ask, my voice on the friendly side of neutral.

'No.' Luke slams the glovebox shut. 'I need music.'

'We'll buy a tape when we stop for gas,' says Karl. 'But just one. We're not wasting money on more than that.'

Only one? This is going to be a long, long drive.

Luke turns and looks at me and I know, in that instant, that questions about my father are about to begin. Again. Great. Just what I want to do first thing in the morning. Make up even more rip-roaring yarns about the grand adventures Arnie and I have had together.

'So why do you have that funny accent, Nick?' Luke asks me, running one hand through his crew cut, out of habit more than anything else I'd guess. 'Your dad comes from Germany, doesn't he?'

'Austria,' I say.

'But you don't sound like Arnie.'

Here it goes again. The inevitable questions. The only unknown is how far Luke will push me in his quest for answers. Some people are satisfied with superficial details. Others want to dig deeper, confident there's some inside scoop they alone can uncover.

(I was surprised this one hadn't come up last night, but I guess it was more exciting for them to ask about Arnie than wonder about me.)

'No,' I tell Luke, 'I don't sound like my dad. I'm a native English speaker. I grew up in England.'

'England? Why didn't you grow up in LA?'

'My mother was English.'

'Was? She dead?' Luke shifts in his seat so he's more comfortable. 'How old were you?'

Holly and Byron have heard this before, back at the training school, so their faces already show sympathy for me. Even Karl is quiet now and I know, however hard he pretends not to be, that he's fascinated too. He can't help himself. I mean, Arnold Schwarzenegger. Who could? (If someone says they're not interested, they're lying.)

'I was only four when my mother was dying of cancer and she made my father promise I'd be raised in England. She wanted me to feel close to her, and she didn't think I'd understand her if I was raised in America, so I grew up at my grandparents' house in London.'

This is part of my usual story, the one I told when I was the Son of Robert Redford, the one I always used, varied slightly, of course, for the specific circumstances of each case. If it's appropriate, I tell my listeners that my parents' marriage was a love match, but that my celebrity relative was tragically widowed very early on, way before he or she was famous. Or if said relative was already famous by the time of my birth, I pretend that a clandestine love affair brought me into being. I've got other ready answers at hand in case my questioners demand further explanations as to why they haven't heard of this marriage or relationship before, but the sorrow in my voice about the supposed death of my parent usually does the trick and few ask for more details.

I'll say anything it takes to keep Karl and Luke believing I am who I say I am.

'And you'd come here for summer vacations to be with Arnie?' asks Luke, frowning a little, watching me. He probably wonders how a boy could bear to be parted from a father like Arnold Schwarzenegger, promise to a dead wife and mother or not.

'Yes, I stayed with my father during all the school holidays.'

True, true, all true. I was always with my father (and my real mother, of course) during school holidays, there's just a little confusion over who they think my father is and who I'm talking about.

Karl's listening. I can see that he is and that's good. Luke's already said he doesn't want me dead — though Karl hasn't promised anything. Now I need to work on Karl and make them both realise they can't kill my fiancée or my friend either. They need to believe that Arnie wouldn't like it. They need to feel closer than ever to Arnold

Schwarzenegger so they won't want to upset him in any way.

'You must be glad to be here,' says Karl, 'away from all that fucking rain and fog you people have in London. I've never even owned an umbrella in my life. It'd be like living in Seattle, only with more rain. I'd hate it.'

Weeks ago I gave up trying to explain that actually it doesn't rain all the time, that the weather in London is similar, though not identical, to that of Paris and no one thinks of Paris as being miserable and grey and wet all the time, do they? Hasn't Karl seen any James Bond films? How about Pierce Brosnan's speedboat chase down the Thames? It wasn't raining then, was it? Although, now I think about it, it might have been cloudy. But it definitely wasn't raining.

Maybe Karl has a phobia about water. That might be good. I could use that. Or maybe it's just that his arsonist's heart is horrified by the thought of all that rain being a natural fire extinguisher.

'Where do you live now, Nick?' asks Luke. 'London or LA?'

'Both, actually. I have a flat in London and a little house in Santa Monica. I do location scouting for studios in both countries.'

'I've never been to Europe,' says Luke.

'Only place I've been is Mexico.' He laughs. 'But I guess I'll be seeing Canada if Karl gets his way.'

'I went to Paris once,' says Byron. 'I loved it. But I was only there for three days before I fell down a flight of stairs inside the Eiffel Tower and broke my ankle. My dad sent me home.' He shrugs. 'He said I'd just slow him down, so he spent the rest of the trip on his own. He went to Rome, Venice, Berlin and London. I'll get there one day.'

'You can come and stay in my spare room,' I say, knowing it won't happen but wanting to give him something to look forward to.

Byron's eyes widen. 'I'd really like that.'

'You should do it,' says Holly. 'London's fun.' She glances at me.

'So, Nick,' says Luke, 'how tall is your father? How big are his biceps? What's his all-time favourite movie? What bands does he listen to? Does he play the guitar? Is there going to be another *Terminator* picture? They could even do a prequel. And what about *Conan*? Arnie looks really cool with a sword.'

MEMORIES:
BACK WHEN I FOLLOWED THE
RULES NO MATTER WHAT

From Chicago's O'Hare airport, I took a taxi to the local driveaway office, leaving Emma's business card lost — discarded — in a black bin-bag that was already on its way to the dump. I drove a Mercedes E-Class to San Diego, stopping only for petrol and to sleep, not in the mood for sightseeing. San Diego was too close to LA and real celebrities for comfort so I stayed only a night. I was tempted to visit the zoo — I'd always heard it was good but I didn't. I wanted to keep moving. I had to be in motion.

From San Diego I drove a Range Rover up the California coast to Portland, Oregon, then a Ford Explorer to St Louis, driving, always driving. In Minneapolis I was the Brother of Bruce Willis, but I only stayed four days, my heart wasn't in it. I drifted on to Memphis, assuming the mantle of the Brother of Tom Hanks after I'd been to Graceland.

I was restless, uneasy, and I knew it was because of Emma. She'd jolted me out of my routine and I had to get back into the swing of things. I was a purveyor of happiness. I had to pull myself together.

ANOTHER WEEK,
ANOTHER RELATIVE

'Hey, guys,' said Joe Jacobs, my new best friend, introducing me to his mates as we joined them inside one of the hottest nightclubs in Dallas. 'This is Jean-Claude Van Damme's brother.'

'No way,' said one, reminding me of a talkative Silent Bob. He had the beard, he had the hair, he had the coat, he had the look.

'Yes way,' said Joe, a smile stretched so wide across his face I feared his facial muscles might tear.

'Cool.'

'Hey, man, how ya doing?'

'I'm Nick,' I said, shaking hands, accepting slaps on the back, politely not acknowledging the looks of adoration and wonder.

Joe Jacobs was the bartender at my hotel. The night I arrived, we'd got talking, and when I'd seen him for my pre-dinner cocktail the following evening, he'd invited me out clubbing. I agreed right away. A boys' night out appealed to me. I was still feeling fragile after my week with Emma and I wanted nothing that would remind me of her. I wanted to be a tough man's man. That's who I wanted to be that week.

I'd only followed the Rules, damn it. I shouldn't have felt like such a heartless bastard, but I did, even though there was nothing I could have done. I, Nick Reed, would have liked to stay with Emma and supported her as she faced her husband and his mistress, as her life was torn apart, but I couldn't. It wasn't my fault; that's just the way it was.

The night went on and I was glad I'd accepted Joe's invitation to the club. We drank and chatted about kick-boxing and karate. They were all disappointed when I said I didn't practise martial arts myself, but they soon forgave me when I regaled them with stories of Jean-Claude's movie stunts and Jean-Claude's life.

'He broke my wrist a couple of years ago when I was helping him rehearse a fight scene. I forgot which way I was supposed to go and walked straight into a round-house kick,' I said, smiling ruefully. 'I thought he'd broken my whole arm it hurt so bad, but he'd only got the wrist. Took a long time to heal, though.'

'He always used to eat pizza the day before a competition. And he loves ice cream. Green beans are his favourite vegetable but he hates cauliflower.' Strangely, food stories were popular with my patrons. I guess people liked to know that celebrities have likes and dislikes the same as the rest of us. Gives them something they can share with their heroes.

'And then there was that time we went sailing in the Mediterranean, just the two of us,' I said. 'It was fantastic. No reporters, no cameras, just two brothers enjoying themselves.'

'He's constantly having parties round his pool.' I smiled. 'And his parties are the best. The women always seem to wear these teeny little string bikinis. Fortunately, the neighbours are always invited so they never complain about the noise.'

The stories went on and my audience loved me. They couldn't get enough of Jean-Claude.

And then it happened. A loud, abusive voice. A sceptic.

'You're not Jean-Claude Van Damme's brother,' said a brawny man, interrupting our loud, laughing conversation. He was holding three full bottles of beer, passing our group on the way from the bar to his own friends.

'Oh, really? Says who?' My face flushed, but I was already warm from the alcohol Joe's friends had been buying me so I don't think anyone else could tell.

'You're English,' said the man. 'Jean-Claude is Belgian.' He turned a scathing look on my new friends. 'Any fool knows that.'

'Fuck you, asshole,' said Joe's friend Sam. 'What the hell do you know?'

The unbeliever's face turned an ugly, mottled red and his eyes narrowed. 'I know he's a liar.' He turned back to me. '*Parlez-vous français?*'

My blood ran cold. I couldn't speak French. I'd barely passed my GCSE at school and that was over ten years ago. I couldn't remember any French except a few rude words, and even then I had appalling pronunciation. I had to go on the offensive. 'Nice accent,' I said, sarcastically, seeking inspiration from my own failings.

If anything his face turned a deeper red. 'I bet you're going to say you don't have to prove anything to me, isn't that right?'

Was I so transparent?

'Look, I don't care what you believe,' I said. 'Just go away.' And I turned my back on him. What else could I do? Say I only spoke Flemish? Oh, yeah, that'd certainly convince him. I didn't want the sceptic to make doubters of my fans. I wanted this night out. I needed a good time. I deserved it. I'd been working hard and that evening was my chance to relax and forget about things. I wasn't going to wimp out and let this one rude man destroy it. 'You remember *Kickboxer?*' I asked my friends, my back to the sceptic, ignoring him, hoping he'd go away. 'Well, you know that scene — '

'Watch out, Nick,' yelled Joe, as he pushed me out of the way.

I whirled and everything seemed to happen at once. The doubter dropped his beer bottles and punched Joe on the nose. Blood went everywhere. Then Joe's friends startled pummelling the brawny man, ganging up on him, but he hit back, with a right hook, a left and then another right. He wasn't kicking and whirling in karate-style, but he knew how to box.

I didn't know what to do. I'd never been in a fight before and it was all happening so fast.

So this is what happens when you pick a relative who lives by the sword, I remember thinking.

Then a hand grabbed my shoulder, spun me round, and someone punched me in the eye. And I hit him back.

After that it was chaos. Fists flying, alcohol spilling, glasses and bottles shattering on the floor. It only went on for a few minutes, but it seemed longer, like it was hours, just blood and sweat and bruised knuckles as we punched and dodged and fought. It was our very own *Fight Club* and I was enjoying it. For the first time I could see the appeal. My fist connected with someone's jaw and I smiled. Blood poured from my nose, my eye was swelling up, but I didn't care. All that mattered was the fight. I was probably losing — I *was* losing, I didn't know the first thing about fisticuffs, let alone bar-room brawling — but I didn't care. It was the fight that counted. The fight that was important.

Then Joe appeared in front of me: 'The cops are coming.'

I blinked, held back the punch I'd been ready to give him, and blinked again. Reality returned. I remembered who I was. I understood what was happening. I knew I had to flee. Immediately. 'I can't let them find me here,' I said. 'This would look bad for Jean-Claude.'

'Come on. I'll get you out of here.'

And we ran, leaving Joe's friends to fend for themselves. We joined the crowd streaming out of the back door. Joe led me down an alleyway then on to a street and we slowed to a walk, heading away. There were sirens in the distance, approaching the nightclub, but we were safe.

EASY DAYS, EASY LIES (THE NORM WAS HARMONY, NOT DISCARD)

The fight had relaxed me, releasing tension and easing guilt. It put everything back into perspective, in a bizarre, brutal way I wouldn't have thought would work if I hadn't tried it for myself. I felt better about everything. I was a purveyor of happiness, I was only doing my job. It was my responsibility to flit in and out of as many lives as possible. I had to be superficial, I wasn't allowed to be anything else.

I left Dallas focused on the future, fully in control of myself, thinking only of the adventures to come, not dwelling on the past. I wouldn't allow myself to think about what had happened to me or what might have been. It was over. This was my life. It's what I'd chosen the day I arrived in Atlanta and spoke my first lie, setting me on this course. I had a duty to myself to carry on. It's what I wanted. I was never going to be famous, but I wasn't going to settle for an ordinary existence. I refused to be ordinary.

I went to Virginia Beach as the Brother of

Russell Crowe and they loved me. Women, men, even children, they all worshipped him — and his little brother too. I was wined and dined. I shared stories of the times Russell and I had camping together in the Australian outback, climbing in Patagonia, scuba-diving in the Red Sea, training for next year's attempt on Everest, playing soccer on the set of *Gladiator*. They adored him. They adored me. It was easy. Fun. I could have done it in my sleep.

It was exactly what I needed to get myself back on track.

RISKS ARE ALLOWED, BUT IN THE END IT'S BETTER TO BE SAFE THAN SORRY

I accepted a driveaway to California, determined to enjoy what the state had to offer and not just travel along its freeways as I had before, even though I'd always thought it was a risky destination for a purveyor of happiness. You'd never know when you were going to bump into someone who knew someone who knew someone who *really* knew someone. But I told myself that most celebrities were concentrated near a few locations and weren't likely to be on every mountain and on every beach. I felt up to the challenge, capable of handling the pressure, so I drove a Chevy Blazer to the San Francisco area.

I took precautions. I wasn't about to go in blind, shouting that I was related to Steve Martin or Kim Basinger. No way. I wasn't a fool. I decided — maturely, logically — that being the relative of a British star rather than an American one would make all the difference.

I decided to become the Son of Anthony Hopkins. That's Sir Anthony Hopkins obviously, but I didn't insist people refer to him by his title. After all, they didn't love him because he was a Sir, they loved him for his talent.

I'd been in Napa Valley only two days, staying at a fine vineyard, enjoying the novelty of not having to explain away my accent as this time my relative was British (nobody picked up on the Welsh/English discrepancy), when the rumours began to circulate. Not the gossip about my visit, no, word had already spread: people knew I was there. Excited speculation about the impending arrival of Nicole Kidman raced through the resort like wildfire.

Suddenly, within an hour of the first whisper becoming general knowledge, the place was swarming with paparazzi.

I had to leave. The staff, the guests, patrons and non-patrons alike, they all knew who I was — who I was claiming to be. It was only a matter of time before the paparazzi learnt of my presence. I refused to become a hunted man. I didn't want to end up like the Incredible Hulk. I did not want to be pursued across the country by an obsessed journalist desperate for my real story as soon as he or she caught my scent. I didn't want anyone poking and prodding and discovering the truth. My truth. I knew that my tale wouldn't hold up to close scrutiny, that if someone with the appropriate media contacts did a little digging they could easily discover that I wasn't who I said I was.

I could allow no one to photograph me. I could leave behind no physical trace of myself.

I had to flee.

Of course I wanted to stay and see Nicole Kidman. I'd have been able to meet her. Just imagine — shaking Nicole's hand, perhaps kissing her beautiful cheek. I would have been able to talk to her, hear her tinkling laugh. A fantasy come true. The Son of Anthony would have met her. *I* would have met her. But I couldn't risk one of those tabloid photographers snapping a picture of me eating breakfast with my patrons or shaking Nicole's hand. The caption would read Nick Hopkins, son of the actor, and someone somewhere who knew the truth, who was acquainted with Anthony Hopkins, would see it and report me as a fraud.

And then it would all be over and I would become the story. I never wanted to be famous for being a con-man, for villainy. I didn't want my family's name smeared across the press like it was so much dung, stinking and unwholesome. I couldn't do that to my parents. They, if not I, deserved better.

So I ran.

I left Napa Valley three days ahead of schedule and it cost me a fortune. I had no patron lined up to pay my bill. Sure, there was a couple whom I'd thought would surprise me with it all paid up when the time came for me to check out, but they were expecting me to stay longer and hadn't made any arrangements that early. They had already covered all my meals and drinks, but I had to pay for the room myself.

I liked the five-star life. I wanted a five-star life, but I couldn't afford it, or not for very long, not if I wanted to keep drifting for a year or two.

I threw my clothes into my suitcase and carried it down to the lobby, not wanting to summon a porter and risk alerting anyone in advance of my departure. No one could know I was leaving. I paid my bill with a straight face, handing over most of the cash I'd been carrying around with me. Thankfully, I was still following the Rules and had my emergency cash supply in case I needed to pay for anything out of my own pocket but was unable, for obvious reasons, to do so with a credit card. I counted out the dollar bills, refusing to cringe at the price, telling the man at the reception desk that a business emergency had arisen and I had to get back to the UK. And then I was gone.

The Son of Anthony slipped away into the afternoon sunshine like a snowflake in the tropics. I floated through the heavens, then came crashing down to earth, melting away and disappearing, never to be heard from again.

PUBLIC OBSERVATION
TEST ONE

I sigh and stare out of the car window, forcing my thoughts back to the present reality of criminals and hostages. I watch the world as it passes in a blur of dirt, rocks, sunshine and emptiness. It's been thirty minutes since Karl said we would stop and we're still driving. There's been no sign of a petrol station, no hint of a town, not even the sighting of a single house, though we have passed a few crossroads.

Suddenly Holly speaks. 'You have to take off our handcuffs.'

'No,' says Luke. 'Then you'll try to escape and Nick might get hurt. I can't believe you're asking us to shoot Arnie's son, I thought you loved him.'

'I do,' she says.

And I feel a quiver in my gut. I know she's just saying that, agreeing with Luke because she's supposed to be my fiancée, but it sounds odd. She can't *really* love me *already*, can she?

'Come on. You know I don't want you to

shoot Nick,' continues Holly. 'I don't want you to shoot any of us, but we can't go to the restroom in a gas station wearing handcuffs. People will notice.'

'She's right,' says Karl. 'Take 'em off, Luke.'

I frown. A second bout of reasonableness in one morning? First he agreed to stop so we could use a real loo and not squat by the side of the road, and now he's taking off the cuffs?

Luke shrugs. 'Okay, but don't blame me if I have to shoot Nick's friend or his fiancée.' He rummages in the bag at his feet. Why he's got our equipment there, in his way, when he could've put it in the boot is a mystery to me. It must be pretty uncomfortable with all that stuff preventing him stretching out his legs, but then what do I know? I'm only a lowly hostage,

Cuffed with our own handcuffs. Ted will never live down the shame of it.

Luke finds seven keys, one for each set of handcuffs. 'You first, Nick,' he says.

I dutifully hold out my hands and Luke tries the keys until he finds one that fits. The cuffs open with that audible snap I've heard on countless television shows. And, yes, just like those TV characters, I rub my aching wrists. Holly's next, then Byron, and we're all free of our shackles, if not actually free.

'Now, you all be good,' says Karl, as Luke dumps the handcuffs and the keys into the pack at his feet. 'Don't forget that if there's any trouble we'll shoot Byron.'

'Could you please stop saying that?' says Byron. 'We know you're going to shoot me if there's any trouble. You've already told us. Could you please just not say it again?'

'Okay, if that's what you want,' says Karl. 'We'll fucking kill Byron if you don't all behave. Does that sound better?'

Byron pales. 'No.'

'Then you'd better hope the lovebirds don't consider your death a fair price to pay for their own attempt at escape, hadn't you?'

We're all silent.

Luke studies us, then finally he sighs and shakes his head. 'You better take off those bullet-proof vests and leave 'em in the car. They'll draw too much attention if you keep 'em on.'

'Good idea,' I say, and slip mine off, then help Holly out of hers.

On the one hand I'm glad to be rid of it, as it's heavy and cumbersome and I'm all hot and sticky underneath, but I can't stop the shiver of fear that hits me. I feel we've surrendered our last defence even though I know that if Karl and Luke do decide to kill us three flak vests would hardly get in the way: clean head shots at point-blank range would do the trick.

The money belt. I'd forgotten about my money-belt. I want to glance down. I need to check it. But I have to resist the urge. I clench my hands into fists. I must ignore it. It feels like my identity documents are burning a hole through my shirt. I wonder if it's visible now, if it's clearly outlined against my sticky shirt, but I dare not look. If the crims can see it I'll know soon enough. Is there a bulge over my stomach? Will they notice? Will they see it? Am I about to be exposed?

Luke turns, shifts in his seat to get more comfortable. 'Do you ever get to hold your dad's props? Are they heavy? Are they sometimes real guns? Or are they always fake replicas?'

'It depends,' I say slowly, not liking to commit myself to answers on technical questions. I adjust my Rolex, tugging my sleeve low, making sure it's still covered.

'Man, you're so lucky. I'd love to hold some of Arnie's movie guns. He gets the best weapons.' And then Luke's off, rhapsodising about how great my father is, asking question after question. I only hope I can remember everything I tell him: I don't want to start contradicting myself later on.

At last we see a petrol station ahead, in one

of those little towns that seems to have sprung up around it with a Taco Bell, a McDonald's, a few houses off in the distance and not much else. It's surprisingly crowded for what little traffic there is on the road, as if all the cars congregate here — and they probably do: we haven't passed anything else while I've been awake.

Karl pulls up beside a free pump and turns off the ignition. 'Right, here's how it's going to work. Luke, you stay here and fill us up. Byron will wait in the locked car. Luke, you also need to keep your eye on Byron and make sure he doesn't do anything stupid like try to write a note to attract someone's attention. He might even attempt to escape so you have to be ready to stop him.'

Luke frowns. 'You want me to shoot him if he tries anything? Right now? Here?'

'Not here. Don't shoot him in public. You just make sure he doesn't get away.' Karl twists in his seat and stares at Byron. 'And don't you try anything or, remember, I'll blow your fucking head off as soon as it's clear. Got that?'

Byron nods.

'Nick and Holly, you'll come with me inside the gas station and I'll take you to the restroom. You don't act strange, you don't speak to anyone, just be natural.'

'Understood,' I say, feeling a vague sense of *déjà vu*, as if I'm back in the bounty-hunting training school and Ted's issuing his orders.

'Right. Let's go.'

Holly and I walk with Karl into the gas station store, strolling, casual — or we would be but for our clothes. Karl's dressed like an ordinary citizen, but Holly and I still have on our black SWAT clothing and look out of place. Without our flak vests we can just about pretend we're following some sort of fashion trend that hasn't yet made it to this part of the world. We avoid the shelves of goods for sale, heading, like many other travellers, straight to the restrooms.

Or restroom. Unfortunately, this is rather too convenient for Karl's plans. There's only one room, a single stall, and it's unisex, so there's no chance to leave a note. Escape, of course, is impossible as they have Byron. I may be a selfish pig, but I'm not so far gone that I'd consider deserting him, thereby condemning him to certain death.

Karl checks out the room, making sure there isn't a window, then allows us to do our business, one at a time. It's his turn next, and I'm wondering what he'll do, if he'll trust us out here on our own — he shouldn't — when he hesitates. 'Shit,' he says, 'you'll have to come in with me.'

337

Holly blushes. 'But — '

'Lady, you think I want you to hear me pee? You think I'm some sort of sexual freak? A fucking pervert?'

'Well, no.'

'You got that right, but we ain't got no choice.' Karl holds open the door and in we walk.

If anyone sees us they'll think some very kinky sex is about to go on. Three of us. In a toilet. Even if it's nearly clean it's still a public toilet and that 'nearly' is a pretty important word. Oh, joy. Holly and I face the wall and then Karl takes the longest piss I've ever heard a man take in my life.

Finally he's done, he washes his hands (good hygiene, Karl) and we leave. Of course, someone's waiting outside the door when we emerge and, inevitably, it's a tiny grandmotherly lady who must be in her eighties. Holly blushes, but Karl only grins and holds the door for her. This must be a cosmic joke, some kind of cruel prank to ensure the utmost humiliation before we die.

'Let's get something to eat,' Karl says.

And I actually smile at him. 'Best idea you've had all day.'

We grab boxes of doughnuts and candy, muffins, granola bars and tortilla chips, soft drinks and bottles of water. It's as if we're on an expedition. Hopefully Karl's planning to share this with us. If not, he and Luke are going to get pretty sick eating it all on their own. And grumpy, hungry hostages as an added bonus.

Our arms laden with goodies, Karl ushers us to a rack of cassette tapes and CDs, mostly compilations and 'Best of' albums from the sixties, seventies and eighties, with Pearl Jam's *Vs.* the sole representative of the nineties and nothing since.

'*Vs.* sold a million copies in the first week,' I say hopefully.

'Eagles,' says Karl, picking up their *Greatest Hits Volume 2*. 'You know where you are with them.'

It's going well until we reach the tills and there it is. An Arizona newspaper. The *Arizona Republic*.

WANTED MEN ON THE RUN.

We've made front-page headlines. Or, rather, Karl and Luke have made the front page. Their names and photographs appear at the top. I can see no photos of Holly or Byron. Or me, thank God. But I don't have time to read the paper, not do I want to pick it up and draw Karl's attention to it. Better if he doesn't know. I'm thinking, maybe he hasn't seen the newspaper, but just at that second Karl reaches out, takes a copy and puts it on the counter.

'And I'd like one of these,' he says to the cashier, cool as ice. I have to hand it to him. He certainly seems to know what he's doing. Has he been on the run before? maybe. Probably. But not on this scale. Or surely he wouldn't have been allowed bail.

Holly and I exchange glances, but the cashier barely looks up as he says the total and Karl slides across a few dollar bills — cash, of course.

I take a moment to scan the other papers: *USA Today*, the *Los Angeles Times*. But there's no mention of us. It must have happened too late to make those papers, or the story isn't important enough to be on the covers, but I bet, if we make it through the day, we'll be all over the nation by tomorrow.

Particularly if they speak to Arnie.

A MOMENT ALONE

Luke takes Byron inside to pay for the petrol as we return to the car. Holly and I climb into the back seat, but Karl stays outside, just standing, unmoving, his gaze turned our way, not obviously staring but keeping us under surveillance. He has a still, eerie look about him that I don't like. I won't make the mistake of assuming he's being kind, allowing Holly and me time on our own. He probably wants us to run so he has an excuse to kill us. Or maybe he's just stretching his legs before we get back on the road. I'd have thought he'd be poring over the newspaper, desperate to read what's been written about him. He's got balls, I'll give him that, standing there looking so nonchalant and at ease when at any second someone might notice him and make the connection.

But, no, it doesn't happen. His luck holds. People don't point and stare or run away in sudden fear for their lives so I'm guessing no one recognises him.

Holly and I sit in the back of the car and read the article. I'm amazed Karl's letting us see the paper at all, but maybe he figures he's not going to have a chance to discuss it in private with Luke, so what does it matter if we see it now rather than in a few minutes?

Holly reads aloud. 'Karl Wright and Luke Russell have three hostages.'

'They don't say who we are?' I scan the article. There's no mention of our names and certainly no photos.

She lowers her voice. 'The police won't know if the crims know your real name, and they won't want to reveal that you're Arnie's son in case they don't.'

'But they do know.'

'Yes, but the police don't know that. Byron told Karl and Luke after we'd left the house. Ted and the others weren't there.'

I nod, barely able to believe my luck. The police must know by now that I'm not Arnold Schwarzenegger's son. The first thing they would have done was contact the big man himself, and Arnie, of course, would have been quick to deny that I'm any relation. So, really, the police are keeping mum because they know I'm not Arnie's son and they're afraid that the crims will think I am. And the police understand that if the crims think I'm Arnie's son then find out I'm not, they're going to be furious, and that would endanger all of us and not only me, the wicked con-artist. They can't risk releasing that information, if only to protect Holly and Byron.

It makes sense in a twisted way.

But con-artist? That sounds bad, doesn't it?

Yet I'm not a bad person. Not really. I make everyone so very happy just by sharing my time, spreading smiles and cheer wherever I go.

Why didn't I listen when I told myself not to get involved with Holly? If I'd just followed the Rules, none of this would have happened. I'd always kept to them before, even when it had been difficult — even when I'd wanted to stay with Emma. Why hadn't I listened to the voice of reason when I met Holly? Is this what I deserve for being a rule-breaker? Doom not only for myself but for those around me?

Well, I did break the Rules and I'm here now and there's nothing I can do to change that. Besides, I should be optimistic, shouldn't I? I should be happy that I met Holly. She's gorgeous and fun and great in bed. And I'm having a grand adventure. It's certainly more exciting than selling insurance, even if it's more dangerous.

Then it strikes me.

'Will the police have given the media our names? Revealed who we are, but told them not to release details to the public?' If so, all hope is gone. Some journalist will dig and dig and discover the truth. He or she won't be able to resist leaking the story somehow, even though they won't intend to get me killed. It'll simply be too juicy to withstand the temptation.

Holly shrugs. Like it doesn't matter. Which, to her, it doesn't. 'Probably not,' she says. 'Not when your father's so famous. They'll want to protect your whole family too, in case the crims use you to try to get at Arnie.'

I feel sick. Arnie's real family. What if Karl changes his mind about the ransom thing? I'll have to keep the crims distracted. I'll have to keep them entertained with my conversational charm so they won't have time to come up with a more devious, cunning plan to use Arnie or his family if things go wrong. I can't let them use his real family.

Why did everything have to get so complicated?

This was supposed to be a happy-go-lucky time full of smiles and joy. It was never supposed to turn out like this.

But the good news — and I'll have to remember to jot down a note about this for a chapter in my book about looking on the bright side even when things are bad — is that Ted's bounty-hunting pal Donnie is alive and stable. He lost a lot of blood, but Holly's quick thinking probably saved his life. So, good news for Donnie. And good news for us.

Karl and Luke are not murderers.

Let's hope they want to keep it that way.

DRIVING, DRIVING, DRIVING

As Byron and Luke leave the petrol-station shop and head towards us, crossing the forecourt, Karl opens the driver's door and slides behind the wheel. Does he not trust Luke to drive? Or does he just like to be in control? Interesting. Or interesting to an FBI criminal profiler. I don't know what I'm supposed to do with that analysis.

When Byron reaches the car he hesitates, meets my eyes through the window, then glances at Karl only to find him staring, watching, waiting, almost eager for Byron to do something. Byron gulps — his neck muscles jerk and he opens the door, scurries inside and fastens his seatbelt. Luke slams his door, sits in the front passenger seat, and then we're off, pulling out on to the road, heading north.

'Give Luke the paper,' says Karl, once we're safely out of sight of the petrol station.

'Paper?' asks Luke.

'Newspaper,' says Holly, handing it to him.

'Cool,' says Luke, taking it, seeing his photo on the front page. 'This is so cool.'

'It's not cool.' Karl frowns. 'By tomorrow every newspaper in the country will have our pictures plastered on the front pages and people will be looking for us.'

Luke scans the article. 'They don't mention Nick's name,' he says, sounding disappointed.

'No, not today. They're just the hostages,' says Karl.

'But I want my picture to be on the same page as Nick's. I want my name next to Schwarzenegger. I want all my friends back home to know I'm buddies with Arnie's son.'

Buddies? Doesn't he mean hostage and kidnapper? But I decide not to make the distinction aloud. If Luke wants to think of us as buddies, then buddies we shall be.

'Nick's photo and name will make it into the papers soon enough.' Karl drums his fingers on the steering wheel. 'And we're going to need disguises.'

As in wigs, fake glasses, big noses and things?

Karl nods to himself. 'We'll stop off at the next major town and get some new clothes and hair dye. Holly will be our hairdresser.'

Holly looks worried. 'But I've never cut anyone's hair.'

'Then you'd better learn quick, honey, 'cause we've all got to look different. You three included. New hair colours, new clothes, everything.'

Byron clears his throat. 'I've always wanted to be really, really blond.'

We drive on, passing a monstrously large caravan being towed by a Grand Jeep Cherokee. The caravan dwarfs the 4×4, making it seem as tiny as tiny as any two-seater MG convertible on the streets of London. It's just another day on the road in America. A happy family exploring their country, camping out in a hotel-on-wheels with all the comforts of home.

'So, Nick,' says Luke, turning in his seat to face the back, 'what's Arnie's star sign?'

I go cold. 'Star sign?' I ask, stalling for time. I don't know Arnie's birthday. I can't remember the date. What if Karl knows the truth? What if he shares the same birthday as Arnie? What if this gives me away? I only checked the year to make sure Arnie could be my dad, I don't remember the month, I don't remember the day. *Shit, shit, shit.*

'I'm a Sagittarius,' says Luke. 'What's Arnie?'

'Oh, I don't know.' I try to look confused rather than terrified. This is it. This is the moment they catch me out and turn against me. This is the moment before the moment that I die. 'I'm not really up with astrology.'

Karl shifts in his seat. But he doesn't look away from the road. He's probably just getting comfortable. He's not reaching for his gun to shoot me.

'Arnie's a Leo,' says Holly, smiling. 'Same as me.'

'I wish he was a Sagittarius,' says Luke, 'but I think Leo and Sagittarius can get along.'

'So what am I?' I ask, pretending that I don't know. 'My birthday's June first.'

'You're a Gemini,' says Luke.

Byron clears his throat. 'I'm a Virgo.'

'What about you, Karl?' asks Holly, her voice bright and friendly.

'I'm a mean son-of-a-bitch who doesn't fucking believe in horoscopes. We make our own destiny, lady. Now, pass me some food, Luke. I'm hungry.'

Luke hands Karl a blueberry muffin, then opens the Eagles tape. We listen to 'Hotel California' while we wolf down doughnuts and chocolate bars, and I turn and watch the scenery. We're passing near to the eastern edge of the Grand Canyon, but we don't stop.

We drive. And drive. And drive.

EVERYONE WANTS TO BE FAMOUS

Was it just a few short weeks ago that I was comfortable and at ease, confident in my abilities as a purveyor of happiness? The novelty had worn off but it definitely had its moments.

Sometimes everything went right, sometimes things went wrong. You win some, you lose some, you get some bills paid, you have to pay others. *Que sera sera*.

Boston. Maybe it was the weather, that damp feeling in the air or the grey sky, but I felt more relaxed and at home there than I did in the bright sunshine I'd experienced elsewhere on my journey. Everyone apologised and said it was the worst week for months, but I loved it.

I was Mel Gibson's little brother and it was great.

'Mel has black coffee and croissants for breakfast. Guinness is his favourite drink,' I said, time and again, telling my patrons what they wanted to hear.

'My brother and Jodie Foster became great friends during the filming of *Maverick*. She phoned me the year *Braveheart* was up for all those Oscars because she wanted to hire a bagpiper to follow Mel around all evening, both before and after the ceremony. Jodie's always concerned with everybody's feelings and she didn't want to do it if he wouldn't find it funny. I told her that he had a great sense of humour and he'd love it.'

'He plays both baseball and cricket. And he loves going to basketball games. He also tries to visit me in London every June and July so we can watch the tennis at Wimbledon.'

Those were the sort of tales I created for my life with Mel.

On the morning of my third day when I was really starting to get into the swing of things in Boston and wishing the *Cheers* of television really existed and I could pop in to see all my old favourites, reality slapped me in the face.

Nothing cold or impolite. On the contrary, it was all done with the utmost politeness and the man responsible does not even know he spoilt my good mood. As a matter of fact, we were quite chummy and that's what brought about the end of my complacency.

His name was Jason Loraxe and he was a waiter at my hotel. It was when he cleared away my breakfast dishes and refilled my coffee that the bombshell struck. So innocently. So unexpectedly. So effectively destructive.

'Mr Gibson,' he said, his voice pitched low so it wouldn't carry, 'would you do me a favour?'

I smiled, always happy to oblige, expecting a request for a signed photograph of my dear brother. Luckily I had a few left in my suitcase upstairs. 'I'll do my best.'

Jason reached into his pocket and pulled out a tape, handing it to me quickly, before I could change my mind or think to refuse. 'I'm a musician,' he said. 'A singer-songwriter. I've performed some local gigs, but I don't have a recording contract, and I'd really appreciate it if you could listen to my stuff and tell me what you think.'

It was like a stab in the solar plexus. Jason wanted to be famous. Jason wanted to be famous through good old-fashioned talent. It had been so long since I'd thought in this way that it seemed a novel approach. Unprecedented, almost. He was about my age and he still had hope.

He hadn't given up on his dreams.

I don't know why he thought I'd have any influence in the music industry, but I suppose he must have been assuming that I was bound to have some contacts, and if I didn't, my brother Mel certainly would.

I listened to his tape in my room that night. And you know what? It was good. Jason Loraxe deserves to make it. Maybe he will if he doesn't admit defeat and abandon his dreams like I did.

But if 'it' doesn't happen I hope he won't become bitter, twisted and cynical. Perhaps he can be happy to keep trying and trying and trying. Maybe he'll never lose hope that his talent will be spotted eventually. He might be one of those single-minded, dedicated ones, who never stop believing in themselves.

We seem to have reached a stage in our society where we all have these expectations that if we set our minds to something it will happen. That if we believe in ourselves and work hard enough success will be ours. And fame, of course, is the ultimate proof of success. Whatever happened to just living everyday life and savouring each little experience? But no, we're not supposed to admit that that's satisfactory, we have to strive harder and harder. Yet not everyone can make it.

And what is 'making it' anyway? Is it always becoming a movie star or a rock star, or does it depend on your background? Maybe my parents thought I'd made it when I became a Grade Eight salesman. It was a decent job and I would have had a decent life, met a nice girl, bought a house, settled down. Perhaps that was enough to satisfy my parents' generation, but I know that people of my age strive for more. My flatmate Richard thought my promotion was great news, but he knew it was only a stepping stone on the way up. The big house and flash car are likewise good, but nothing is ever enough. No one is ever content. We want more, more, more.

Images of dotcom millionaires, young actors, popstars and supermodels fill our screens and magazines. Fantasies are rammed down our throats, sold like just another consumer product until our heads are bursting with dreams and we will not settle for anything but the best. To do otherwise would be giving in, surrendering, accepting failure and mediocrity as our due.

We want it. We want it all.

My parents are content. That does not necessarily mean they are happy, although I think they are.

For me contentment is not enough. I probably would have been content, most of the time, with my life in Wimbledon, bar a mid-life crisis or two. (And all this, I suppose, probably counts as the first.) But I'm not cut out for that. Maybe, for me, it's better to be miserable than content.

And it's not just me. It's my generation.

Jason the singer-songwriter doesn't want to settle for a job and a car and a normal life. It's not enough. It's never enough.

Yet here I am. My dreams were surrendered long ago so maybe I'm more like my parents than I thought. This whole purveyor of happiness business was only ever supposed to be temporary. It's only now that I realise I can't ever go back to being a seller of bizarre insurance policies to international businesses. Where's the purpose in it? What sort of meaning or life satisfaction could it give me? Who cares if companies want to insure against sandstorms, piranha attacks or their satellites dropping out of the sky? It might matter to them, but it could never matter to me.

I'm a failure. I've walked away from normal life, but not to follow some grand dream on the route to fame or artistic notoriety. No, I've walked away from a decent, normal job to become a scrounger, to lie and cheat people out of small favours and money. Even if the pleasure I gave outweights the gifts they bestowed upon me I'm nothing more than a con-man. I'm a cheat. A rogue.

And I'll never be famous. I'll never be the rock star or actor I wanted to be. I'll only ever be nothing.

Jason Loraxe may become famous. Do I

console myself with the knowledge that I'll be able to say I knew him when? No, I won't even be able to say that, not when I go back to being Nick Reed, for Jason Loraxe won't know me. He might recall the Nick Gibson who didn't help him out, who never put in a good word for him to his famous brother, but Jason won't know Nick Reed. No one knows Nick Reed. (Except family, friends and ex-colleagues, but that's not what I mean. Nick Reed is not famous. Nick Reed doesn't know anyone famous.

It was in Boston I realised that other people still had dreams. They thought talent would be enough.

And I was jealous.

BEING A PURVEYOR OF HAPPINESS ISN'T ALL SWEETNESS AND LIGHT

Another town, another hotel, another city, another resort, another meaningless conversation. Okay, I admit it: it's not all glamour and glory. A lot of the time it's downright boring. You feel like you're doomed to repeat the same dialogue over and over again. It's as if you're in some hellish loop, trapped in your very own *Groundhog Day*, condemned to relive the same day over and over and over again but you can see no way out because it isn't really the same day. It isn't all exactly alike and there's no way you can make it perfect because it just isn't possible while you're doing this job.

You can never be entirely noble and good when you're a liar. And doing this postpones the search for true purpose. It's a delaying tactic. A last desperate stab at youth before the onset of middle age and the realisation that you're all grown up and you have no valid excuse for such an aimless existence. You reach a certain point and it's no longer cute if you're messed up and uncertain; it's uncomfortable for everyone else. They've all made their peace with life and the world, and your restlessness upsets them, so it's time for you to settle down. You just have to accept that you, like everyone else, are on the inevitable path towards death, and that childhood and young adulthood can't last for ever. They don't like it any more than you do, but they're getting on with their lives.

They're getting on with their lives.

And I was trying to put off the inevitable. That's what all this was about. Jealousy, unhappiness and a macabre realisation that I would not live for ever.

But I did have a good time on my travels.

Mostly.

I wouldn't have stayed working as a purveyor if the happiness hadn't extended to me as well as my patrons.

It just wasn't the Answer to the Meaning of Life. And that's really what I was looking for.

THE ENDLESS JOURNEY NORTH
TOWARDS CANADA AS SEEN FROM
A PRISONER'S PERSPECTIVE

I'm feeling bloated and sick after all those doughnuts and chocolate bars. Everything just tasted so good and I was starving. Then, when I was starting to feel contented, I realised it might be my last meal. Maybe Karl had some devious plan in mind to murder us all and was being kind in his own warped way and ensuring that our last meal was a pleasurable feast of sugar and fat. The last meal of the condemned.

And then I couldn't stop eating. I mean, did I really want a jam doughnut to be the last thing I ever ate before I died? I thought I should have a KitKat and a Twix to be on the safe side, and when I'd scoffed both of those I saw a cinnamon Danish with my name on it and before I could help myself I'd eaten that too. All washed down, of course, with as many fizzy drinks as I could hold. And then there was that container of cheese Pringles, and who can say no to Pringles? I knew that once I'd started I'd never be able to stop until they were gone.

Now, wanting no more than to curl up on a sofa, hold my stomach and moan, I almost wish I was dead. At least then I wouldn't feel so ill. This is the first time oblivion has looked tempting. I could confess my sins, tell them my real name and that I'm nothing but a no-good liar, that I don't know Arnie, that I've never even met him, and Karl would put me out of my misery soon enough.

Put like that it's not so appealing. I don't want to die in a hail of bullets. I just want a long sleep so my stomach-ache will go away, then maybe I could wake up to find that this has all been a dream.

But it doesn't work that way. The world doesn't stop spinning because I want it to.

We seem to have been travelling for days, but it's still early, barely mid-morning, and we haven't even left the state, though we are — at last — nearing the border with Utah. We drive into Page, Arizona to the sounds of 'New Kid in Town'. Page has houses and everything and isn't just a strip of motels and burger joints for tourists, though there are plenty of those. There are signs advertising whitewater rafting, camping, hiking, horseback riding, helicopter rides over the Grand Canyon, boat trips on Lake Powell, you name it. If Holly had wanted a normal assignment, we could have been somewhere like this, experiencing everything the area had to offer rather than being stuck in a car with a couple of desperadoes.

Karl ejects the Eagles tape and switches off the stereo.

'We're going to stop at a Wal-Mart or someplace like that, get some disguises and stock up on supplies.'

'We're going shopping?' asks Byron.

'No,' says Karl, his eyes on the road. 'We're not going shopping. I am going shopping. And Holly's coming with me. Everyone else stays in the car.'

'Now wait just a minute,' I say. 'Holly's not going anywhere without me.'

Karl ignores me. 'Luke, you'll stay in the car with Nick and Byron.'

I won't put up with this. 'No — '

'You shouldn't worry, Nick,' says Luke. 'We're not going to kill her just for the hell of it. We're not going to kill anyone for the hell of it. You're here to protect us from the cops. If you behave you'll all be fine. You know we don't want to shoot Arnie's boy.'

'Take me,' I say. 'Leave Holly out of this.'

Karl rolls his eyes and glances at me in the rear-view mirror. 'Stop playing the hero. This isn't one of your father's movies. I'm taking

Holly because she's a woman and I need help getting clothes and hair dye. We'll be less suspicious if we're a couple. A pretty woman at my side will smooth things over.' He grins. 'Holly can pretend to be my girlfriend.'

'But — '

'I'll be fine, Nick.' Holly takes my hand and strokes my fingers with her thumb.

'I don't like it,' I say.

Karl stops at a red light, turns in his seat and stares at me. 'Are you going to make me shoot Byron to teach you a lesson?'

'You're not supposed to talk about shooting me,' whispers Byron.

'Oh, yeah, that's right,' says Karl, turning to Byron, his expression snapping from icy calm to fuck-you-and-your-entire-family-including-the-dogs-and-the-hamster.

'It wasn't shooting, it was killing, wasn't it?'

Luke glances around the car. 'Just do what Karl says and everything will be fine.' His voice is soothing, cajoling, trying to smooth things over.

I don't like it. Truth is, I hate it, but I'm not ready to force a confrontation. There's two of them and they both have guns, so even if I could hit Karl over the head there's still Luke, and he wouldn't hesitate to take me out if it came down to him or me, Arnie's son or not. I can't risk Holly and Byron. And, really, who do I think I am? I'm not a military man — those days with Ted proved that. We're in the back seat of a car. I'd need *Buffy* strength to get us out of this one.

It's all very well for Karl and Luke to say they won't kill us if they don't have to, but who knows what reasons will be enough for them? Maybe they'll decide they need to get rid of us so we can't talk to the police. They won't want the law looking for them in Canada, and if they let us go we'd reveal everything we know. Maybe all this buddy-buddy business is really to put us at our ease. They could be planning on killing us anyway. They might not mind murdering us in Canada when they no longer need us as human shields. Perhaps Canada doesn't have the death penalty and they're waiting to cross the border to wipe out the eyewitnesses. Or it could be that Karl's the only one planning to execute us and Luke is sincere — but killed by one of them is still dead.

Yet what can I do? I can say no twenty-nine times, a hundred, a thousand even, but Karl's not going to listen to me. He's the one in charge and he wants Holly to go with him, so Holly will go with him. There's nothing I can do about it.

If I thought I felt sick after eating all that food, it's ten times worse when we find a place to stop and Karl and Holly leave the rest of us in the car.

The wait is dull. I know I should be using this time to work on Luke, to cement that let's-be-best-chums bond, but I don't have the energy, not while Holly is alone with Karl.

Byron fidgets in his seat, sighs, then clears his throat. 'I never thought it'd be like this,' he says.

'What would be like this?' I ask, tearing my gaze away from the store exit: I've been watching it for Holly and Karl to reappear.

'Being a hostage.'

Luke laughs. 'What did you expect, then?'

'When I used to play cops and robbers as a kid we always tied up and gagged our prisoners. And we always kept them locked away out of sight so they couldn't be rescued.'

Great, Byron, I think. Why don't you give him some more ideas about how to make us uncomfortable?

'You saying you want me to handcuff Arnie's boy and stuff him in the trunk?' Luke shakes his head. 'No way. Arnie'd never forgive me.'

'I don't want you to do that. It's just different than I expected, that's all.' Byron smiles a little half-smile. 'My dad wanted me to experience the real world. He said I lived in a dreamland. I don't think this was what he had in mind, but I guess this counts as a genuine life experience, huh?'

Luke shrugs. 'Things never work out like we plan.'

I nearly make some comment about losing your dreams and taking a break from it all, but I can't. Nick Reed was fed up with the everyday, with normality, but I can't be Nick Reed. Not here.

We sit in silence for a moment, then Luke says, 'I need music.' He stares at us. 'Now, I'm going to take the spare key out of my pocket and put it in the ignition so we can listen to our tape, but I don't want either of you doing anything that we'll all regret. You with me on this?'

Byron glances my way, then we both nod.

'Good.' Luke turns on the stereo and we listen to the Eagles while we wait for Karl and Holly to return.

I stare out of the window, thinking, plotting, remembering, admitting a few harsh truths to myself.

ONCE THE THRILL IS GONE
(A WELL-GUARDED SECRET OF THE PURVEYING LIFE)

I've kept it all hush-hush up till now, of course. It wouldn't do to give the game away early on, but perhaps I've exaggerated a tad. No, not exaggerated exactly, but my earlier confidence and wild assertions of success might have led to unrealistic expectations of the purveying life. Truth is, you'll be adored, but, after a time it can get rather lonely.

Your conversation is, by necessity, superficial. You meet lots of great new people but all they want to talk about — indeed all you can talk to them about — is George Lucas, Bruce Willis, Jean-Claude Van Damme. You can speak to your family and friends on the telephone, but you can only tell them where you've been, not what you've been doing. You have to keep it all secret. To be a purveyor you must be gregarious, but you need a quiet side too or you'll never survive.

At first the novelty and excitement keeps you going, but you have to like spending time on your own. You travel from place to place, constantly shedding and changing your identity, becoming someone new at least once a week. You start to make connections with people, but then it's time to move on.

It isn't the perfect way to live. It never leads to a happy-ever-after with you remaining rich and popular in a five-star world for the rest of your days. You wouldn't want to do it for ever. But so what? It's still a bargain way to travel and it's mostly fun.

It's been good to do.

For a time.

LESSONS FOR THE
WOULD-BE PURVEYOR

To fill out my how-to guide and make it long enough to be a proper book, I'm going to need lots of anecdotal evidence and examples, not just lengthy explanations of the Rules. It's only fair that I share my experience with my readers. Yes, that's what I need to do: think up stories of things that happened to me, but twist them around so that everything has a point. I can use them to illustrate the Rules. Hmm. I can see this idea is going to need some thought. It'd be difficult to write an instruction manual without giving away my secrets.

Maybe the whole thing is a bad idea. If I write a book, my past patrons might see it: they might realise that it was only me they met and not Brad Pitt's brother or Harrison Ford's son. And that would not make them happy. That would make them sad, embarrassed, angry, humiliated. It would defeat the whole justification for my work.

Providing happiness is the only thing that stops me being bad. It's what keeps me on the side of Robin Hood, even if I haven't technically been stealing and I'm not exactly sharing my bounty with the poor. If I reveal my past deeds it would destroy all the goodwill I've built up and it would negate my excuses for doing this in the first place.

Everyone would hate me — Holly would hate me, Ted would hate me, Byron and the other wannabe bounty-hunters would hate me. Karl would turn against me like a rabid dog and he'd start muttering about the need for retaliation. Luke's chumminess would evaporate, mutating into an over-zealous need for vengeance — strong enough to make him come out of hiding and hunt me down. Even Emma would despise me: she'd probably rate me alongside her lying, despicable soon-to-be-ex husband, and I don't want to be like him. I don't want to be anything like him.

I can't do it.

DISGUISE:
A FASHION LABEL FOR MEN AND WOMEN ON THE RUN

Thirty-three minutes later we're still sitting in the car listening to the Eagles, tapping our feet to the music, watching, waiting. Karl and Holly have yet to come back. The money-belt feels tight against my bloated belly and I'd loosen it if I could, but I can't risk it.

When 'Life In The Fast Lane' comes on, Luke turns up the volume and Byron and I exchange grins and start playing air-guitar. Luke glances back at us, smiles and joins in. My stomach's not aching as much as it was, so I enjoy the moment. I'm alive — I'm still alive — and I'm celebrating that fact.

Our strumming motions become wildly extravagant as we compete with one another for the most spectacular-looking playing. We accompany the riffs with shaking heads, tapping feet and frantic movements of our hands up and down the necks of our imaginary guitars.

We're all cracking up with laughter, when

Karl and Holly finally return, Karl pushing a trolley filled with carrier-bags. He frowns and we stop goofing around.

Byron's the last to realise, and his hands freeze midstrum as he sees Karl. Holly appears unharmed. My eyes meet hers and she nods at me, mouthing, 'I'm okay.'

Still smiling, Luke turns down the music and opens his window. 'Got everything we needed?'

'Yes,' says Karl. He hesitates, then opens my door and gestures to Holly. 'Get in.'

Holly climbs over me into the middle seat. When she's in Karl slams the door shut behind her, eyes narrowed as he stares at me. I feel a spasm deep inside my gut. Does he know? Has he seen something? Heard a newsflash regarding my identity? I meet Karl's gaze, willing myself to remain calm.

But he can't know. If he'd heard something Holly would have heard it too and she wouldn't have smiled at me so sweetly as she got into the car.

Karl and I stare at one another, then he raises one hand, forms a gun with his index finger and thumb and slams his thumb down, pulling the imaginary trigger. He watches for my reaction. For three or four seconds his eyes bore into mine. Then he walks away, behind the car, and unloads the bags into the boot. When he's finished, he pushes the trolley into a nearby empty parking space, then gets into the car behind the wheel. 'We'll stop and change clothes when we find somewhere secluded,' he says, starting the engine and driving off.

Luke shrugs and fastens his seatbelt. I hold Holly's hand as we leave Page, Arizona behind us. Byron glances back over his shoulder, watching the last building fade from view. His face, when he looks forward again, is pale, his eyes hooded. I wish I could say something to cheer him up, to give him courage, but there's nothing I can do except keep reminding the crims of the Arnie factor.

Soon we cross the state border into Utah. By the time Karl pulls off the road into a deserted picnic area at the Grand Staircase-Escalante National Monument I'm desperate. I'd known all those fizzy drinks I had with breakfast weren't a good idea. Karl lets us use the toilet one by one. It's one of those smelly pits with no running water, but I don't care.

When it's my turn I'm struck by a brainwave. This might be the only chance I have to get rid of my money-belt and the incriminating papers inside it. I look down into the toilet. The waste is a good four or five feet below the rim of the seat and I don't hesitate. I strip off the money-belt, take out

372

my wad of dollar bills and shove them into my pocket, then drop the belt into the pit. It doesn't sink, the gunge below is too solid for that, but I rip off fistfuls of toilet paper and manage to cover it with enough so my unusual addition doesn't look suspicious and you certainly can't tell what it is. After a minute or two it's all blended in, Karl and Luke will have no reason to suspect anything when they check it over to make sure we haven't left any messages pleading for help.

I feel a moment's unease for the loss of my passport, driving licence and credit cards, but they're all replaceable and I know it's necessary. I've nothing left on my person that declares me to be Nick Reed. I am a man without a confirmable identity.

Once we've all finished, Karl inspects the toilet. I try to act nonchalant and have to keep reminding myself to breathe, in and out, in and out, in and out. What if he sees the money-belt? What if he wants to find out what it is? What if he looks for a big stick to scoop it out of the pit? What if he can't find a stick and insists that Byron be lowered head first into the hole to grab it? What if he holds it, sees it, reads my papers and finds out my real name?

A couple of minutes later Karl emerges into the open air. He doesn't look upset. And

I know I'm safe. Nick Reed is gone. Nick Reed is not me. I am Nick Schwarzenegger and they can't prove otherwise.

At least, not without some help from the press.

I glance around, acting casual, trying not to draw attention to myself. Byron's staring at the ground, while Holly's studying the picnic area, probably even now thinking about her articles. Karl is distracted, opening the boot of the car, but Luke stands watching us. It's not time, not yet, but I'm ready now, waiting. When the opportunity arises, I'll grab Holly and Byron and we'll take off. We have to.

Karl starts pulling clothes out of the carrier-bags: jeans, T-shirts, shorts, two pair of white trainers, packets of white socks, five baseball caps and three pairs of flimsy flip flops. (What better way to prevent the hostages escaping than giving them inadequate and impossible-to-run-in footwear?)

'We had to guess sizes,' says Holly. 'When in doubt we went for big and baggy.'

'You can thank Holly for the clothes. She paid for them.' Karl smiles at her, winks, then turns back to the group. 'Now, I'm giving each of you a choice,' he says, holding aloft a pair of scissors and a packet of home hair dye. 'A haircut or a new colour. Holly is our designated beautician.'

Holly shifts uncomfortably. 'But I've never — '

'Honey, you're a woman. Just do your best. We don't have to look perfect, we just have to look different. We're not going to Hollywood to meet Nick's dad.'

I have to stop myself sighing with relief. He must be sticking to his original plan and have no immediate intention of trying to involve Arnie. Boy, am I glad to hear that.

'I don't want to cut my hair,' says Holly. 'I love my hair.'

'Then you can dye it,' says Karl.

'It'll ruin it.' She tries to smile at him, but the pleading, seductive look is ruined by a lone tear running down her cheek. 'I don't want to be ugly when I die.'

'You're not going to die,' says Luke. 'Just co-operate and you'll be fine. I explained all that earlier.'

'But I love my hair,' whispers Holly, her eyes filling with tears.

'Come on,' I say, trying to be reasonable when all I want to do is punch Karl or hit him over the head so we can escape. 'Let's all just wear the baseball caps. It'll take too long to do everyone's hair, and if we don't know what we're doing we'll look even more suspicious.'

Karl sighs. 'She can wear a baseball cap as

long as she keeps her hair tucked up inside.'

'Thanks,' says Holly, smiling at Karl, her eyes no longer swimming with tears. She turns to me and winks.

I blink. She doesn't look the least bit upset now. Was she seeing how far she could push them?

'The rest of us,' says Karl, his voice sharp, 'will be having new haircuts. Is that understood?'

'But I don't want my hair cut,' says Byron. 'I want to be blond.'

Fast as fast can be, Karl draws his gun and points it at Byron. 'This isn't a fucking democracy. I don't want another word of protest. The lady is to be the only exception.' He glares at Byron. 'Is that understood?'

Byron nods.

'Good.' Karl holsters his weapon. 'Holly, I've decided against the hair dye. We don't have enough water anyway. You're just going to have to use the scissors instead. Okay?'

Holly takes a deep breath. 'If you're sure that's what you want.'

'Practise on Byron. Then Nick. Luke and I will go last.' Karl smiles at her. 'I'm kinda hoping you'll learn what you're doing by the time you get to me.' He holds out the scissors to Holly, who she steps forward and takes them. 'And, Holly, please don't think of doing anything silly. I'd sure hate to have to kill Arnie's boy. Luke'd never forgive me.'

'We're not killing Nick.' Luke runs a hand through his crew-cut. 'And I don't need a haircut. There's nothing you can do to change this style.' He smiles. 'Guess you get to go third, Karl.'

So Holly performs the first three haircuts of her life. Byron's got two bald patches, but I'm pleased that I've only got one and it'll soon grow out. Karl fares even better and he's the only one who looks remotely different — his was the only hair that was long enough for real change.

When Holly's finished, Karl takes the scissors from her, riffles through the shopping-bags and pulls out an electric razor with a pack of batteries. Then he shaves off his goatee. As disguises go it's not perfect, but it's a start.

'Time to complete the makeovers.' Karl turns to survey the clothing. As expected, he chooses a pair of the trainers. He also picks up jeans and a T-shirt with a Budweiser can on the front. 'I'll change first,' he tells Luke. 'You stand guard. And, remember, if they act up you're not supposed to shoot Byron, you're supposed to kill him.'

Byron gulps. 'I guess it's okay just to shoot me,' he says. 'Forget I said anything.'

Karl stares at Byron but says nothing. (If he's trying to intimidate him I'd say it's working.) After a long, silent moment he strides off with his bundle of clothing and changes out of sight behind the outhouse. When he's finished Luke goes, and when he reappears in shorts, a *South Park* T-shirt and the other pair of trainers, it's our turn.

'Byron and Nick, you change here where we can see you,' says Karl. 'I don't want to waste any more time.'

'I'll turn away,' says Holly, and does so.

As I'm stripping off my black bounty-hunting clothes, I slip my hand into my pocket and grab my wad of dollar bills, transferring it to the pocket of my new outfit as soon as I can. Byron and I each end up in shorts, matching Grand Canyon T-shirts and plastic flip-flops. With our patchy, just-out-of-bed haircuts we look like tourists who've been travelling two months too long.

I leave on my Rolex. The brief thought of Emma that always comes with a glimpse of my watch leaves me feeling uneasy. Thank God she's not here. My heart skips a beat as it hits me. If she'd been here, Karl would have taken her into that shop with him. Emma would have been alone with Karl. I shudder, pushing the thought away. She's not here. She's safe at home. She'd never have been stupid enough to get into this situation in the first place.

'We're finished,' I tell Holly, and she turns back. I stare at her, mentally willing her to make a run for it when she goes behind the toilet to change. I want her to get away. If she can hide and Karl can't find her immediately he might just give up and let her escape. Surely he wouldn't waste too much time looking for her when we've got such a long way to go before we reach Canada. (I know he'd search for her, he wouldn't want her to warn the authorities about the Canadian plan, but I can hope. I have to retain a hint of that purveyor optimism.)

It's as if Karl's reading my mind, for he says, 'You'll change here too, Holly.'

'No way.' I shake my head. 'Absolutely not. She's not going to undress with everyone staring at her.'

'Okay,' says Karl, walking to my side and drawing his gun again. He presses the barrel against my temple. 'Luke, Byron, you heard the man. We're all turning around and not watching the lady. Keep your back to her. Holly, you go ahead and change. We won't watch, but you better start humming and keep humming 'cause if I can't hear you I'll think you're running. And if I think you're running, I'll pull this fucking trigger and lover-boy's brains will splat and get all over me and that would not make me a happy man. Do you understand me?'

Holly, white-faced, nods. 'Yes.'

'You can't kill Nick,' says Luke. 'Use Byron instead. I don't want to be responsible for causing Arnie to lose his boy.' He turns to me. 'Are you the eldest?'

'Yes,' I say. Does being the eldest make me more important? Please, God, make him think the eldest is the most important.

'We can't kill Arnie's eldest boy. He'd hate us for ever.'

Karl sighs. 'And he'll love us for kidnapping him?'

'Use Byron,' Luke insists.

'Holly, choose your clothes and start humming. I'm so fucked off right now it won't take much for me to pull this fucking trigger and I don't give a shit who's at the other end.'

So I stand facing the barren landscape with a gun to my head while behind me Holly hums the various Eagles melodies we heard this morning all jumbled together. Presumably she's changing.

I listen to Holly humming, I feel the cold metal barrel against my skin, and it hits me: I'm not in love with Holly. Yes, she's as gorgeous as Liz Hurley, she's exciting and sexy and I *like* her, but I don't love her. It's just superficial lust between us. It's never been anything more.

I went on a bounty-hunting course for a woman I don't love. I blink, then blink again. Holly's still humming and I let the sounds roll over me. I don't love her. And that's the truth.

I'm in love with Emma. I just wouldn't admit the truth to myself.

The timing wasn't right. Emma's circumstances, my circumstances, it was all wrong. It was too early on in my purveying days, too near the beginning of my adventure, and I wouldn't — couldn't — face facts. But I can now. There's something remarkably clarifying about having a gun held to your head and knowing the man whose finger is next to that trigger won't hesitate to pull it.

Wow. I'm in love with Emma.

It should have been so clear to me. It's obvious now. Of course I'm in love with her. That's why purveying was never the same after I left her.

I'm in love. That's what this feeling is. I've never been in love before, I know that now, that's why I didn't recognise it, why I couldn't recognise it at the time. I wasn't expecting love. I wasn't letting myself think of love. I wasn't even supposed to think of friendship. But it's true. It's love.

A while later, Holly says, 'You can turn round now.'

Karl removes the gun from my head and reholsters it. I turn and see Holly now sporting shorts, a plain blue T-shirt and a Detroit Tigers baseball cap with her hair hidden beneath it. I look at her with fresh eyes. She's incredibly beautiful. But I don't love her. I think some part of me has known that all along.

I don't love her, but I am going to save her. I'm going to save her and Byron both. That's why I'm here, why I went on the bounty-hunt. It's my destiny, my fate, and if I'm required to sacrifice my life for a woman I merely like and a man I've only known for a few days then so be it. I'm ready.

Karl nods approvingly at Holly's new look, then instructs us to gather up all the old clothes and hair clippings and stuff them inside empty plastic bags that he tosses into the boot. He doesn't want to leave anything behind. Then we're climbing into the car and it's only as Luke shuts my door that I remember I was going to try to help us all escape. Damn. Why does Karl have to draw his gun at the least sniff of trouble? We didn't stand a chance.

I'll have to wait for Karl to make a mistake. I'll have to wait until his and Luke's backs are turned at the same time and neither is paying attention, but in the meantime there is clearly a need to cement our teetering buddy-buddy relationship.

Surely they don't *want* to become murderers. Do they?

ON THE ROAD AGAIN

To cover his crew-cut and provide a limited form of disguise, Luke puts on a baseball cap with Las Vegas written in large gold letters on the front. We leave the picnic area and travel on. It'd be enjoyable — the scenery is spectacular and I've always dreamed about taking an American road trip with my American friends — if we were just sightseers and if we were actually friends. We drive on flat roads, then tortuous mountain roads until finally we reach a freeway, the I-15, and head north.

I watch the landscape and the other vehicles as I think of Emma. The Eagles tape plays over and over and over again. Eventually, on what must be the tenth repetition of 'Hotel California', Luke starts singing along. He's about as tuneful as Cameron Diaz's character in *My Best Friend's Wedding*, but he seems completely oblivious to this. Not only can Luke not sing, he is the worst singer in the world. No, in the known universe. Even beyond. He cannot carry a single note. If we had a faithful hound dog travelling with us it would be baying in pain, trying to drown out the noise.

Holly and I exchange secret smiles and suddenly I feel better. Everything's going to be all right. I have to keep telling myself that. I have to believe. I have to make it happen.

And then, as one, Holly and I start singing too, partially to drown Luke's voice, but also because we're in this together and we've been in this car for hours and there's nothing else to do. Luke seems pleased and he carries on singing, with even more gusto. After a moment or two Byron joins in, quietly at first, then gaining in confidence. Karl's just sitting there, driving, staring straight ahead at the road, but the rest of us are all singing along together and we're smiling and relaxing and I think, Yep, survival is possible.

STUCK IN A RUT (IT CAN HAPPEN TO PURVEYORS TOO)

There are only so many times you can reveal Meg Ryan's favourite food or Sandra Bullock's favourite dessert as if it's a great big secret and be able to maintain an expression of interest. At first I used to stick to sensible choices, healthy things, like raspberries or cherries or sometimes kiwi fruit, but when that got dull I made up more exciting culinary creations. Ordinary people like hearing that beautiful sexy actresses like celery smeared with peanut butter or pizza dripping with five varieties of cheese.

And if I happen to speak in a whisper as if I'm sharing a confidence with my patrons, they're even more delighted. They like to know that Hollywood stars eat real food too. They like to know that hot fudge sundaes can occasionally pass those perfect lips. I don't know what diets my supposed relatives really follow, but I know what my patrons like to hear.

Does that mean I'm shallow? Did I like flitting about without forming any real connections apart from the one with Emma? Did I tell myself that Holly was perfect because I was bored? Because I was lonely? Because I'd met Jason Loraxe, singer-songwriter, a couple of weeks before and was still reeling with jealousy and inferiority? Had I been ready to stop and used Holly as an excuse to do so?

But I'm not only concerned with image, power and wealth. I truly believe that it's all about happiness.

Yet I look back over my life and I wonder what was real. I was smooth, suave and charming. I was generally successful with women. I've had a number of six-month relationships but nothing longer.

Was it all just about sex and self-serving pleasure-seeking?

But I've always had friends. People like me. I'm a likeable bloke.

I sneak a peek at Holly, not wanting to attract her attention. What if she loves me? What if I fooled her, like I fooled myself? What if she's expecting us to ride off into the sunset together? What if she doesn't care whether I'm Arnold Schwarzenegger's son or not? I don't want to hurt her feelings.

What a bloody mess. And I've no one to blame but myself.

THE ENDLESS MILES

We drive on winding mountain roads through stunning landscapes, but no matter how many times I tell myself that it's beautiful I still don't feel I'm appreciating it enough, not when this might be the last day of my life. No amount of awe over the breathtaking views could ever be enough. Not if we're going to die before the sun sets. I try to focus on the vistas, instructing myself to delight in nature's panorama, but it's virtually impossible to do so without thinking of what the future might hold.

Byron and Holly stare out of the windows too, and we're all subdued. Even Luke is quiet now, just listening to the music and watching the road as the miles pass by. I yawn and yawn again.

Karl drives ever onwards. We stop only for petrol, having to co-ordinate our toilet trips with these breaks and buying whatever food and drink we can find on the shelves to keep us going. Each time we're allowed out of the car, Karl tells us, 'Keep your head down. If anyone talks to you just tell 'em we're headed to Yellowstone to see Old Faithful blow.'

We certainly look the part of tourists now, Byron and I with our matching Grand Canyon T-shirts and flip-flops, Holly and Luke with their baseball caps, Karl shorn of his recognisable shaggy hair and goatee. All of us casual and crumpled and looking like we've been camping and haven't showered or slept in a proper bed for days.

'What's Arnie's favourite colour?' asks Luke.

'Green,' I say, yawning.

'Green?' Karl glances at me over his shoulder and raises an eyebrow. 'I thought you said it was blue.'

Shit. I did. I told them it was blue.

'It's both,' I say quickly. 'He likes both colours. Blue for clothes. Green for cars.'

'Ah.' Karl says nothing more.

'Blue's better,' says Luke, then lapses back into silence.

Karl doesn't challenge me again and I'm tense, waiting, but time passes and eventually I start to relax.

I think about escape constantly, but Karl doesn't let any of us hostages leave the car together. And we're never left alone to plan. One of the crims stays with us at all times.

Finally Karl lets Luke drive, so that he can get some sleep, and after that they take turns.

They seem determined, at whatever cost, to remain fugitives and free. I can only hope they won't resort to doing a Thelma and Louise if we get cornered.

'Prison,' says Karl, shoulders back, head high, voice firm, like he's the hero in some action film and not the bad guy, 'is not an option. I will never surrender.'

EMMA ON MY MIND

I've never been in love before. In like, in lust, infatuated: yes, I've experienced all of those to varying degrees, but never love like this. I've only ever known love for my parents and grandparents, and a general feeling of fondness for the rest of my relatives: an aunt, a couple of uncles, a few cousins. But that's not what I mean.

How could I not have realised that I'd fallen in love with Emma?

I have no idea what she feels for me — if anything, beyond a fondness for my part in a week's escape from the torment of her real life.

It's been over two months since I last saw her. Two and a half months in which she's heard not a word from me. Not a phone call or even a postcard.

She might be divorced. She might be reunited with her bastard husband.

I don't even know if she'd want to see me again but if I live I'm going to Chicago. I have to see her.

NATIONAL NOTORIETY

Once it's dark and there's nothing to look at, we hostages pass uneasily between sleep and wakefulness as the miles go by. We talk occasionally, and it's often Luke asking another question or two about Arnie, but mostly we're silent. We've used up the obvious conversation, and even I am infected with a strange feeling of desperate urgency, that we must hurry, hurry, hurry.

In the early hours of the morning we see the new editions of the national newspapers. The good news is that the hostages are not identified by name. The bad news is that our faces are splashed all over the front page.

Wow, we're famous. I've always wanted to be famous. I've always wished that people would be able to recognise me on the street.

Large photographs of Karl and Luke — the police mugshots Ted showed us back at the training school — are accompanied by drawings of the three hostages. Those of Holly and Byron are very accurate. I wonder why they didn't use the snapshots Ted took, but I guess photos of the poor, innocent hostages posing with guns and dressed in SWAT-team clothing aren't appropriate when you're trying to make the kidnappers seem bad.

I, on the other hand, look more like a younger, non-muscular version of Arnold Schwarzenegger than myself. Sure, the features and general outline sort of looks like me, but it's as if Arnie's image has been superimposed across my face and it's ended up as some bizarre mix that isn't me. It's no doubt what I would have looked like if my genes were crossed with Arnie's genes, but it's definitely not me.

I wonder if Holly and the others will notice, or if that's how they see me too.

And then it hits me. Will my patrons who cherished me when they thought I was John Travolta's son or Russell Crowe's brother, recognise me? Will they phone the police and identify me by name, patting themselves on the back for being so helpful to the law? Will the police string together all my activities of the last few months? Will I be arrested alongside Karl and Luke if we're apprehended?

Then everything would be ruined. The joy I'd spread throughout my travels would be wiped out, obliterated, curdled to hate and humiliation.

At least there's no mention of Schwarzenegger. Yet.

And maybe no one will recognise me. The drawing in the paper looks more like Arnie. Maybe, in my patrons' minds, I appear like Brad Pitt or a male Goldie Hawn. That's probably true. So the question becomes, does it look enough like me to jog a memory here or there?

Holly reaches for my hand and I hold hers, squeezing lightly, stroking her cold fingers.

I just want this to end. One way or the other I want Karl and Luke to go on their way and leave us behind. We must be getting close to the border now. We've been in this car for a lifetime. Three lifetimes.

I don't want another day's headlines. It's only a matter of time before my story comes undone.

We drive on, ever northwards.

Isn't being famous fun?

RULE 33:

YOU OWE IT TO YOUR PATRONS TO KEEP THE TRUTH TO YOURSELF FOR EVER

Rule 21 already instructs you not to tell the truth to anyone, but it could be interpreted — wrongly — to apply only to the duration of your purveying trip. Rule 33 is meant to buttress the previous rule and to remain in force for all time. You can never reveal the entire story to anyone. Not even to the woman you love. To her and her alone you can tell a partial truth. You can say that you've been masquerading as the Son of Arnie or the Son of Robert Redford, but only if it's necessary, only if you've met your love during the course of your travels and have to tell her your real name as a confession. And, if that's the case, you've obviously been a slipshod follower of the Rules and you need to take yourself in hand and learn some self-discipline. Rule 33 is a good place to start.

It's not that you don't want your love to

know the whole sordid truth, though not having to point out that you were a minor con-man is a bonus: it just wouldn't be fair to your patrons. People, even those in love, can fall out and argue. Indiscretions happen. Unintentional revelations can give the game away. Whispers and rumours spread. It's *unlikely* that your patrons would hear, as you don't move in the same circles, but they *might*, and that makes it too big a risk. You can never do anything that could potentially threaten your patrons' happiness. It wouldn't be right.

Letting them live off the tales of how they met Drew Barrymore's or Gwyneth Paltrow's brother, or the son of Anthony Hopkins, is your gift to them. Payment for all the adulation and goodies you received. Keeping mum is not optional, it's a requirement.

THE END OF THE ROAD

In Montana we quit the freeway and head on to mountainous roads that get narrower and more deserted. Karl turns, leaving what had previously seemed a dangerous route to drive along a dirt and gravel single-lane track that makes the last one seem positively flat. Indeed, with a sheer drop to one side and the steep, nearly vertical incline of the mountain to the other, it's more like a goat track than a road. Karl must have a thing for roads that aren't really roads.

He keeps driving, not talking now concentrating on the winding bends as we climb higher and higher into the mountains. An hour later, perhaps two, he stops the car. We've seen no hint of civilisation for hours: no houses, no shacks in the gaps between the peaks, no other vehicles, no litter, not even tyre tracks in the dirt to declare that humans have passed this way before. We're alone in the vastness of the wilds. Three hostages with their criminal captors. There's no need to worry about witnesses. There won't be any.

Karl turns off the ignition and stares straight ahead. The silence is tense and I know that this is it, decision time. This is where we say, 'Goodbye, life.'

I wonder if we've crossed the border into Canada without my knowing it. I've never been there, but I've always wanted to go.

Finally Karl speaks. 'Everyone out of the car.'

'Hey, where are we?' asks Luke. 'Are we in Canada? Have we made it?'

Karl shrugs, not answering, turning to the back seat. 'Everyone out. Now.'

I slip on my flip-flops and open my door. We can't run away: there's no place for us to hide. No way to escape. I climb out of the car, then assist Holly. She's shivering and her hands are shaking and I'd bet it's not just with the cold. Byron slams his door. He avoids looking at Karl. I meet Luke's eyes and whisper, 'Help us. Please. Don't let Karl kill us.'

Luke steps out of the car too. 'Now, hold on a minute. What's going on here?'

'Nick, Holly, Byron, you three stand over there.' Karl points to the middle of the road, a bit too close for my liking to what looks like a thousand-foot drop.

We hesitate.

Karl frowns. 'Move,' he says, drawing his

398

gun, pointing it at us. 'Fucking do as I tell you to do.'

So we do. I hold Holly's hand and we walk slowly towards the edge. The three of us stand in a line in the centre of the road, facing our captors. Byron reaches out and holds Holly's other hand.

Karl holsters his weapon, opens the boot of the car and takes out a shovel.

My stomach plummets as if we've just crested the tallest hill of the world's steepest roller-coaster. Why didn't I attack Karl the second I climbed out of the car and tell Holly and Byron to run? That's what I should have done. They could have escaped. I could have given them time to get away.

Byron moans and Holly's hand grips mine fiercely, squeezing so hard it hurts.

'What's going on here, Karl?' demands Luke.

'It's time to get rid of the fucking hostages. You didn't think we'd keep them for ever, did you?'

'What exactly are you saying?'

Karl shrugs, shifting the shovel to his left hand. 'It's time. You knew it would come to this.'

'But Nick's Arnie's boy. And I like Nick.'

'We're getting rid of the hostages.'

'I don't want to die,' whispers Byron.

Luke frowns. 'We're not killing Nick and his friends.'

'Yes, we fucking are.'

'We're not killing Arnie's boy.'

'Nick is not Arnold Schwarzenegger's son,' says Karl.

'Yes, he is,' says Luke.

'He's lying.'

'But he told us about Arnie's shark attack and his flying lessons.' Luke glances at me. 'He's told us about all about Arnie.'

'Nick didn't even know Arnie's star sign,' says Karl.

'I'm not very good with astrology,' I say.

Karl glares at me. 'Shut the fuck up, Nick. When I want to hear from you I'll let you know.'

'But he *is* Arnie's son,' says Holly.

Karl stares at her. 'Honey, he's a fucking liar. Hell, maybe you all are. I don't know. I just know Nick's been fucking with our heads.'

'I think you've got it all wrong, Karl,' says Luke. 'Look at him. He's Arnie's boy. You know he is. He has to be.'

'Then why did Nick say Arnie's favourite colour was green when he'd said blue before?'

'Because he was tired. Because he's not slept for two nights. Because Arnie has two favourite colours.'

'Who are you going to believe, Luke? Him or me?'

'Come on, Luke,' I say. 'I am Arnie's son. And we had a great time, didn't we? Surely you believe me. You can't let Karl kill us.'

'I, er, I, uh — ' Luke hesitates.

'While he's deciding, you can make yourself useful and start digging, Nick.' Karl lifts the shovel, preparing to throw it.

'Now, just a minute,' says Luke, 'we're not killing Arnie's boy.'

Karl lowers the shovel. 'I'll say this one more fucking time. Nick is not related to Arnold Schwarzenegger.'

Karl and Luke stare at one another, and then in the blink of an eye, they've both drawn their guns and are pointing them at each another.

'We're not killing Nick,' says Luke.

'Yes, we are,' says Karl.

'No.'

'Yes.'

'You know I won't stand for killing Arnie's boy. Arnie would never forgive me. No one would forgive me. We're not doing it. We're not killing any of them.'

'Don't be a fucking idiot,' says Karl. 'If we let them go, the cops will know we've gone to Canada. The Canadians will be looking for us too. We should just kill them and get rid of the bodies.'

Luke's eyes narrow. 'No.'

Karl gestures at us with the shovel. 'We can't let them tell the fucking police where we are.'

'We don't know where we are,' I say. 'We can't tell the police anything. Just leave us here and drive off.'

'It would take us days to walk back to civilisation,' says Holly.

'Shut the fuck up,' says Karl, not looking at me, not looking at Holly, not moving his eyes from Luke's. 'I wasn't talking to you two.'

Luke shakes his head. 'We can't kill Arnie's boy.'

'He's not Arnie's boy.'

'Well, I think he is,' says Luke.

Holly, Byron and I are still, frozen, not wanting to annoy Karl, not wanting him to whirl and shoot us all dead in a haze of fury. We're quiet, hoping, praying, not wanting to be noticed.

'I don't want to have to hurt you, Luke. I like having a partner.'

'We're not killing Nick Schwarzenegger,' says Luke. 'And that's final.'

Karl and Luke stare at one another.

'Nick, you go on and get out of here,' says Luke, his gun centred on Karl's chest. 'Take your friends and run.'

I hesitate for half a second, then nod. 'Thanks, Luke.'

'Fuck that,' snarls Karl, as he raises the shovel and whacks Luke in the hand, sending Luke's gun flying through the air. It lands with a thud on the dirt road.

Luke howls in pain and cradles his hand to his chest as he stumbles backwards.

Karl smashes the shovel into Luke's stomach. Luke doubles over. 'I don't want to hurt you,' says Karl. 'I don't like it. But I'm not letting you get in my fucking way.' He raises the shovel again, preparing to hit Luke over the back of the head. 'I'm not going to prison.'

I don't think, I don't pause for reflection, I just move. One, two, three running steps and I am there, beside Karl, my right foot kicking the back of one of his knees, both hands grabbing his gun hand.

'You're not going to fucking kill us,' I shout in his ear.

'Wanna bet?' yells Karl. He squeezes the trigger and a shot rings out. But the barrel's pointing upwards and it's harmless. The shovel hits me on the calf with a loud whack and I grunt in pain. Bastard. But I don't release my hold on his hand.

I'm yelling, Karl's yelling, and I'm careful to keep the gun pointed away from me. Keep it pointed up, I tell myself.

Suddenly Holly and Byron are there too,

ganging up on Karl. Holly pulls on Karl's free arm, wrestling for the shovel. Byron drops to the ground and wraps himself around Karl's legs, trying to hamper his movements.

Karl twists and bends suddenly, like a boxer doing a feint, and he elbows Holly hard in the stomach, causing her to lose her grip and fall back. Instantly he throws the shovel to one side and punches me in the jaw with his left hand. My head snaps to one side and I feel a tooth loosen.

I'm holding on to Karl's right hand with all my might, trying to wrest the gun away from him, trying to keep him from pointing it at me, when another shot rings out. It takes me a second to realise it wasn't from Karl.

'Everybody freeze,' says Luke. He's reclaimed his own gun.

Karl stops fighting, I stop struggling, Holly and Byron stop too.

'I've always wanted to say that,' says Luke. 'Karl, let go of that fucking gun and let Nick have it.'

Karl hesitates, then relaxes his grip. I take the gun and step away, rubbing my jaw. I flick my tongue past my sore tooth and feel a jolt of stabbing pain. The tooth's definitely loose. Holly stumbles to my side and Byron stands slowly, moving gradually away from Karl.

Luke sighs. 'So, now what are we going to

do, Karl? You hit me.'

'I didn't want to.'

'But you did. You hit me with a fucking shovel. You could've killed me if Nick had let you hit me over the head.'

'Come on, Luke, I was just trying to knock you out so I could get rid of the hostages. You know we have to.'

Luke glances from Karl to me. I'm holding Karl's pistol, but I keep it dangling at my side, pointing at the ground, not wanting to seem a threat. Luke stares at me, then shakes his head and smiles. 'Go on, Nick, get out of here. Take your friends and get out of here.'

'Don't do it,' says Karl. 'They'll — '

'They'll what? Be able to identify us? We posted bail, Karl. Everybody already knows who we are. I'm not killing Arnie's boy. And that's final. Go on, Nick.'

'Thanks, Luke.'

We leave the road, heading for the incline, scrambling up seems a better option than tumbling down into the void below. After a few steps I take off my flip-flops and stuff them into my pockets, deciding bare feet give me a better grip. I hold Karl's gun in my hand. I'd like to get rid of it, but I'd better keep it. Just in case. I let Holly and Byron go in front of me and hang back, staying between them and the crims.

As we reach the top of the first section of scree-covered slope, our feet slipping and sliding as we ascend, Luke calls out from below, 'You tell your daddy we're real proud to have met his son, Nick.'

I look down, see Luke still pointing his gun at Karl. 'Good luck, Luke,' I yell. 'And thanks.'

I turn away and move out of sight of the road. And just like that we're free.

We've no food, no water, no blankets, no coats, nothing but a gun with one bullet already gone, but I don't care. We're dressed in shorts and our only shoes are flimsy, but it doesn't matter. We're alive. We're alive and we're free.

IN THE MIDDLE OF NOWHERE (WE'RE NOT LOST, WE JUST DON'T KNOW WHERE WE ARE)

We push on, heading away from the road, fiercely determined to survive. We're gasping for breath, unused to the altitude, our faces pink with exertion as we climb, but we have to keep going. We have to put as much distance between us and the crims as possible, in case Karl overpowers Luke or persuades him that they have to hunt us down. I've got Karl's pistol, but I have little faith in my ability to use it effectively. And we don't have any spare ammunition. The gun wouldn't hold them at bay for long.

Holly, Byron and I keep glancing at one another, jubilant and subdued at the same time, almost unable to believe we're escaping. We've heard no gunshots so we don't know if Karl and Luke have settled their differences and are now *en route* to a new hideout or if they still might come after us. But we will live through this. I won't allow anything else.

Half an hour later we stop, unable to go

further without catching our breath. My bare feet are sore, unused to walking without shoes, so I slip on my flip-flops, deciding they're better than nothing now that the climb isn't so steep and there's less gravel.

'Aren't there bears in these mountains?' asks Byron.

'Yes,' says Holly. 'Grizzlies. Maybe black bears. Definitely mountain lions.'

Byron shudders. 'I hate predators. I'm not food.'

This is real mountain-man country and it's a pity my interest in becoming a forest ranger hadn't lasted long enough for me to take any classes. I haven't a clue what to do in a situation where it's us versus the elements. Wish I'd read that SAS survival handbook my mother gave me for Christmas last year.

After a short rest we press on, ascending more gradually now, then the land flattens and we're able to head away from the road without having to climb over the top of the ridge. An hour later we're all uneasy, flinching at every little noise. The snap of a twig is enough to make us jump. Ted would be disgusted with our city folk fear, but we can't help it. We're not modern-day Daniel Boones or Davy Crocketts eager to explore new frontiers, we're just tourists on a holiday outing that went dreadfully wrong. Ideally, we'd prefer to sit down, stay here and wait to be rescued, but that's not going to happen. No one who could save us knows where we are, so it's up to us to find our own way to deliverance.

A few minutes later I stop, gasping for breath. Holly and Byron are breathing heavily too. They come to a halt beside me.

'It's going to get dark soon. Maybe we should stay here,' I say, tucking the handgun into the waistband of my shorts. 'We could set up a shelter for the night, then tomorrow morning head back to the road and follow that down to the highway.' This area doesn't look any better or worse than the places we've already walked through: it's merely far enough off the road to make things difficult for Karl if he tries to hunt us down.

'Or we could look for a river and follow it to safety,' says Byron. 'That's what they always do in the movies.'

I wonder for a second whether to discuss my *Hollywood Guide to Life* idea with Byron. He obviously has a bit of the old vision thing if he thinks like that, but I don't have the energy. I have a confession to make.

I know I'm bending Rule 33 already, that I'm not supposed to breathe a word of truth to a woman I don't love, but I have to make Holly understand about Arnie. Telling Byron wasn't part of the plan. I hate to disillusion him, but I can't send him off on a short hike for an hour or two so I can have some privacy with Holly. It wouldn't be fair on him. Or, in all probability, safe. So Byron will hear my revelation too, and that really is going against the spirit of Rule 33, but I have no choice.

And, actually, there's a logical reason why they must both know. I don't want them blurting out the name Nick Schwarzenegger as soon as we're rescued. The fewer people who know about that fiasco the better.

We might be attacked and eaten by grizzly bears or mountain lions in the night and I don't want to go to my death without Holly knowing the truth. I thought I'd want to wait until we were safe to tell her, so I could explain it all quietly, but there might not be a better time. She might be in love with Nick Schwarzenegger and I can't let her remain in the dark any longer. The time to tell her is now.

I clear my throat, open my mouth, stop. How can I say it? There's no way to make myself sound anything other than the scoundrel I am. They'll probably both hate me and want to shove me off the edge of the mountain. But they won't. They'll just huff and puff and be angry. They'll hate me, but they're not stupid. They need me to survive this ordeal. If we were in a city, back in our normal lives, they could spit on me then leave, never have to see my face again, but here they have no choice: they'll have to listen and listen and keep on listening to me.

I clear my throat again, ignoring the throbbing of my tooth.

Holly looks at me, eyes quizzical. She's been peering around our immediate area, searching for a suitable place to build a shelter while I've been trying to find the courage to confess. I wonder if she was ever a Girl Scout.

'I have something to tell you,' I say.

I have her full attention now. Byron's too.

I decide just to come right out and say it. There's no way to cushion them from the blast of cold, sober reality that's heading their way. Not when the fundamental fact they think they know about me is false.

My mouth is dry. I lick my lips, swallow and take a deep breath. 'I'm not Arnie's son,' I say. 'My name's not Nick Schwarzenegger.'

'What?' says Byron, his mouth dropping open, his eyes wide as saucers.

Holly just stares at me.

My eyes gaze into Holly's. I take a few steps towards her, closing the distance between us. I want to take her hands in mine, but I don't touch her. 'I'm not Arnie's son,' I

411

say again, softly. 'I'm so sorry.'

'I know that, you bastard,' she says, eyes narrowed. 'You think I didn't?'

Now it's my turn to gape. 'What?'

Vaguely, out of the corner of my eye, I notice Byron staring at her too. He's gawking at both of us, confused, not understanding, possibly wondering if he's hallucinating, if the fear of a grizzly attack has left him weak in the head.

Holly glares at me. 'I know you're not Arnie's son. I've always known you're not Arnie's son.'

'You have?' I don't understand. 'How? And why didn't you say anything?'

Wait a minute. She kissed me. She shagged me.

Why did she go to bed with me if she knew I was lying?

It doesn't make sense. None of this makes any sense. Maybe I'm the one who's mentally weak. Maybe I'm the one who's imagining things and we're still standing in the road waiting for Karl to shoot us. This might be some elaborate scenario my brain has concocted to block out the terror I'm experiencing.

But I don't really think we're still with the crims.

Holly knows I'm a liar. She's always known I'm a liar.

I feel so stupid.

Holly ignores my questions. 'So, Nick, who are you?' Her voice is laced with scorn. 'And is Nick even your real name?'

'My name is Nick. I'm just a guy. I'm no one.'

That's right. I'm a nobody. I'm back to being me.

'You're not Arnie's son?' asks Byron.

I glance at him briefly. 'No. Sorry, I'm not,' I say to him, then turn back to Holly. 'But we kissed. We had sex. And you knew I wasn't related to Arnie?'

'Let's just clear one thing up here, Nick. I'm a journalist.'

Byron mutters weakly, 'You are?'

Holly ignores him and continues looking at me. 'I told you I was a journalist. You knew that and you still stuck with me. And, yes, I did kiss you for the story. Yes, I led you on so you'd want to go on the bounty-hunting course with me, but I had sex with you because I liked you. Because I wanted to. You were already exactly where I wanted you to be. I didn't have to fuck you. Got that? I don't fuck anyone for my job.'

'But how did you know? When did you find out?'

'In Phoenix,' she says.

'Back at the resort? When I first met you?'

413

'No, Nick, I knew you were lying even before we met. I'd heard that someone claiming to be Arnold Schwarzenegger's son was staying at the hotel and I did a bit of digging. It was pretty easy to find out you were lying. I am a reporter, Nick. I have contacts.'

'You knew who I was when I sat next to you in the bar?'

'Yep. You've got it in one, Nick. Why do you think I was so friendly? Why do you think I was so keen on spending time with you? I knew you'd give me a great story. I worked hard to get you to fall for me. If you hadn't approached me, I would have made sure one of the hotel bartenders introduced us.'

'But we had a fantastic time. I liked you.'

Holly flushes. 'Yes, I liked you too once we got talking. You're a fun guy to be around.'

'If you were using me to get a story, why did you tell me you were a journalist? It doesn't make sense. I was more wary of you after that.'

'I know. But you would never have come on the bounty-hunting course with me if you thought I was doing it just for kicks. You'd have run in the opposite direction.'

'You wanted me to come with you?'

'Of course I did. I didn't know if I'd tie the bounty-hunting and the Arnie's son thing together, but I thought I'd keep an eye on you and see how things went.'

'But I volunteered to go with you on Ted's course.'

Holly smiles and bats her eyelashes. 'Oh, poor little woman, me, I need a big strong man like you to keep me safe.' She laughs. 'And you fell for it. Why do you think I said my expenses could cover your tuition fee? I needed to make it easy for you to come along.'

'But we had sex.'

She sighs. 'Look, Nick, I like you. There's a sexual-chemistry thing between us — you know that. And it was good fun while it lasted.'

'You're going to write a story about me? But you promised you wouldn't write about me.'

'No, I promised I wouldn't write about Arnie's son. I think you can see the distinction I made, Nick. I never said anything about you.'

I feel sick to my stomach. 'You're going to expose me?'

'What you did was wrong, Nick. Can't you see that? You can't go around telling people you're related to Arnold Schwarzenegger. It's just not right.'

'I didn't mean any harm.'

'Didn't you?'

'No.' I swallow, hesitate. 'So you're going to expose me?' I ask again, after a pause.

'I was. Now I don't know.'

'You don't know?'

'Oh, I'm still going to do the story, Nick. You must see that I can't resist. But I don't know if I want to expose you, as you say. I know that you did your best to protect us from the crims, and I appreciate that, I really do. You're a nice guy, in your own twisted way. You saved our lives. I know that.' She smiles at me. 'But the story will break with or without me now that it's turned into this huge kidnapping thing. Wouldn't you rather have it revealed by a reporter friendly to your side than one determined to dish the dirt on you?'

'I'd rather not be in the papers at all.'

She shrugs. 'You should have thought of that before. It's too late now. Tell you what, I'll promise to try to portray you in a reasonable light and I won't even use your real name.'

'You don't know my real name.'

'No, but I know where we met. It wouldn't be that difficult to track it down and find out just what else you've been getting up to lately, would it?'

I sigh, defeated. There's nothing I can do to

stop her. 'Okay, do your story.'

'Oh, I intend to.' She smiles. 'I can see the headlines. But don't worry, it's not that big a story. If I do the coverage the hype will die down soon enough. If I didn't do it someone else would, and they'd keep on digging because they don't like you and what you stand for. And I bet they'd find out a whole lot more about you than I'm planning on printing.'

I'm not sure if she won't stick it to me once my back is turned, but I know I have little choice in the matter. 'Okay.'

And then it hits me. Holly doesn't love me. She's never loved me. I didn't break her heart.

I'm thinking I should be a little more upset that she used me, that she knew I was lying all along, but I'm so relieved not to have broken her heart and not to be the only treacherous one here that I don't care. I'm free. Free of the crims. Free of guilt over Holly. Free to search for Emma.

'I'm sorry I lied to you.' I turn to include Byron in my apology. 'I'm sorry I lied to both of you.'

Byron stares at me, frowning. 'You're not Arnie's son?'

I give him a rueful smile, abashed. 'No. Sorry. I've never even met him.'

417

'And Holly knew this and played along with you from the start?'

Holly shrugs and grins, not in the least apologetic. 'I couldn't tell you the truth. I had to keep Nick thinking he'd fooled me.'

'But what about all those stories you told us?' Byron asks me. 'What about Arnie's favourite films? His favourite fighting moves? His skydiving trips? Your mother dying of cancer?'

'I made it all up.'

'None of it was true?'

I shake my head. 'No, it was pure invention.'

'But Luke — ' Byron stops, gulps, the colour draining from his face. 'Karl. Karl was right.'

'I did what I had to do.'

Byron looks confused. 'But why did you say you were Arnie's son in the first place?' he asks.

I think about it for a long moment, and then I say, truthfully, 'Because I was bored.'

BACK TO THE REAL WORLD

The retirement of Nick Schwarzenegger has left me strangely invigorated and free. It's the way you feel after that last exam when you're leaving school or university or at the end of your final day at a particular job. You've been working so hard, and suddenly you're finished and you have this overwhelming glow of euphoria and relief inside you, as if great chains have been lifted from your shoulders and you're so light you could float. That's what I experience as we build our shelter, using pine branches to try to make a space that offers some protection from the elements. It's going to be a long night and we'll be cold, thanks to Karl's lightweight disguises, but we do what we can to make it easier on ourselves.

My tooth still hurts, but it's subsided to a dull ache. I'm going to have to get it sorted out when this is over.

Byron and Holly keep asking me questions about why I did what I did. They want to understand, they want to know the whole story, but I tell them nothing. I don't want

Holly knowing that I was a purveyor of happiness or finding out about the Rules. I don't want her becoming intrigued with my travels and unable to resist writing about my days as Goldie Hawn's and Brad Pitt's brothers. I don't want to ruin the memories of those whose paths I crossed. Yes, this happens to tie in quite nicely with my selfish desire to keep my true identity secret, but I'm not doing it just for me.

And I'm not having Emma learn the truth about me from some newspaper article or news report. I'm going to tell her myself. I'll be the one to confess — in person — that I'm not Robert Redford's son.

I'm first lookout — although I have no idea what we'll do if a grizzly bear comes our way — and after that we take turns, keeping watch through the long hours of darkness. We huddle together, needing to share our body heat as our shorts and T-shirts do little to keep us warm, trying not to flinch at all the night-time noises. Eventually we sleep.

Soon it's morning and I wake to a rustling in the undergrowth. My heart thumps in my chest and I know I should be scared, that it might be a bear, mountain lion, wolf, or some unknown denizen of the forest come to eat us for breakfast, but I don't care. I've confessed my deepest sin — well, partly, but it's a start

— and I'm happy. It's almost as if I've bared my soul and in return I've received the nearest non-priestly equivalent to the Last Rites. So if something should happen to me now at least I know I'll get a fair trial at judgement and won't be sent straight to hell for my deceit.

I still don't know what I'm going to do with my life. I don't even want to think that far ahead, all I want to do is concentrate on getting out of the mountains. We need to find a town or a city, or even a lone ranch house, just somewhere with a phone so we can be rescued.

Holly wakes. There's another rustling and I feel her stiffen in alarm so I sit up. Byron's gone. I stand, pulling Holly up with me, but then I see him. Byron is walking back towards the shelter. He's the one responsible for the noises. My heart slows to its normal rate.

'Morning,' I say.

'Good morning,' says Byron. And he smiles. He's disappointed in me, sad that I'm not Arnie's son, but he's not one to hold a grudge. He's just happy to be alive.

And then I stretch and Holly stretches and we all smile foolishly at one another, our fears of the night seeming silly in the full light of day.

'We'd better get moving,' says Holly. 'I'm

not spending another night here.'

Byron shudders. 'Me neither.'

'Yes, we'd better go,' I agree, but I'm strangely reluctant. When we're back in civilisation we'll have to return to real life. I'll have to face up to what I've done, I'll have to decide what to do in the future. And it's not all going to be sunshine and palm trees.

But I won't worry about that now. What's important is that we're here and that we didn't all die. I know we're not safe yet, that this isn't going to be a simple stroll across a park, but I don't mind. We've survived a bounty-hunt, we've survived a kidnapping, our odds are improving and, for the first time since this all started, I truly believe that survival is possible. Not only possible but likely.

So we set off, walking and walking, trying to ignore our growling stomachs and thirsty throats, our flip-flops snapping and flapping with each step. We head back to the dirt and gravel track, then follow that as it winds and twists down the mountain towards the main road.

We walk for five hours, six, seven, eight, nine, and I'm starting to worry that we'll have to spend another night in the wilderness, when at last we catch sight of the road through the trees. Its paved greyness is comforting to the eyes.

'What are we going to do with the gun?' I ask.

'Give it to the police,' says Byron. He's very matter-of-fact. 'Tell them how we got it when we escaped.'

'I'll take it,' says Holly, holding out her hand. 'I'll hide it underneath my shirt so we don't scare off any would-be rescuers. I hardly look the sort to carry a gun.'

I hesitate, then nod. I certainly don't want to have it on me when we meet other people. Taking the pistol from my waistband, I wrap my shirt around it, carefully wiping the fingerprints from its surfaces. I just don't like the thought of my fingerprints being on any gun. When I'm finished I hand it to Holly, being careful only to touch it through my shirt. She smiles and shakes her head at me, but says nothing.

Another fifty minutes and we reach the road. We're wondering which way to head, right or left, to retrace the path we drove yesterday, or to set off in a completely new direction, when a vehicle approaches and we flag it down.

It's a pickup truck with a Montana plate and as the driver stops and pulls over one simple fact becomes clear to me: I can't go to the cops. I can't go with Byron and Holly to the police station and make a report. I will not risk giving myself into police hands. I can't answer their endless questions. They'd know all about the Son of Schwarzenegger thing, they'd know I've been lying, they wouldn't settle for a partial truth. I just can't do it.

The driver lowers his window. He's wearing a red flannel shirt and looks to be in his fifties. 'You folks need a ride?'

'Yes,' says Byron, 'we've just been — '

'Our car got stuck up that dirt track,' I interrupt, cutting Byron off, pointing up the gravel road we've just walked down. 'Could you give us a ride to the nearest town?'

He thinks a moment, looking us over, his eyes dwelling on Holly. Then he nods. 'I'm headed to Missoula. I can drop you folks off at one of the small towns on the way, or you can come all the way to Missoula with me. I'd let you use my phone to call for help, but it doesn't work in these hills.'

Missoula. Does he mean Missoula, Montana? Are we still in the US? I want to know, but I can't ask. I'll have to wait until I see some road signs.

I glance at Holly and Byron, my eyes pleading with them to say nothing. 'Missoula sounds good,' I say.

Holly stares at me for a moment, then her

face relaxes. She gives me an imperceptible nod and smiles. 'Sure does.'

The man's dog, a Labrador cross, is clearly used to being the front passenger, so we all climb into the back seat. Our knees press into the seats in front of us and I experience a shimmer from the past. It's like the night we were first kidnapped, the three of us crammed into the back of a truck.

'You folks on a road trip?' asks our rescuer, knowing without having to ask that we're not locals.

Holly glances at me, her eyes falling on my Grand Canyon T-shirt. 'Yes,' she says, smiling broadly. 'We've seen the Grand Canyon, the Arches in Utah, and even Yellowstone. We were on our way to Glacier National Park when our car broke down.'

'Uh-huh,' says the driver. 'Not a good road you chose. You doing the map-reading, pretty lady?'

Holly's hands clench but her smile doesn't falter and her voice is as sweet as ever. 'How'd you guess?' She giggles for good measure. 'The boys were trying to teach me, said the best way to learn was just to do it, but I guess we all learnt a lesson today.'

Byron's not very talkative and neither am I. I just sit there and fiddle with the Rolex on

425

my wrist and he stares out the window, but Holly more than makes up for us. She's utterly charming as she laughs and tells our driver all about our trip across the country. And as she tells the tale, it sounds such fun that I almost wish we'd done it. I can see why I fell for her lines in the resort at Phoenix. She's good. She's so good that I feel a vague regret for what might have been. My trip to America could have been like that, just a simple drive, sightseeing and exploring. But it wouldn't have been such an adventure, and I certainly have memories to keep me going in the years ahead.

A couple of hours later our knight-in-a-pickup-truck drops us off in Missoula, Montana, USA. (Karl didn't take us to Canada after all.) We're left outside an auto mechanic our driver recommends. He accepts only heart-felt words of thanks as a reward before he drives away.

Once he's gone, before Holly or Byron can say or do anything, I pull them aside. 'I'm going now,' I say.

'What?' says Byron. 'But we have to go to the police and tell them we're safe.'

'You know I can't go to the police.'

'But — '

'He has to go, Byron.' Holly smiles at me. I return her smile. 'Thanks.'

'Good luck,' she says.

'Good luck with your articles.' I kiss her cheek. 'You give 'em hell.'

She laughs. 'Oh, I will.'

'I'm glad we're not going to be around Karl and Luke when they find out the truth,' I say. 'I don't think we're going to be their favourite people.'

'You certainly won't,' says Holly.

Then I shake Byron's hand and I turn and walk away, my flip-flops flapping with each step. I need to get out of town. Quickly. I walk to the side of the road and stick out my thumb. I look unshaven and unkempt, but I reckon I don't look too unsavoury in my shorts and T-shirt.

Luck must be with me today because, not three minutes later, a huge lorry is just about to turn out of a gas station when the driver sees me, stops and waves me over.

He's a big man, in his early forties, and he looks friendly enough. 'Where you headed?' he asks.

'East,' I say.

'I'm going to Minneapolis. Hop on in.'

And as I climb up into the cab and slam the door shut, I glance back. Holly and Byron are standing where I left them. I wave as the truck driver turns on to the road, heading for the freeway, and then they're lost from view. Gone for ever.

The driver glances at me. 'I'm Bob. You got a name?'

'Nick,' I say, smiling. I don't tell him where I'm going. I can't, I have to cover my trail. But I know my destination. I'm headed to Chicago.

THE FUTURE

I'm going to Chicago to find Emma. I don't know what will happen. I don't know if anything will happen. We met at the wrong time in both our lives, but I'm in love with her. I have to give it a chance.

And I need a new passport. I have no identity documents. Not even a credit card. Just that wad of dollar bills I took from my money belt and shoved in my pocket when we stopped to change into the outfits Karl chose for us. I know there's a British Consulate in Chicago. I'll go there, say I was robbed and request new papers, and while I'm waiting for those, I'll search for Emma.

I don't know where she lives. I threw away her card so I have no contact details, but I know her name and her husband's name. I know he's a plastic surgeon too. It won't be that difficult to track her down.

I'll find her. And I'll see what happens. I'd be willing to relocate to Chicago if that's what she wants. Or she can move to London with me. Or we can even go somewhere new for both of us. I don't mind.

What about my future? My career? Well, I need a proper job, but I'm going to reclaim my dreams. I'm going to start up another band. I'm going to write a low-budget movie, direct it, act in it, film it, and then I'll see. I'll get a real job to keep myself in money, but I'm not going to work in insurance. I'm never going to work in insurance again. I'm a salesman. I can sell anything.

If I never make it, well, that's fine too. At least I'll have tried. I won't have given up. And I like being creative just for the sake of it: it's good therapy, good for the soul, good for happiness. If I do happen to get famous later on, I'm not worried about my purveying days. My patrons might think I look familiar, but their memories will fade with time and Nick, after all, is a common name.

But, whatever happens, I'll know that I've finally lived a life worth living. I've done something, been something, I've reclaimed my passion. And what adventures I've had. The tales I could tell. But I won't. It's my secret.

THE END